THE PLAYLIST

A SPICY CHILDHOOD FRIENDS TO LOVERS
ROMANCE

SPRINGBROOK HILLS SERIES
BOOK 5

MORGAN ELIZABETH

To the Swifties who found themselves somewhere between the bridge and the chorus and let that shape how they see love and life.

Long Live.

vacations.

Little rocks we found and painted.

A gumball machine ring that makes my heart squeeze just a tiny bit looking at it.

A ticket stub from a concert we went to.

And a stack of two papers that I distinctly remember.

"Oh my god, no way," I say, snatching them off the top.

"Do you remember making those?" Luna asks with a laugh. "We went through like thirty tries to get it just right."

"And we burned all the rest so we couldn't get confused," I say with a laugh, picking Luna's up.

God forbid we put the wrong ideal future into our dream box.

At the top is MASH in big, bold letters.

It was a game we played as kids where you'd decide all of the aspects of your life with a single sheet of paper.

Who you would marry.

Where you'd live.

What your job would be.

How many kids.

What kind of pet you'd have.

You put options under each topic and then meticulously and seemingly randomly cross them off until you have your "future life" all mapped out.

Reading Luna's makes me laugh.

Marry: Tony Garrison.

"Well, you got that right, I suppose. And you're living in a house in Springbrook Hills. Though . . ." I look at the top. "I think techni-cally you were destined for a shack. I suppose the great universe decided you were due for an upgrade." I smile at my best friend. "You wanted to run a business, another match."

"Because I didn't want anyone to boss me around," Luna says with a laugh, snatching the paper back. "Oh, god, I wanted four kids! God, help me."

"What, is four too many?"

"I think three, max," she says with a dreamy smile. "Tony wants a setup like I had growing up. Two boys and a little girl he can spoil."

Jealousy cuts through me at the look and the realization that Luna is well on her way toward her dream life.

And I'm . . . existing.

"He so would spoil a little girl," I say with a smile. Her voice goes low as she directs her eyes back to the paper, not meeting mine.

"He wants to start soon," she whispers, and again, there's that stab to my gut.

Fuck.

Fuck.

"Soon?" I ask, my voice a little higher. I clear my throat. "You want to start soon?"

"I'll be thirty this summer."

"You just got married!" She shrugs.

"It's a ways away still. We'll see. You never know what will happen."

It's not the idea of my best friend having kids with the man she's loved since she was seven that has my stomach in knots.

It's that we had always planned to do it *together.*

"Let's see what you put into the universe," she says, changing the subject and picking up the other paper, scanning it over.

It's not hearts and laughter the way it was for hers.

I lick my lips and reinforce my mental shields before reaching over and snatching it.

"House," I say, remembering the image I had built in my head of a big white home with a wraparound porch and a playground in the backyard.

Instead, I live in a shitty apartment in the city.

"Interior designer," I say, and I remember my passion for picking things out for my room, for getting it just right and balancing useful-ness with design.

I'm trying to climb the corporate ladder, working in marketing for some corporate asshole who never remembers my name.

"Springbrook Hills," I say, remembering how Luna made me promise we'd stay in our tiny hometown together and how a little over a year ago, I left, needing a change.

I told myself I needed more.

"Two kids," I say. I wanted my kids to have siblings, unlike me. I wanted them to have other people to rely on and not feel the pressure to be everything to their parents.

The way I feel every damn day.

"Zander Davidson."

Luna's older brother.

Because I was in love with him, and we wanted to be real, legal sisters and thought that would be the best way to make it happen.

Now I'm dating Jeffrey, a guy I met on some dating app who checks just enough of the boxes.

I stare at the paper, and it becomes hard to breathe, the room closing in on me.

"Zoe?" Luna says, looking at me funny, but I can't stop staring at that piece of paper yellowing on one corner, pink hearts doodled all around.

This was what I wanted from life.

This was what I thought my ideal world would look like, enough so that I put it into a box that, in my heart of hearts, I thought would give me whatever I dreamed for.

And looking at it, I can't *breathe.*

"Zoe, are you okay?" my best friend asks, and I shake my head.

"It's just a silly piece of paper, right?" I ask with a laugh, but when I look at her, she's worried.

It's clear.

She's worried because I'm slowly having a meltdown.

"Right?" I ask again, this time with panic clear in my words.

"Yeah, of course. Right," she says, then she takes the paper from my hands, placing it back in the box. "This was silly. I shouldn't have even . . . It was just—"

God, now Luna is feeling guilty because I can't keep my shit together, and I'm having a crisis of faith in realizing my life isn't anything I thought it would be.

"No, this is fun, Lune. Let me see what else is in here." She stares at me, concern clear on her face, before pushing the box in my direction.

"I think . . . I think I'm gonna make some more drinks," she says, her face saying things only a best friend can interpret.

Let me get us some drinks because I foresee a long night.

"Good idea," I say, digging around in the box.

I smile at the friendship bracelets and keychains we made together at camp. I let my fingers run over the thin, flat rock that would have been perfect for skipping if it wasn't for the fact that it had a white line in the shape of a 'Z' on it, meaning it instantly turned into a prized possession for a ten-year-old girl.

An old, dead Tamagotchi is at the bottom, along with a picture from Luna's 14th birthday, all four of us in the photo.

Tony on one side, his best friend and Luna's brother on the other, Luna and me in the middle.

I remember us deciding we'd redo the photo one day when we were all married.

A knife that I haven't even acknowledged in years twists.

What is wrong with me? I think, continuing to dig.

And then I find it.

My playlist.

Or, really, my *Love Story Bucket List*, as I called it back then.

It started in 2014 with *Debut*.

We added to it in 2018 with *Fearless*.

And for each release after that, until the box went missing, we added to it.

I look at the list, the knife twisting more as I see my girly handwriting start to change over the years, along with my expectations.

I never stopped writing that list, even after it was lost, keeping a secret "love bucket list" as a joke in the notes on my phone.

I'm opening the app when Luna comes in with two drinks—ones

I know will be sweet enough to temper the large amount of alcohol in them because Luna has that face.

That *let's drown your sorrows in liquor and then have Tony take us to the diner for hangover food in the morning,* face.

I don't let myself acknowledge that I *want that.*

And then I admit to myself that *I* want someone who will drive me to get hangover food in the morning at my favorite local diner in my hometown, a place where they never even give me a menu because I know what I want at any given time of day after years of trying everything.

"Do you have a pen?" I ask, grabbing the paper and leaning over it.

"What?"

"A pen. Do you have one?"

"Zoe, are you okay?" she asks quietly, like I'm a feral cat and she needs to approach me carefully.

But I *am.*

I'm better than I think I've ever been.

Except for the fact, of course, that my life is literally *nothing* like I thought it would be.

Because I think . . . I think my life is *boring.*

Safe, even. And not in a good way.

Young Zoe would be disappointed.

But I can change that, right?

"I'm great," I say. "I just need a pen."

Because the right place to start when having a mental breakdown is with a killer fucking playlist.

ZOE'S LOVE STORY BUCKET LIST

Only me when I'm With You

        Go stargazing

Our Song

        Shotgun with crazy hair

Fearless

        Dance in a parking lot

Love Story

        Throwing pebbles at the window

Sparks Fly

        Kiss me in the rain

Treacherous

Drive through the night on a trip

You Are In Love

My best friend

Dress

Wear a dress I know he'll want to take off

I Think He Knows

His hand on my thigh in the car

Daylight

Watch a sunrise together

Cardigan

Makes me feel special when I feel average

Invisible String

It has to feel like it was always meant to be.

Gold Rush

Wander a little beach town in love

Sweet Nothing

Someone who wants sweet nothing.

TWO
YOU BELONG WITH ME
-ZANDER-

One week later

The first time I fell in love with Zoe, she was scream singing a Taylor Swift song in my parents' living room while my sister Luna laughed at her.

At least, I think that's the first time.

It's happened so many times now.

That's what's running through my mind as I stare at my phone.

I'm standing in the back room, waiting for the clock to hit five.

It's been a long day.

A long day that included following a man who was supposed to be visiting a sick aunt to a strip club, helping a woman who locked her keys in her car in a parking lot, and my sister sending me this frantic text to tell me a fact that, to be honest, I'm not quite sure what to do with.

> RED ALERT! ZOE BROKE UP WITH
> JEFFREY.

I don't know who Jeffrey is.

Not really, at least.

But I definitely know who Zoe Thomas is.

Sometimes, the world gives you people that, from the start, you know they'll be there forever.

For my sister Luna, that's Zoe Thomas.

Which means, like it or not, Zoe is in my life forever, too.

So, of course, I know who Zoe Thomas is.

She's my sister's life-long best friend.

My boss's daughter.

The woman who, over multiple occasions over multiple years, I thought there was a chance I'd eventually end up with her.

And now she's single.

Allegedly.

> And?

My sister is four years younger than me, the biggest nuisance of a sibling you could ask for, and, ironically, married to *my* best friend.

> And now is your CHANCE, Zander!

Now is my chance.

> I don't know what the fuck you're talking about, Lune.

I'm lying, of course.

For the first time in a lifetime, or at least for the first time since Zoe was eighteen, we are both unattached at the same time.

> You're single. She's single. Please, for the love of fuck, make me a sister-in-law.

I don't tell her she's wrong.

I don't tell her I have no idea what she's talking about this time.

Instead, I stare at the screen of my phone and remember everyone who has found someone in the last three years.

Hunter Hutchins, Springbrook Hills golden boy returning to town and marrying his sister's nanny.

My sister and Tony being forced to admit they've always been it for each other when she had a *stalker*.

Tanner Coleman finally dropping that hand he held up all the time, keeping everyone at a distance, and letting in the most unlikely of people.

Fuck, even Dean got over all of his fuckin' trauma, giving Cal a dad and knocking up Kate again.

And with each one, I hated to admit it, but my brain would go just a little haywire, a little unhinged.

That should have been us.

It should have been Zoe and me. We should have stopped fighting this shit by now, finally given in to it.

But it never lined up.

She always had a man, and when she didn't, I was dating some woman I had found to fill up space, to take up time.

And the one time I offered to give it all to her, she told me to go home.

And now she's single.

Goddammit.

"You off the clock?" a deep voice asks, interrupting my mental haze.

Joseph Thomas.

My dad's best friend since high school.

My boss.

And Zoe's father.

"Five more minutes, then yeah," I say casually, as if I weren't just daydreaming about his daughter, before tucking my phone back in my pocket. I can deal with that later.

It's strange looking at your boss and knowing you've jacked off to the thought of fucking his daughter more times than you can count.

"You got plans?" he asks, his voice gruff.

And then I notice.

I'm not as in tune with reading body language as Tony is, but I notice this.

The look is nervous, like he's about to say something uncomfortable.

Still, I answer his question.

"Nah. Just gonna hunker down, try and avoid the cold."

Maybe he's going to ask if I can pick a few extra shifts? I have the next three days off, but I'd be willing to cover for one of the guys if needed.

They all have lives, after all.

Wives and families to spend time with.

I just have a couch and a takeout menu that's calling my name. There's no real reason to be excited for a three-day weekend—these days, Tony is too busy fucking my sister to go out, and I refuse to date the admittedly dwindling pot of eligible women in town.

And not just because news always gets to the wrong ears in a small town, and there are a particular set of ears I don't want to be listening.

"She's free, you know," he says, kicking his boot onto the linoleum.

"Who?" I ask, my blood freezing.

There's no way.

"Don't play stupid, Davidson. You gonna grow a pair and put a ring on my little girl's finger?"

The breath stops in my lungs. I smile, laughing a hoarse, forced sound. I choke on it, coughing a bit before I rub the back of my neck and look at Joseph.

"I think you might need to go to the doctor, sir. Zoe? Zoe and me? A ring?" Another forced laugh, a lie, because I've thought about it.

I've thought about it a lot.

"Not sure if that's how it worked when the dinosaurs roamed, but these days you need to actually date a woman before you put a ring on her finger." He rolls his eyes at me, a look he would give Tony and me when he'd catch us drinking underage, telling us to sober up and get home before he had to rat us out to my dad.

To be fair, he always ratted me out to my dad, meaning Tony and I would catch a list of chores to do while hungover, but he did it quietly, so my mom never got wind and reamed me out.

Thomas is a good guy.

"That's because when you were young, you were too busy being an idiot, spreading your seed or whatever the fuck. Wouldn't have let you near her with a ten-foot fuckin' pole five, six years ago. And anytime you had your head outta your ass, she was dating some loser she'd never settle down with."

"I don't think it's fair to call her exes—"

"So, should I call one of them up? Ask *them* to take her away for a week, make her see reason?"

I don't answer.

I don't want him to call up one of her exes.

God, I'm fucked in the head, aren't I?

"Look, she told Mary Ellen she's got some kind of interview in a week. Big fancy thing, an office in the city. She's back for now but told her mother if she gets the job, she's leaving again, staying in New York. Not far, but too far for Mary Ellen to see her regularly. You'll get it one day, but when you marry a good one, you don't like watching her struggle. I don't want my wife upset that her only child is too far to see every day."

Silence fills the small space as I try to figure out what he's saying.

Is he telling me . . .

"You're off this week."

"I'm off for three days," I correct.

"You're off for a *week*. You've got a week to change her mind."

"Joe, I—"

His eyes go firm and soft in a strange confusion of emotions.

"You think I want to do this? Want to pawn my daughter off on some fuckin' boy? No. But I know she's been in love with you since she was a little girl, back when she still thought she was my princess, and I know sometime around when she was in college, you started lookin' at her differently. Around then, she stopped being your little sister's best friend. Why you two never tried to make it work, I'll never know, but I'm telling you now, you need to *make it work*."

Strangely, the breath stops entering my lungs.

I'm stuck where I'm standing, frozen in place.

My mind moves to a night over ten years ago, when I gave her that offer and she told me to go home.

"Are you telling me . . . You're telling me to run off for a week to God knows where, take your daughter with me, somehow convince her to be with me, and . . . what? Ask her to marry me?"

"Your reputation precedes you, so yeah. And make the wedding snappy so Mary Ellen and your mother can plan some kind of shindig."

A shindig.

Absolutely nothing in this universe makes sense right now.

But also, I'm not mad about this gift I've been given.

I can play with crazy.

I grew up with fucking *insane*.

"I've never even dated her, sir," I repeat, giving him a, *You know this sounds fucking insane, right?* kind of face.

"Does that even matter?" he asks, and deep brown eyes look at me, reading my soul.

Joseph Thomas has always been able to look at you and read you, to know when you're lying and what your true intentions are.

I thought I hated that trait when it meant him realizing I was lying about not toilet papering the police station when I was 15.

But right now, I really fucking hate it when it comes to him determining how I feel about his only daughter.

But still, I think.

I think hard about the way people used to always laugh when I helped Zoe out of some stupid situation, like when she climbed too far up a tree and I was the one to help her down.

Zoe and Zander. One day that boy will get the hint.

And then I got the hint, and I don't know if it was too late or she wasn't ready, but the answer was no.

And then I spent ten years watching her date assholes. Spent ten years dating women who I always hoped would give me the thrill Zoe does, but they never did.

And then I give Thomas his answer.

"I'm not sure it does."

Because I'm not.

If Zoe told me tomorrow that she wanted to be mine and wanted to make it official, I'm not sure I wouldn't take her to Vegas on the next flight.

"Great, perfect," he says, slapping me on the back. "You've got a week."

And then he leaves the room, off to do God knows what, leaving me standing right where he left me, confused beyond belief.

I'm not sure how long I stand there thinking over the past and the present and a potential future before I shake my head, grab my shit, and head out.

And then I go to the only place I can think of that might help me make sense of this mess.

THREE
ANTI-HERO
-ZOE-

"This is so depressing," I say into my phone, staring at my ceiling. Two days ago, I lost my mind and atom bombed my life.

I broke up with my boyfriend of a year, a man I'd been living with for three months, because he made me feel just . . . blah.

I quit the soul-sucking job I'd been working to climb to the top of. For four years, I dedicated nearly every moment of my life, and it ended because my best friend showed me a box from my childhood.

Who the fuck am I right now?

"Why? I'm so excited you're back home!"

"Lune, I was literally a forty-five-minute drive from you."

"So? Now you're *here*." I sigh. "Now you can come over for sleepovers or drink at the bar with me any day."

She has always been the optimist of the two of us.

I wouldn't call myself a pessimist, though. More like a realist.

The world isn't all sunshine and rainbows and happily ever afters once reality sets in.

Why set myself up for disappointment by assuming otherwise?

"Luna, I'm lying in my bed, staring at a goddamned One Direction poster on my ceiling." Luna chokes out a laugh.

"Is Harry hot?"

"In the photo, he is quite literally a child, so no."

"He was hot even as a child."

"You're really fucked in the head, you know that?" I say, but there's a smile on my lips.

This is the perk of being back home.

My friends are here.

Sometimes, they feel like a lifeline.

Back in the city, everyone I knew had a persona—a perfected version of themselves they felt comfortable sharing, and I can only assume the real part was hidden away the same way mine was.

But here in Springbrook Hills, I've known most of these people since the day I was born. None of them have a secret personality hiding.

"Whatever."

"Being here is just . . . depressing," I say. "It's like I never grew up. It's a time capsule from my childhood."

"That's because if your mom changed anything, you'd go apeshit on her," Luna says with a laugh.

"I would not," I say, my brows furrowing.

Okay, maybe I would.

Maybe that's my problem.

Maybe that's why I can't find a man, why I can't settle down, why I can't stick with a job that I love.

Maybe I'm broken.

The neurotic Type A in me that slowly started to take over my entire being in my twenties has only gotten worse with age.

But why am I so worried about this now?

"I think I'm going through a midlife crisis," I say, and Luna laughs, the sound carrying despite the noise of the bar. She's setting up for the day before she heads home to spend the night with her doting husband, who is also off the clock.

Because when Tony's not working, Luna does everything in her power to be home with him.

I try not to let the tiny tug of jealousy on my soul pinch too badly.

"You're not having a midlife crisis, Zoe." I roll over onto my stomach and sigh, a giant Squishmallow under my belly.

"I have all the key markers," I say. "I quit my job with no other job in mind. I dumped my boyfriend of a year—"

"He was *boring,*" Luna says. "So, not your forever guy."

She's not wrong.

Last week, I woke up in Luna's guest room, just a bit hung over with the smell of bacon in the air. I lay there, listening to my best friend and the love of her life giggle quietly, my mind going over the night before.

The box.

MASH.

The realization that ten-year-old Zoe would be unbearably disappointed if she saw me right now. In that bed, I decided I needed to break up with the man I'd been dating for a year and living with for three months.

Jeffery was . . . fine. He was nice. He was handsome. He didn't need to be reminded seventeen times to lift the seat every time he took a piss.

But he wasn't . . . life-altering.

I didn't look at him and feel my soul change a tiny bit each time he smiled at me.

When I tried, I could picture a future for us—two-point-five kids, probably in prep school. Two yearly vacations, some kind of family aesthetically pleasing dog that would be in all of our Christmas cards.

I could picture him giving in and agreeing to go to my family's house for holidays, rescheduling the ones with his for another day because splitting holidays would be out of the question for my mom, but I didn't see it as a point of tension.

We would have had a good life together.

But I don't want a *good life.*

I want a *spectacular* life.

I want to know to my bones that whoever I finally land with was meant to be mine from the day I was brought on this Earth.

I want our kids to watch us dancing in the kitchen when we think they're not looking, smiling as we do.

I want what my parents have—surety and love and a hint of frustration, but never doubt.

I want what Luna and Tony have—history and adoration and arguments that end in spectacular make-up sex.

I want what Hannah and Hunter have—trust and loyalty and kindness and the kind of man who would create an entire summer camp for me just because I mentioned it once in passing.

I want *extraordinary*.

And Jeffrey was . . . ordinary.

"And now I'm back to living in my childhood freaking bedroom, questioning all of my life choices," I say, rolling to my back again and staring at Harry and Niall and trying to ignore my best friend's words.

"You're not having a midlife crisis, Zoe. You're not even thirty."

"Maybe quarter-life crisis?"

"That would mean you'll live until you're 120."

That seems old.

"Third-life crisis?"

"I mean, that works better, I guess." The line goes muted and she must move the phone as she shouts to someone to grab her a new keg. "But I think you're not giving yourself enough credit."

"I'm *living in my parents' house at thirty,* Luna."

"No, you're not. You're figuring out what you want to do. Go online and search around. Honestly, Zo, I think Sadie is looking for someone to help her revamp Rise and Grind. Maybe go talk to her."

"For what, marketing help?" I ask. "She's doing just fine with that." And she is. The coffee and coworking space in town is always full of customers and silent workers.

"No, Zoe. God. With her decor. You were always so good with that, picking colors and themes and patterns. Designing."

My stomach churns at the idea alone.

It was what I wanted to do when I was a kid.

In fact, when I went to school, I spent six months with it as my major before I decided it was too unrealistic and I needed a more stable career.

A sure bet.

Marketing.

Marketing would always be needed. It was an in-demand skill to have, and I could climb the corporate ladder.

My parents only have one child to push all of their pride and expectations on, and that's me. I knew I'd have more of a chance of succeeding and "making it big" if I went with something safe.

Except I'm miserable . . .

"I don't know. That's not—"

"Not what, Zoe?"

"Reasonable. Interior design isn't reasonable."

Luna scoffs out a laugh. "Jesus, when did you get so damn boring, Zoe? All reasonable and safe."

My gut drops at her accusation, one I've made in my head so many times, but hearing it out loud . . .

"Shit, I didn't—" she says before I can say anything.

"You're not wrong," I say quietly. "It's just the way I am."

Silence, and I think she's moving now, going somewhere quieter.

"You weren't always, you know," Luna says. I sigh.

"I just . . . I grew up, Luna."

More silence, a silence that hangs on the phone line.

A silence I freaking *hate.*

"Are you sure, Zoe? Or did you just do what you thought people expected of you?"

Well, fuck.

Fuck, fuck, fuck.

"Luna—"

"Not gonna get into it. I know you have that interview in the city. You have a week to think about it. Would it really be so bad to take a year to try it out? Try something you're passionate about instead of something you think you're supposed to be doing?"

God, I hate my best friend.

I sigh, stewing on her words.

"I'll think on it, okay? No promises."

I can almost hear the smile she makes, the kind that fills her whole face.

"Alright. Good. I like having you near, Zo. I'm selfish like that, but also, soon Tony and I will start trying . . ." My gut twists again when I think of how everyone is moving on with life and I'm stuck. "I want Aunt Zoe nearby."

"Got it, babe," is all I can say through the lump in my throat.

"Okay. I love you. I'll support you even if you want to have a boring corporate job working for the man for the rest of your life. I gotta go, though. Gotta help open then get home to Tony."

"Yeah. Okay. Love you."

"Bye, Zo."

And then I'm alone once again, staring at my childhood room I painstakingly decorated and designed so many times and wondering where the girl who once lived here went.

FOUR
MARY'S SONG (OH, MY, MY, MY)
-ZANDER-

"Hey, man," my best friend says when he meets me at his front door. He steps back, opening the door for me and welcoming me in without saying the words *come in*. "You wanna beer?"

I run a hand over my hair, looking around. Tony bought this place years ago and completely gutted it. Halfway through, my sister moved in with him and helped him finish. It's intriguing to see Tony's stoic style alongside Luna's hippy-dippy one she got from our mom.

But mostly, it's the photos that always hit me in the face when I walk in.

Luna decorates in memories, and no one who walks into their home doesn't know it.

Photos of Tony and I growing up, of Luna, our little brother Ace, and me. Photos of all four of us on fishing trips with our dads.

Photos of Zoe.

Her best friend since the beginning.

So many photos of Zoe.

The girls when they were little, in matching preschool outfits, Luna's light, straight hair a stark contrast to Zoe's dark curls.

High school graduation, hugging in matching caps and gowns.

At Tony and Luna's wedding just a few months ago, Zoe in a gorgeous light-green dress, (sage, my sister corrected, as if that held any fuckin' significance to me) standing on my sister's left while I stood on Tony's right.

I was angry that entire fuckin' wedding, except when the best man had to dance with the maid of honor.

Then my grimace melted because fuck, I got to hold her.

Then she walked off the dance floor to some prep school douche who lived in the city with her.

"You good, man?" Tony asks, staring at me a bit confused. I shake my head, trying to swipe away memories I don't need right now before speaking.

"Yeah. I, uh, I gotta talk to my sister. She home?" I ask as if I didn't see her Beetle out front, as if I don't know her schedule because it hasn't changed in nearly two years.

If Tony's off, Luna is off. If she needs to go into the bar, Tony sits in his seat there, calling one of us to keep him company or just watching his girlfriend.

Fuck. Wife. His wife.

And tonight, Luna goes in at eight, and Tony will drive her there, sitting at her bar until she closes.

"You wanna talk to Luna?" he asks, his brows furrowing.

"Yeah, man. I just gotta talk to her."

He doesn't believe me.

I don't blame him.

"Everything good with your parents?"

"Parents are fine," I say.

"Ace?"

"Jesus, Ace is fine, Tony. I just want to talk to my sister." He looks at me, confused, but it's not like I *never* talk to my sister.

I just . . . never go out of my way to go to the Garrison household to see her. If I want to talk to her, I see her at family dinner, or I head to the bar on a night she's working.

Or, you know, I call her, like a normal person.

I should have just called her.

And when I see it, I *know* I should have because here in my best friend's presence, his detective skills go into overdrive, and he sees through whatever exterior I put up.

Fuck.

"Oh my god," he says, and the smile on his face starts to grow.

"What?"

"*Oh my fucking god.* Lune, darlin'! Come here!" he shouts to my sister, somewhere in the house.

"What?" Luna calls.

"Come here, Luna!" he says, and now the smile is taking over his face.

"Why?" she yells, which is so Luna. Her husband is yelling for her to come and she doesn't. Instead, she just has a full-blown conversation from across the house.

"Zee's finally realized he wants Zo!"

"No fucking way!" I hear my sister yell, and then there's thumping, things being thrown aside before I hear her feet on the hardwood floors. "*No fucking way!*" she shouts, running in our direction. Her blonde hair peeks around the corner, and her face is completely split with a smile. "Are you for real?"

"I don't—"

"He came here to talk to you."

"To talk to *me?*" she asks, confusion crossing her face. "Why would he come *here* to talk to *me?*"

"Because he wants to know how to win over your best friend."

"You think?" she asks.

"You know I'm *right fuckin' here*, right?" I say, waving my hands as if I've somehow gone invisible. Both of them look at me.

"I'm gonna go get you that beer, man. You're gonna need it," Tony says, disappearing toward his kitchen. My sister crosses her arms on her chest and looks at me like I'm about to disappoint her big time.

"Are you serious, Zander?"

"I don't know how I could be serious or not serious, considering I've not gotten more than three words in."

She stares at me.

I stare back.

She raises an eyebrow at me.

The problem is, I know this girl can hold this stare down until she dies and turns to dust.

And I only have a week.

I sigh.

"Joe Thomas gave me a week off." She furrows her brow, not understanding my words. "Told me to figure out how to keep Zoe in Springbrook Hills. How to convince her not to take some fancy new job in the city."

Luna pauses.

She's got a face on like there's a puzzle in front of her and the pieces aren't fitting.

Finally, her face clears, and her eyes go wide. *"The box,"* she whispers like it all makes sense.

Absolutely *none of it makes sense.*

"Lune."

"The box, Zander! The damn box I found the other day when Tony forced me to clean out that guest room."

"Because it was a fuckin' trash heap," Tony says, walking in with a beer and handing it to me.

"Not now, Tony, Jesus." My best friend rolls his eyes at my sister, and I try not to heave thinking about them being together.

It's a fine line between *happy they're happy* and *barfing everywhere because they're together.*

Such a fine fucking line.

"The box. We made this box when we were kids—one of Mom's manifestation nights."

"Oh, I remember that box. It was under your bed," Tony says, and Luna's eyes shoot right to her husband.

"What?"

"Oh, we went through your shit as kids. All the time," I say, remembering the pink bedazzled box. "Really, under your bed isn't a great hiding place."

"Neither is your sock drawer," Tony says, and the looks they give each other make me dry heave.

"Can we please move on? I'm still here."

Luna rolls her eyes, and Tony smiles.

"So, we made this box and added to it over the years. You know, little shit. Friendship bracelets and pictures."

I look at her with an *okay and . . . ?* look.

"I found it, and when Zoe came over for a sleepover the other night—"

"You guys still have sleepovers?" I ask, staring at my sister. They're both thirty and apparently do little-girl shit regularly.

"Shut the fuck up, Zee." She throws a pillow at me before she continues. "Anyway, when she was here, I pulled it out. I was laughing because we had this little game we played where it would predict your future. And we put our perfect one in the box to try and make it happen. Mine was pretty much dead-on minus four kids."

"*Four kids?*" Tony says with a smile.

Tony wants a big house and a big family.

"I was young and stupid. Shut up."

"Just saying. Big family sounds like your dream, not mine," he says, and she glares at him.

"Okay, look, you two can be all lovey-dovey and talk about *making babies* when I'm not in here with a task to make Zoe stay in Springbrook Hills in less than a week. Can we please finish this damn thing?"

My sister rolls her eyes but continues on.

"Anyway, when we looked at Zoe's, it was very much *not* her life now."

"What was it?" I ask, and Luna's eyes get . . . guarded.

"This is best friend shit, Zee."

"Yeah, and I'm being tasked to win over Zoe by her father."

"Why?"

"What?"

"Why? Why are you being tasked with that?" my sister asks, crossing her arms on her chest.

"No idea. He says that his wife is tired of Zo being so far, and he needs her to have a reason to stay."

"But why *you*? There are a hundred people he could have asked."

"I . . . I don't know," I lie. "I was free? He's got control over my schedule?"

"I don't think that's it, Zander," she says.

And for some reason, the way she's looking at me has me willing to spill.

She's right.

I move to the couch in the sitting room next to the front door and plop down, Luna and Tony following suit.

"Because he knows there's always been something there between us."

"Ding ding ding," Luna says. "But why didn't you ever do anything about it?"

"The time was never right. She always had some boyfriend or was living out of state, or I had some girl."

"No girl you've ever dated has been serious," Luna says. "Why not dump them when Zoe was single?"

"Like it's that simple, Luna."

"It could have been." I sigh.

"I tried once. When she was nineteen. There was . . . There was a thing, and I offered to dump my girlfriend at the time." Luna groans.

So does Tony.

"Jesus, man," he says under his breath, running a hand over his face.

"What?"

"You just don't offer to break up with your girlfriend like that. Fuck, man, use your brain."

"Why not?"

"Because women read into shit."

"What the fuck could you read into that other than I wanted to be with her?"

"Uh, maybe that you easily drop girlfriends?" my sister says. "Or that you're a cheater?"

"She's known me my whole life, Luna. She knows I'm not like that."

"In high school, you were always with a new girl." I roll my eyes and look at the ceiling.

"That was high school!"

"That shit sticks with women, Zee," Tony says, his voice low.

He had his own shit with my sister years and years before they got together that made Luna do everything in her power to avoid Tony, so he would know.

I sigh again.

Looking at it from a different point of view, I can see how that would make me seem like a piece of shit.

Fuck.

"So what, I fucked up when I was 23 because I was young and stupid and some crazy shit had just gone down, and now there's no chance?"

I don't like the way my gut seizes at that thought. At the way I feel sick just thinking I ruined my shot with Zoe.

It's Luna's turn to sigh.

She looks around the room like she's trying to figure something out, trying to find some kind of guidance or permission, before she finally nods.

"Look. I'm going to share something with you, but if you ever tell anyone, I can rightfully be flogged publicly."

Tony's eyes go wide, and a smile crosses his face, and my stomach churns for an entirely different reason. My sister, thankfully, throws another throw pillow at her husband.

"Anthony Garrison, stop it. You're making Zander nauseous."

Tony just smiles.

I hate this. Her being married to my best friend makes shit so uncomfortable.

"Do you agree to never, ever, in a million years, tell Zoe what I'm about to show you?" Her face is stoic and serious.

"Will it help me?"

She goes quiet for a split second before nodding.

"Then yeah," I say, because this is not the time for egos.

"Okay," she says, then she stands and walks out of the room.

Tony leans back in the couch, putting a foot on one knee before leaning back with a smile.

"So, Zoe?"

"Shut up, man."

"It's not like we didn't all know."

"Shut up, man."

He laughs, but then Luna walks through the entryway holding a very familiar box. It's worn with age but I could pinpoint it anywhere.

Their stupid wish box.

The box Luna hid terribly; the box Tony and I riffled through more times than I could count as kids just to fuck with my sister.

And now it might hold all of the answers.

She sits down with it in her lap and I grab for it. She moves it out of my reach, staring at me.

"Look. I'm not doing this for you. I'm doing it for Zoe."

"Babe, you're revealing your best friend's hopes and dreams *for her*?" Tony says with a smile, and I want to punch him.

He's supposed to be on *my* side, not Zoe's.

"She's having a midlife crisis."

"She's thirty."

"Third-life crisis. Shit, I've already had this freaking conversation once with her. I don't need to have it again." Tony smiles, and I watch as nearly instantly, Luna's frustration melts off.

Magic.

I hate that the first thing I think is that I fucking want that.

I've *never* wanted that.

I've watched my parents stay happily married for forty years.

I've watched my best friend fall for my sister.

I've watched all of the people I grew up with fall in love with their better halves.

I've never wanted it, not really.

At least not in a way I let myself grasp.

But now that it's maybe a sort of, far-off possibility with Zoe?

Fuck. *I want it.*

I shake my head.

"Luna, what's in the box that's so Earth-shattering?" I feel like a 1990's Brad Pit meme.

"All of my little girl hopes and dreams and more importantly, all of Zoe's. Showing you this willingly is a huge break in the sisterhood of lifelong best friends. I could go to jail for this."

"Pretty sure you couldn't," Tony says.

"Girl jail, which is a million times worse than real jail, trust me."

Tony sits back with his hands in the air and smiles. Luna rolls her eyes and shakes her head.

"As I was saying—" She glares at her husband. "This holds everything Zoe wanted in life from age ten to like, twenty. And when she looked at it again, I think . . ." She sighs, trying to find the words. "I think she shocked herself. I think it shook her to the core knowing what she saw in here wasn't even close to the life she was living." My gut drops in concern for Zoe.

"I think . . ." Luna sighs again, leaning into a hand on her chin. "I think if she knew the life she was living was giving her all-consuming joy, that she was living a life even better than her ten-year-old brain could have thought up, she'd be fine. But she's miserable. She's not where she wants to be. I know because just days after our night together, she quit her job and dumped her boyfriend. I think . . . I think this was her wake-up call." She lifts the box.

"Okay . . ."

"So I'm just saying, showing you this means something. It's not just something funny to laugh about."

"I wouldn't—" Luna gives me a look because I totally would.

I totally would laugh at the girlish thoughts and memories and desires of my sister.

"It's silly, but it means something. I'm only going to show you because I think it's time you both stop playing this weird game, time you both admitted shit. It's freaking time you gave me a sister-in-law because I need someone to gossip with."

"You're acting like you can't gossip with Zoe on any other given day. Like you *don't* gossip with her daily," Tony says, and she glares at him before looking back at me.

"It's not the same. But that doesn't matter. All that matters is that you need to take this seriously. Do you understand?"

I look at her and see how earnest she is, then I nod.

Luna smiles then lifts the lid, handing it over to Tony.

"Oh, I guess I get a job too, cool." She glares at him and *fuck*.

I want *that* too.

Who the fuck am I right now?

"This is my MASH card," she says with a smile, cutting into my mental reverie. She hands it off to Tony.

"See, Luna. Four kids. The universe has spoken." She shakes her head then moves to hand another piece of paper to me.

"This was Zoe's. This was . . . This was what shook her up, Zee."

And then I see it.

All laid out, Zoe's childhood dreams are in the palms of my hands.

A cheat sheet, in a way.

A house.

An interior designer—I remember how much she loved to mess around with the furniture when she and Luna would have sleepovers, always talking about her visions and colors and vibes.

She'd be good at that.

Two kids. Makes sense, since she was an only child and basically lived in our chaotic house.

Live in Springbrook Hills.

Keep her here, Thomas's voice says.

And married to . . . Zander Davidson.

To be fair, this is not the first time I've seen this paper.

I saw it and laughed at it when I was 15 and a douchey kid looking for dirt on his sister.

Back when this was some kind of fairy-tale daydream for Zoe.

But now . . . Now she looks at it and is reevaluating her life.

I look up from the paper, my finger touching where her girly handwriting wrote my name, and I ask the question I'm actually scared to ask.

"Do I have a shot?"

I'm terrified because by asking this, I'm admitting things I don't want to put into the world unless it's reciprocated.

I grew up with a feminist hippy and I'm not too shy to admit that my masculinity is as fragile as glass right now.

Being rejected—again, I might add—by Zoe Thomas after everyone hyped me up would hurt more than I'd like to admit.

Luna smiles.

Tony smiles.

"Yeah, Zee. You've got a real chance if you do it right." I sigh, nod, then place the delicate paper on the coffee table.

"Okay. What do I do?"

And that's when Luna smiles.

"I've got just the thing."

FIVE
LOVE STORY
-ZOE-

Hours after I get off the phone with Luna, hours after I take a shower in the tiny bathroom attached to my room, using the same drug store shampoo and body wash I used when I was nineteen, and after my mom brings me up food, I hear it.

For a moment, I think I'm going insane, or maybe it's just been so long since I slept in this room that I don't remember the creaks and noises of it.

But then it happens again.

Ping.

I stand, moving around the room, waiting for it to happen again, trying to track the source of the sound.

I probably look psychotic as I do, but then it happens again.

Ping.

I move toward my window where I think it came from, waiting for the noise.

Something hits the window.

Looking down, there's a shadowy figure standing out front. Quickly, I duck, trying to get out of view of someone who is clearly here to murder me.

What did I do to get a stalker?

This is not the kind of experience I thought I'd share with my best friend, who once had a stalker of her own.

Fumbling and attempting to stay below the window, I scramble to grab my phone which just lit up with a new text.

It's probably Luna.

Thank God.

My dad's at work and I don't want to freak Mom out—maybe Luna can send Tony around? Scope out the area?

I read the text and get even more confused.

> Did you just fall?

What the fuck?

> Go to your window.

My window.

My window?

There's another ping on the glass, this time louder now that I'm directly under the glass.

> Are you my stalker?

A moment passes before another text comes through.

> If by stalker you mean the person throwing rocks at your window, then yeah.

What the actual fuck?

I look down at the lawn and see a figure, my eyes focusing until I recognize the form.

He waves at me.

Zander Davidson is outside my parents' house throwing rocks at my childhood bedroom window.

Why?

Open the damn window, Zoe, Jesus.

I want to argue.

I actually *live* to argue.

But instead, I move, peeking out to try and see the street and, yup —there it is.

Zee's car is parked at the corner.

And he's throwing rocks at my window.

Another hits right where my face is and I finally stand, opening the heavy window and sticking my head out.

"What are you doing, Zander?"

"Let's go," he says, calling up to me.

I blink at the man who is barely four years older than me. The man I've known since before I could cogitate what it means to *know* someone. His sister and I have been friends since we were in Mommy and Me classes, our mothers making it a mission for us to be best friends forever and, well, it worked.

"Zander, what the fuck are you doing outside my window? It's like, forty degrees out. Aren't you freezing?"

"Yes, now come on. Let's go," he says with just a hint of exasperation.

"Where are we going?" I shout down at him.

"A road trip."

I blink, the cold stinging my eyes, but I don't respond.

I don't know *how* to respond.

"Jesus Christ, Zoe, just come outside. Pack a bag and come downstairs."

"Zander, what—"

"Alexander Davidson, you stand out in that cold much longer, you're going to get sick. Stop shouting up at her from down there and come inside," my mother's voice says from the front step. "You can come upstairs and shout at her in a warm house."

My mother.

The reason I moved out all those years ago.

Zander smiles, the flash of his teeth reflecting in the front light of the house before he starts moving to the door.

What on Earth is happening?

Voices from downstairs travel up to me in the old house, Zander greeting my mom. My mom offers him a soda as if having my best friend's older brother in my living room *without* my best friend present is normal before I head toward the stairs.

"Joey called. He knows the plan," she says of my dad, and I hear Zander's laugh boom through the living room.

"Should have known," he says.

"Should have known what?" I ask, staring at Zander and my mom.

Zander just smiles at me.

"You pack a bag?" he asks, and I furrow my brow at him in confusion and frustration.

"For *what?*"

"I'll leave you two alone," my mother says, raising her hands and backing into the kitchen. "Just remember, Zoe. Zee's a good boy. And some adventure would be good for you!" I glare at her before she lifts her hands in a placating manner and leaves the room.

"Come on, babe. Go pack a bag," Zee says once she's out of the room, but probably not out of earshot.

Babe?

A bag?

"What on Earth is happening?" I ask in near panic. I don't do well with surprises. I don't do well with *spur-of-the-moment.*

Not anymore at least.

I grew out of that long ago.

"We're going on a road trip," he says like this happens all the time.

Like Zander coming to my house at nine at night and telling me to pack a bag for a road trip is *normal.*

"A road trip?"

"Jesus, yeah, come on."

"Come on *where,* Zander?!" My pulse is rising with the lack of an answer.

He steps closer, entering my personal space, and my heart skips a beat.

There has never been a time I can remember when Zander Davidson didn't make my heart skip a beat.

"On that road trip we planned."

"I would remember planning a road trip with you, Zander. I don't —" He stops me with his words.

"You were twelve and I was sixteen. You said when I got my license, we should go on a road trip. We never did it. I'm off for a week and so are you. Let's go. I'm tired of the cold. Let's go somewhere warm."

It all comes back to me in a rush, the memory that was buried in cotton, kept safe from the harsh reality of the world.

───

I'm at Luna's for a sleepover and Mrs. Davidson is ordering us a pizza. Luna has run upstairs to grab her magazine to show me some new picture of the Jonas Brothers, and Zander walks in the door.

"Did you get it?!" I ask, jumping up onto my knees and bouncing on the worn-in couch covered in old quilts.

"Get what, pipsqueak?" he asks with a smile. His blond hair is spiked and his tan from the summer makes him look like a surfer boy.

He's my dream man.

Every time I play MASH with Luna, I add his name. The only reason Luna hasn't completely banned it as an option is because she says if I marry her brother, we'll be sisters for real.

"Your *permit,* you jerk. And stop calling me that." He walks past the back of the couch, using a hand to mess up the top of my hair, and I swat at his arm. As he moves to the front of the couch, my body moves, turning to face him like he's north and I'm a compass needle.

He flops next to where I'm sitting cross-legged, the couch bouncing, and throws a piece of paper in a plastic envelope at me.

"Got it," he says with a smile.

It's so freaking cool, is all I can think. This piece of paper means that freedom is *so close* for Zee.

I wish I were 16.

And not just because a permit would be cool.

Because then I wouldn't be his kid sister's best friend.

I wouldn't be a *pipsqueak*.

"Only took you three tries," I say with a smile, refusing to ever give into his teasing.

"Shut up!" he shouts, false shock on his face. "I can't believe you said that to me."

"You failed the written test three times and made two instructors quit. I feel like I'm allowed to remind you of that." His blue eyes roll but he keeps smiling at me.

"You saying you wouldn't trust me in a car?"

I think about that.

My dad would never in a million years let me get into a car Zander Davidson was driving.

But still . . .

I hop back up onto my knees, moving to face him.

"Take me on a road trip."

"A road trip?" he asks with that smile that's totally given him pick of any girl at Springbrook Hills High.

"Yeah! We can go to where it's warm. Disney!"

"You want to take a road trip to Disney?" he asks with another smile.

It's then I remember sixteen-year-old boys don't like Disney World.

They like cool stuff.

"Or, you know. The beach. Or we could buy fireworks! Or—"

"Disney would be cool, pip," he says with a smile.

God, I think I'm in love with Luna's big brother.

"So you'll take me?" I ask.

"One day, we can go on a road trip, pip."

———

"You remember that?" I say, my voice low and shaky.

I barely remember that.

And I only do because back then, I was so incredibly head over heels in love with Zander Davidson that every interaction we had is burned into my subconscious.

"I remember everything that has to do with you, Zo," he says.

His voice is low when he says it, a shock to my system.

I stare at him, silence filling the space as I try to understand.

I don't know what to say.

I don't know what to do.

This new information could drastically change, well . . . everything.

"So what do you say?" he asks, staring at me. "Road trip?"

"I don't—"

"You busy?" he asks, cutting me off.

"What?"

"Why am I asking, already asked Lune? You've got nothing going on for a week. Your job interview is on the ninth, yeah?"

I'm going to kill his sister.

"Uh, yeah . . ."

"Just get a bag, fill it with shit, and let's go."

"I—" I start but then my mom's head pops in.

"Jesus, Zoe. Go with the boy! When was the last time you did something fun? Something spontaneous?" She does a shimmy when she says *spontaneous* and I think I might die.

"I don't like spontaneous. I like plans. I like structure—"

"A week won't kill you. If you don't go, you'll be stuck here with your father and me. I think he's taking time off, too, so we'll both be around the house all day."

"Fine," I say, knowing there is no world where I want to be stuck in my childhood home with *both* of my parents. She smiles a smile like she won some kind of war and I know then.

She planned that.

My father isn't going to be here all week.

I don't know why I fell for it. It's the oldest trick in the book.

"You gonna back out?" Zander asks, staring at me with a smile.

And he also knows I can't back down from a challenge.

At the same time, my mind runs through all of the reasons I'm back home.

My life is too safe.

I've gotten too comfortable.

In a way, I've forgotten the girl who once loved adventure and thought for sure she'd settle down in Springbrook Hills with Zander fucking Davison.

So I answer.

"No," I say, turning toward my room so I can pack. I look over my shoulder before I start up the stairs. "But we're taking my Jeep."

And when he smiles, I wonder for a moment how much I'd let him get away with to see that smile directed at me all the time.

SIX

ALL TOO WELL (10 MINUTE VERSION) TAYLOR'S VERSION FROM THE VAULT

-ZANDER-

An hour later, we're standing in Zoe's parents' driveway, staring at her Jeep.

I know Zoe better than she thinks I do.

I know that her dad does regular maintenance on this despite the fact that it's been sitting in their driveway since she moved to the city.

I know that Zoe has a crazy fuckin' kit in the trunk that she calls her *emergency* kit, and I know that taking her vehicle will give her some kind of comfort.

I know that she will be ten times more likely to go on a trip with me if she has that comfort.

But standing on the front step, staring at her little red two-door Jeep with its daisy tire cover and the mirror ball in the rearview mirror and a fuckin' bumper sticker that reads, *Honk if you love Taylor*, I change my mind.

"I'm not going on a fuckin' road trip in this, Zoe," I say, crossing my arms on my chest.

"Then I'm not going on a road trip because I'm not going in *that*," she says, tipping her chin to my car.

I stare at her.

I'm *offended*.

That car might be an old ass Mustang, but I take better care of that thing than some people take care of their dogs.

"Why not?"

"Because it's disgusting and smells like boy." I tip my head back and laugh full-out.

"What?" I say with a smile when the laughter settles and she's staring at me like . . . like she saw something special for the first time. "What?" I ask, my brows furrowing.

Her head shakes.

"I'm not going in your car, Zander. Mine is clean, it's bigger, and it has my stuff in it."

"Your stuff? Your bag is right there."

"Yeah, but that's my bag. My *emergency bag*. It's got . . . everything."

"Ahh, your Type A is showing, Zoe."

"Just because you Davidsons were raised on chaos and good vibes with a hint of football from your dad, does not mean that I need to live that same lifestyle."

I smile again because she's not wrong.

My mom is one hundred percent chaos and good vibes, and my dad is definitely a hint of football, leaving most of the child-rearing to Mom.

I stare at her, weighing my options.

I need to get her on the road.

I've seen that look before—there is no way in Hell this woman is going anywhere with me in my car.

So I nod.

"Fine. But I drive."

Her smile turns cat-like.

"Fine, but my music."

"No phone," I say, one of the few things I actually thought of ahead of time.

"No phone?"

"No phone."

"What do you mean *no phone,* Zander?"

"You have your phone, you're off texting Luna and your girls and not taking a fuckin' road trip. We're going old school. No phones."

I can see it now: the battle.

The new version of Zoe is Type A to the fucking core—the idea of not having her phone to check directions or weather or restaurants in the area will drive her insane.

Good.

Zoe can use a little bit of chaos and good vibes in her life, and I'm going to be the one to give it to her.

"But I'll let you have it for your music."

She blinks at me a few times, working to make a decision at rapid-fire speed.

To give in or not to give in. That is the question, isn't it?

"Fine," she finally says, then she tosses me her keys before walking to her Jeep.

I hold them in my hand, staring at the old-school red hotel keychain with the words *fuck the patriarchy* on it.

"Are you kidding me right now?" I ask, and she turns with a smile, definitely knowing what I'm talking about.

"What?" Her words are sugary sweet.

"Fuck the patriarchy?"

"Is your masculinity so fragile that you can't admit the patriarchy is in place to keep women down and that as a woman, I might believe that said patriarchy should get fucked?"

And I think she says the words forgetting who raised me.

I shake my head at her before looking to the sky, begging God to give me the strength to deal with this handful of a woman.

A goddamn handful.

But a handful I'll hold on to as long as she'll let me.

SEVEN
HOLY GROUND
-ZOE-

As I move to the trunk my car with my stuff, I turn to Zander.

"We need to go to Luna's before we leave town," I say, hefting my bags up off the ground to put them in the trunk.

"Why? Also, what the fuck is that?" he asks, eyes on the two bags I'm holding and the third on my back.

"Because Luna . . . has something for me."

I don't tell him that the "something" is my sanity.

If I'm going to be phoneless for the next week, I need the pep talk to end all pep talks before I run off with Zander.

"Something that's not already in three bags?" His eyebrow is raised, but I'm already out of my comfort zone. I won't be doing this without all of my stuff.

"Look, you want me to go with you to some undisclosed location, fine. But I have no idea what to pack. I just know you said *warm*. I need my stuff."

"Three bags of stuff?" I just stare, hands on my hips. "Okay, okay, three bags it is," he says with a smile. Then he takes them out of my hands, arranging them in the tiny trunk before putting a hand on my lower back and maneuvering me out of the way so he can slam it closed after putting in his own small bag.

My skin tingles where he touches me even though there is a tee shirt and a hoodie between his hand and my back.

God, this is a terrible idea, I think, but I don't have time to sit on how terrible of an idea is it.

Because once the trunk is shut, he moves me, pinning me to my car with his body.

Not hard.

Barely even touching, really.

But it still makes my heart go fucking wild.

His hand moves up, touching the tips of my hair in my ponytail, and he looks at the sleek strands and shakes his head like he can't believe something.

"What?" I ask, my voice confusingly breathy.

"Nothing." Then he looks into my eyes and my breath leaves me completely. "You gonna let me take you on a trip, Zoe?"

"What?"

"Are you gonna let go of the stranglehold you have on every moment of every day and let me lead?" My brows furrow and my mouth opens to speak before he continues. "Are you going to relax and be spontaneous with me?"

"I don't—"

"Asking a simple question. I've got a plan up here," he says, tapping his head, and I can't help but smile.

It's a cute move.

"And your overthinking mind with your need to plan is going to mess with it. We do this, I take the lead."

I pause, unsure.

I don't like this.

The not knowing.

It eats at me.

But also, where has living comfortably gotten me?

Where has always knowing what's next and being safe gotten me? Right back to square one.

"You won't lead me somewhere crazy?" I ask, and even to my own ears my voice is nervous.

"Never," he says, and I believe him.

I believe him.

I don't know why, but I do, and that means something to me.

My dad taught me to always trust my gut. The few times in my life that I haven't, it's never gone well.

So, I trust my gut now.

"Yeah. But I need to stop at Luna's first." And then he smiles like he knows something I don't before he nods and steps back, jingling my keys in his hand, walking to the passenger door, and opening it up for me.

EIGHT
BEGIN AGAIN
-ZOE-

"Zoe!" Sadie yells when I walk into Luna's Full Moon Cafe, the bar my best friend opened when she was barely even old enough to drink.

Following her dreams of owning her own business, even if it terrified her.

"What are you doing here!?" Luna says, walking around the bar. Hannah and Sadie are in their normal spots, seats no one sits in beside our crew, facing the front door. Kate waves from where she's working behind the bar and on the other side, the men can be seen, watchful eyes on their women.

Hunter and Tanner are there, Tony and Mitch on-call, I assume. If Kate's on, it's a good guess Dean is home with Cal and baby Jesse.

She doesn't work many nights at Luna's anymore now that she's full-time at the coffee shop, but a few nights a month, she's still here, serving and hanging out.

"I needed to stop in for, uh, that thing," I say, my eyes shifting to Luna's brother. He smiles before winking and walking over toward where the men sit.

There's no way he knows.

There's no way he knows that I'm here for advice and moral support, right?

I race over to my friends either way, hugging everyone hello.

"I didn't even know you were in town!" Hannah says with a smile.

"You're too busy trying to get knocked up," Sadie says with an eye roll. Hannah's mouth opens to retaliate with some barb to her best friend, but I cut them off.

"I have no time for this shit. I need advice."

"Advice?" Kate asks, walking over, a glass and a bar towel in her hand as she dries it.

"Zander. He just came to my house. He wants to go on a fucking road trip."

"I'm sorry, *what?!*" Sadie says in a shriek, forcing eyes our way.

"Sadie, *shut up!*" Jordan says.

I love Jordan.

She wasn't around when I was in love with Zander as a kid, but she is a girls' girl through and through and can always read a room.

"What?!" Sadie repeats, quieter this time. "Why?"

"Because when we were kids, I told him he had to take me on road trip when he got his license." Eyes go wide.

"How old were you?" Kate asks.

"Twelve."

"And he still remembers that?" Hannah questions, shocked. I sigh, frustrated.

I have no time to figure out these tiny details.

"I guess. I have no idea, but I'm freaking the fuck out. We're leaving tonight."

"No fucking way," Hannah whispers. I nod.

"You're going, right?" Luna asks, and I look at her, slightly confused.

She should be confused.

Or shocked.

Or anything but . . . cautiously optimistic.

"I mean. He told me I was too Type A to want to go—"

"Valid," Kate says, and I glare at her.

She smiles.

My friends suck.

But I don't have time to bring up just how uptight she was before she settled back in town and got with Dean.

"So, I said yes because I was kind of offended. Still, I figured, you know. I have a week to try and be more fun, to live life a little less . . . safe before I start any new job."

"You mean boring," Sadie says.

"You've been perpetually single since you were twenty. You wanna dig into that one?" Hannah asks with a raised eyebrow.

"We don't have time to talk about both of our trauma!" I say in a quiet whisper. "Zander is taking me on a fucking *road trip* for no reason *right now*!"

"What if there is a reason?" Luna asks, keeping her eyes away from mine.

What does she know?

"What on Earth could the reason be?"

"You are single . . . ," she says.

"And how would he know *that*, Luna?" I ask, and her cheeks go pink.

"I mean, your dad works with him. He could have mentioned it. Or Tony. Tony has a huge mouth."

Tony does *not* have a huge mouth.

I glare.

"Did you do this?" I ask, and she instantly gets a stern look, shaking her head

"No, this is all Zee, promise." She lifts a pinky in one half of a pinky promise, but I don't have to complete it—we made the rule that even *implying* a pinky promise is legally binding as kids.

Silence covers our group.

"What do I do?"

"Well, you go," Sadie says, taking a sip of her drink. "Duh."

"Well, yeah. I can't back out now. But like . . . what do I *do*."

Luna stares at me and her eyes go soft.

"You don't play it safe, Zoe." I know what she means. She was there for my mental breakdown, after all. "Remember what we were talking about, Zo."

"I have a job interview in a week."

"Zee knows?"

I nod. "He said he'd have me home before that."

"Then you go. You go and you live life. Let it be . . . your taste of freedom. What it would be like without the confines you've set up for yourself, A time to be . . . you. Or figure out which version of you makes you happy.

"I don't have *versions* of me."

Jordan chokes on her drink and we all look at her as she coughs, a finger in the air telling us she has some kind of commentary.

"Look, as someone who has been multiple people for the cameras and then another person behind them, you so do have multiple versions of yourself. Sorry, babe." My gut drops.

Have I been this obvious all along?

"But you need to find the version that makes you happy, Zoe."

Having good friends really, really sucks.

"Trying out versions of you while you're young is normal. Trying to balance who you were as a kid, who you're going to be in the future, who your parents want you to be? It's a process. But eventually, you're supposed to land on a version that you can be happy with. You're not supposed to settle on the version that you think will be the most impressive," Luna says, and I bite my lip.

She knows me too freaking well.

She also knows me well enough to turn her serious face into a smile and nod like the conversation is already over.

"Alright, let's get you a shot for the road," Luna says with a wink, seeing the anxiety on my face undoubtedly.

And with that, I circle back to loving having good friends.

NINE
NEW YEAR'S DAY
-ZOE-

We leave the bar at eleven and after two more shots. Zander stayed away from where I stood with the girls, didn't drink anything but water, and never once asked what I needed when I walked out empty-handed.

And barely even thirty minutes into the drive, I start to feel that sleepy haze take over me.

I've always been a car sleeper, and my normally regimented routine means I'm usually in bed by nine, asleep by ten at the latest.

I've always been a morning person, up with the sun and ready to accomplish my task for the day once I roll out of bed.

God, how did I never notice how regimented and boring my days were?

I shake my head, trying to knock out my overthinking and the exhaustion that's slowly consuming me.

"I'm so tired," I say with a yawn. "Should we stop? Or maybe we should go back and start tomorrow." Zee laughs and shakes his head.

"Not a chance we're turning back until we have to," he says.

I didn't think he'd go for that.

In fact, I don't think anyone could ever talk Zander out of anything when he has an idea in his head.

"We should stop. Get coffee or energy drinks or something."

"We will eventually. Taking the long way, I'm sure we'll find some places. But you sleep," he says, his voice soft.

Soothing.

"What?"

"You sleep. I'll drive." I shake my head in the negative.

"That's not fair, Zee. That's not how road trips work."

"They do when I'm driving."

"You're driving *my Jeep,* though," I say, feeling myself getting unintentionally self-righteous. He smiles, reaching over and grabbing my hand.

God.

I like that.

His hand in mine.

He squeezes it, once, twice, three times.

A reassurance of sorts.

"I work nights, babe. It's all good. You think I'd put you in any kind of danger?" I look at him and know the answer, of course.

"No, you wouldn't want to deal with my dad if something happened to me."

He looks at me, staring for a long moment despite the moving car.

"Zander!" I say, tipping my head to the road.

Maybe I was wrong about him not putting me in danger.

He shakes his head but looks back at the road all the same.

"You don't get it," he says under his breath.

"Get what? That you're insane?" I say with a laugh.

His lips don't tip up as I expect.

"You don't get that the need I feel to keep you safe has absolutely nothing to do with your father, Zoe."

The way he says it has me questioning what it *does* have to do with, even if my subconscious can probably answer that question.

I don't think I'm ready for that answer.

I'll probably never be.

A minute or two passes in silence, the radio singing about a mirror ball low in the background before I speak, breaking the silence.

"I'll stay up," I say, trying not to let out a yawn. Zee fights a laugh, a boyish smile replacing the frown.

"Sure you will." I furrow my brow in confusion.

"What does that mean?"

"Means when we were kids, Tony and I always knew you'd pass out first. You woke up in the middle of the night, but you'd pass out first. Once Luna was out, we could sneak in and pull some kind of prank, go into Lune's hiding spots and go through her shit—"

"You went through her shit?" I ask, freaking out over what he could have found.

The box?

"Oh yeah. All the time. Luna was terrible at hiding things."

I sit on that, panic infiltrating my bones.

"Nothing about you, Zo. Only Luna's shit."

Like he can read me, always.

And honestly, he's probably lying. He was a big brother, after all. But he doesn't have to know just how deep those little girls' wishes went, or how they've impacted my very recent decisions.

"Go to sleep, baby," he says in a low voice, and I want to question that, too, the sweet pet name, but instead, my eyelids get heavy, my mind focuses on the constant stroke of his thumb on the back of my hand, and I fall asleep.

The car is dark when I wake up, and it takes me a moment to realize what woke me.

My hand is engulfed in Zee's, his callused fingers squeezing mine in a rhythm.

One, two, three, then a pause.

One, two, three, then a pause.

His gaze moves to me quickly before he looks back at the road.

"Everything okay?" I ask, my voice groggy.

"It's midnight," he says. I blink slowly, sleep still so close, but I try and form real sentences.

"Okay?"

"Can I ask you a question?" he repeats.

"A question?"

"Yeah. A question." I blink at him still, trying to understand.

"What kind of question?" He shakes his head at me and smiles.

Zander has a good smile.

He's *always* had a good smile. Even when he got drunk and broke his front tooth in half, his smile was still great.

"Yes or no, pip?"

God. I love that too, the nickname he used to call me because I was so much smaller than him when I was five and he was nine.

A *pipsqueak.*

Even when I grew into the height I inherited from my parents, towering over half of the boys in high school, he still called me that.

Pip.

"Yeah," I answer, because what else would I even say? I've trusted him this far, far enough to drive to some undisclosed location with him.

"How many kids do you want?"

The question shocks me.

"What?" I say, my groggy mind still not totally there. Maybe I misunderstood.

"Just a question, pip. How many? Four? One? None?"

"Three," I answer without guarding myself.

"Three?" he asks, curiosity in his words.

"Yeah. Three. You guys . . . You guys had it good. With three of you, there was always someone to play with. Always someone around."

There's a pause while he thinks.

"Yeah. Three is good."

Silence takes over the car again, but his hand doesn't let go, his calloused thumb continuing to brush over the skin of my hand, a silent metronome that sends me back to sleep.

TEN
DAYLIGHT
-ZOE-

I wake a few times in the night as Zee takes back roads to wherever he's headed to, following him into random gas stations for coffee refills and bathroom breaks, but mostly snoozing the rest of the ride.

But the next time the car comes to a stop, Zee putting it into park, I keep my eyes closed, my head against the cool window, caught in that space between asleep and awake.

Then I feel it.

One, two, three.

Pause.

One, two, three.

Zee's easy, unobtrusive way of waking me.

My eyes open slowly, looking through the dash to see the ocean, the sky a dark blue. Not night, but not morning yet.

"Morning," he says, and I look over at him, his eyes solemn as he takes me in.

I get the feeling he's been staring at me for a while, like he's been watching me drift and snooze, his own mind moving through some far-off thoughts as he does.

"What?" I ask, confused and delusional.

"Morning, pip."

"It's not morning," I say, even though when I look at the screen, the time tells me it's just past six.

Normally, I'd be up thirty minutes before this, ready to take on the day.

"Almost." He tips his chin to the sky in front of us. "Sunrise."

"What?" I ask, a parrot.

"We're watching the sunrise on the first day of our road trip."

"*What?*"

"You've always liked the sunrise."

I don't respond because he's right.

I just don't know what to say.

I don't know how he knows that, either.

"When we'd stay in that cabin in the Poconos, you'd wake up first, nudge Luna until she woke up, and her grumbling would wake everyone else. You'd sit on that front deck with whoever you could con into sitting with you, watch the sun rise."

"You never woke up for it," I say, remembering how he would pull the blankets over his head and tell me to, "Go away, pip."

"Not a morning person."

"It's morning now," I say. "You seem pretty chipper."

"You are a morning person," he says as if that explains it.

I guess it does, in a way that, again, I don't want to look into too much.

We sit there, long minutes passing as the dark blue starts to turn and the soft waves in the bay begins to become more and more recognizable as light hits them.

"Why did we never work, Zo?" Zander asks, his voice quiet. I'm still groggy from shitty car sleep, but not too groggy to understand what he's asking.

Still, I play dumb.

"What?" I ask, feigning confusion. We're sitting in the Jeep, staring at the water, waiting for the sun to rise. The sky has started to lighten, but it's still a milky mess of blues and grays with the faintest hint of an orange.

"Everyone thought it would be us. It never was," he says as if I didn't say what.

As if he knows I'm faking not understanding.

I can't keep pretending.

My voice goes low as I answer.

"Zander. We never . . . I never . . ." I don't know what to say, how to put it, how to explain.

And fuck, I'm *scared*.

A conversation like this . . . it could change everything.

But aren't we already, in a way? Changing everything?

We're just a handful of hours into this road trip, and I've never been more confused in my life.

"But I did," he whispers, the words so soft I almost don't hear them. I open my mouth to answer, but nothing comes out. Words swirl in my mind, variations of the same, safe answer and new, scarier options. Confessions and explanations.

"Look," he says, louder now, interrupting my thoughts and tipping his chin to the ocean as the sun finally breaks over the horizon.

When I look, the daylight hits the sky, turning it into a vibrant mess of cotton candy colors—pinks and blues and oranges and yellows.

"God. It's beautiful," I say, letting myself relax, to move on from the conversation.

To pretend it didn't happen.

I need that, to pretend. Because I don't think I could handle the hope of it, the hope of him.

"Yeah, it is," he says, and when I look at him, I realize he isn't looking at the sky at all.

His eyes are on me.

ELEVEN
JUMP THEN FALL
-ZANDER-

We don't stay long, just long enough to watch the sunrise and for Zoe to wake up before we start to head out. I drive inland, far from the coast, wasting time, liking sitting next to her as she wakes up, as she reads some book about creating habits and routines that I kind of want to throw out the window, as she dances when a song she likes comes on.

Eventually, though, we need to stop for some kind of sustenance.

"You hungry?" I ask, and just then, like the words brought forth action, her stomach rumbles.

"Uh, yeah, I guess. Do we have time to stop for food?"

"It's a road trip, Zo. We'll stop at some junk food place and stock up, eat while I head back east."

"East?"

"Yeah. I booked a room in a little town on the water." She stares at me, and I expect more questions.

Asking where.

Or why.

Or, what I most dread—*can she pay for half?*

I would say no to all of them.

The point of this trip isn't even a destination.

It's about forcing her to spend time with me and getting the opportunities I need to show her what this should be between us.

"Why not sit down and eat?" she asks, and I shake my head.

"Nope."

"Why not?"

"Told you. It's a road trip. We'll have plenty of time for real meals, but the first day of a road trip means junk food in the car, period."

"We can't eat in my car," she says, crossing her arms on her chest.

"Why not?"

"Because . . . crumbs." She looks at me like *I'm* the insane one for even thinking about doing such a thing. I laugh and shake my head at her as I change lanes.

"You gotta live a little, Zo. Maybe *that's* your problem."

It's most definitely her problem.

I don't quite understand the *why* of it—how she became this way, why she went from the carefree girl I grew up with to this regimented and, quite honestly, boring version of herself, but I plan to find out.

"What?"

"Your midlife crisis or whatever," I say, referencing her breakup and the sudden quitting of her job.

"I'm not having a midlife crisis," she says, but her cheeks go pink.

I remember Luna telling me otherwise—that something snapped in her mind that night they spent together, and she up and changed everything about her life nearly overnight.

Personally, I don't think it's a midlife crisis, though.

I think it's the real Zoe finally taking herself back and realizing the life she'd been leading wasn't fulfilling her.

And while I think there's a huge chance she'll slip backward, fall back into old habits if she lets herself, go back to a boring life with a safe job that she doesn't like, I'll do everything in my power to make sure she gets every wake-up call to stop her from doing that.

"I know that, but do you?" I ask, looking at her.

She stares at me, trying to read between the lines. I smile and shake my head.

God, the woman can't let anything be, can she?

"Were you happy?" I ask point blank, staring at her.

She doesn't answer, so I keep talking, filling in the quiet.

"Were you happy in the city? Working for some giant corporation, dating some boring fucking douche, living your regimented little life?" I pause, waiting to see if she'll answer. "Because if you were, if you were happy in that life and you didn't drop it all when you realized you were miserable, I'll take you back home right now. If you didn't start to panic a bit because you want something new, something that lights your soul up, and just don't know how to get it, we'll go right to Springbok Hills, and I'll stare at the apartment listings in the city for you until my eyes cross."

She bites her lip. *She can't say it. Can't say she was happy.*

"But if you want me to help you figure out who you are, who you want to be, then we do things my way. We go on a trip with no real itinerary; we make random stops to look at some big fuckin' yarn ball or pickle store or a damn petting zoo because it seems fun. We shut off our phones and we drive. You give yourself the time to figure out where you are and where you want to be."

This time, I stop for good.

I let her think.

And I pray she doesn't tell me to go back home, that her safe life is what she wants.

I don't know how I'd react, to be honest.

But thankfully, she sighs.

"How have we gotten to this? We were just talking about eating in my car, not my life and how I am or am not enjoying my current path."

"Because it's all the same. Your problem is you're not *living*. You're spending every second of every day trying to fit some weird mold you think your mom and dad or whoever made for you, and it's clear to everyone but you that you're miserable."

Her eyes go wide, and some color leaves her face.

"I don't think . . . " she starts, but her voice trails off, unable to finish.

"Why'd you quit your job, Zoe?" I ask.

I don't mention the boyfriend.

I don't care about the boyfriend, not really.

"I . . . I . . ."

I don't fill in. I don't take over.

I know she wants me to, wants me to fill in the gap so she doesn't have to answer.

But I don't. Instead, I keep driving, eyes on the road.

Minutes pass before I hear her.

During that time, I think she's let it go, that she doesn't plan on answering, that I pushed her too hard, too fast.

But then she speaks, her voice low and almost scared.

"I was bored."

There it is.

"You want to work on living life, Zoe?" I ask.

There's a pause, a long one while I wait for her to answer once again. And then she sighs, tipping her chin toward a sign for a rest area at the next exit.

"Let's go get some junk food and eat in the car."

And it's small—infinitesimal, really—but it's a win.

TWELVE
I'D LIE
-ZOE-

"I'm gonna run to the bathroom first, okay?" I say to Zander as we walk into the big rest area. "I want to wash my face and whatnot." He smiles at me and nods.

"I'll be here, grabbing snacks and drinks."

I fight the urge to tell him not to pick anything that is too messy, instead walking back to the bathroom with my toiletries bag in my purse and trying not to let my mind stay on our strange situation for too long.

I fail, of course.

I fail hard.

Because *what on Earth is happening right now?*

How has my life changed so drastically in just a week?

In eighteen hours, even.

And what the hell is Zander's plan?

My mind flits through a million and seven things he could be working toward, and none of them feel right, except for one that I will never let my mind sit on too long.

What if his plan is me?

What if he is finally being the brave one and jumping on the first time I can remember when we're both single? What if he saw an opportunity, and he's making a break for it?

It couldn't be that, I think as I wash my hands, staring into the mirror. The hair around my hairline is going curly again. My regular blowout is not built for humidity and salt air, but I'll have to worry about that later.

Because as I dry my hands, all I can think about is what Zander said when we waited for the sunrise.

"Why did we never work, Zo?"

———————

"You good?" Zee has three stuffed plastic bags on his arms.

"What's that?" I ask, confused, tipping my chin to the bags.

"Provisions. You good?"

I glare at him. "You got all of that while I was in the bathroom?"

"No idea what you were doing in there for fifteen minutes."

Having a mental breakdown, I think to myself.

Zander just smiles.

"I want to get a coffee," I say, rummaging in my purse to grab my wallet.

"Got it," he says, turning to where he has two coffees sitting on a shelf—one hot, one iced.

He hands me the iced one.

I stare at it like it might bite me if I accept it.

"Take it, Zo," he says. "Let's get on the road."

"What is it?"

"What?"

"What is it? I'm very particular—"

"Upside-down caramel macchiato with almond milk." I blink once, twice. "Though the barista chick informed me that an upside-down macchiato is just a latte."

I stare at him again.

"Are you ready to go, Zoe?" He's looking at me like he doesn't understand what's going on, doesn't understand why I'm so confused.

To be fair, I *also* have no idea what's going on.

But I guess that's all part of his plan. So instead of arguing, I just nod, grabbing the coffee he somehow knew exactly how I would order and heading back to the car, confused but refusing to even ask.

Because I decided in the bathroom that while we're on this trip, I'm going to go with the flow. Not something I do well or even *like* doing, but it feels right in this situation.

And Zander feels like the right person to do it with.

"These are yours," Zander says once we get settled in the car after he drives over to the gas pump part of the rest area. He hands me one of the three bags, and I stare at it like it might bite.

"What is it?"

"Jesus, Zoe, just take it." I do, the bag dipping with the unexpected weight. He reaches for the door once he lets go, hopping out and stopping only when I call his name.

"What are you doing?" Again, he looks at me like I'm insane, tipping his chin to the gas pumps.

"Gotta fill the tank, babe."

Ignore it, my mind tells my heart when it flips with the name.

"Just . . . wait," I say, tipping my head toward the little stand where the attendant stands.

He smiles big, that one he makes when he thinks Luna or I am being slightly dumb and he knows he'll be able to use it against us for eternity.

Oh fuck.

"We're not in Jersey anymore, pip. Gotta pump your own gas here."

"Oh," I say, looking over and remembering. I've never needed to fill up in the city because my car was never with me, and anytime it was, I filled up in Jersey since it was usually cheaper.

"Wanna learn?" he asks, grabbing the pump and holding it up.

I kind of do.

But the bag in my lap is begging me for attention, and honestly, I'm kind of embarrassed already, so instead, I shake my head.

"No, not this time." He just smiles and nods, slamming the door and leaving me with my music and this bag.

But I almost regret it when I start to look through it.

Magazines.

Home design and decor magazines. Four of them.

My fingers tremble just a hair as I open one, flipping through to see this year's trends, what colors are expected to be popular in the next four years, and what's "out."

My mind goes to the MASH card, to the days when I thought this was my destiny.

When I'd clip pictures and make mood boards and bring them to my mom. When she'd smile and take me to the store so I could redo my room or the living room or the sitting room for the fifth time.

Before reality and common sense and "safe careers" were even on my radar.

I'm still lost in thought when Zee hops back in.

"Ready?" he asks, looking at me.

He doesn't even see that my hands are still slightly shaking.

"What are these?"

"Uh, magazines?" he asks, turning the key in the ignition.

"I know they're magazines, Zander. I'm not an idiot," I say with a roll of my eyes. "I mean, why did you get them?"

"Because the book you're reading looks so fucking boring, it's putting *me* to sleep."

"What? No, it's not. It's very interesting," I lie. "It's about how to add habits into your life to become more productive."

"Right there. That's your fuckin' problem," he says with a shake of his head.

"Excuse me?"

"That's your problem. You're so damn worried about being productive and creating habits and routine that you've forgotten how to live life."

"I have not. I—"

"What do you do for fun, Zoe?" he asks, hands on the wheel but looking at me.

I stare back.

"I—" I start, but then my mind blanks.

What do I do for fun?

"I—" I try again but come up blank *again.*

No, I definitely have things I do for fun.

He raises an eyebrow, and the act basically makes my brain blank even further.

"You're putting me on the spot. Of course, I can't think of something."

"Fine, ask me."

"What?"

"Put me on the spot." I roll my eyes.

"What do *you* do for fun, Zander?"

"I fish. I run. I watch the game with the guys. I go hiking with Hunter even though I hate the fucking bugs. I sit at the bar with Luna and talk shit. I work on my house. I work on my car—"

"Your car is a piece of shit," I say as if that makes my lack of hobbies any less glaring.

"Doesn't matter. I spend my time working on it because it makes me happy. Now tell me. What do you do to relax yourself?"

I can't tell him that I use my vibrator, right?

That's a terrible, horrible road to walk down with this man.

I give a safe answer.

"I read."

"Read about how to make your life even more boring, predictable, and safe."

My jaw tightens.

"I go for walks."

"What kind?" he asks, looking at me, and I don't know how, but he caught me again.

"Treadmill walks," I say quietly.

"And what do you do on them?"

I look at my calendar for the day and plan out my to-do list.

He shakes his head before I can say anything.

"You need hobbies, Zo. You need to stop reading and worrying about bettering or streamlining or whatever-ing your life. Instead, just go *live* it. That's what this is, Zoe. This is a week for you to remember how to live your life. A week of no plans, no phone calendar. No fuckin' self-help books. A week of making crumbs in your car and cleaning them out when we get home because it will not make or break your life. A week of doing spontaneous shit just because it's fun." He stares at me, and his eyes look so genuine, I almost can't breathe. "You need that, Zoe. You need that wake-up call."

"Why are you the one to give it to me?" I ask quietly. "What makes you so qualified?"

"Because from the time you were five, I could always convince you to do crazy shit with me. I just spent the last ten years or so forgetting that that was my self-appointed job."

I remember the time he's talking about instantly, of course.

It's one of my earliest memories.

We were at the community pool, and Luna and I just passed our swimming lessons, meaning we were now allowed in the deep end without swimmies on.

And we could finally jump off the diving board.

It was a big moment for two little girls living in a small town.

Luna was so excited, having watched her brother do it for years, but I was *terrified*.

I spend two weeks that summer walking over to the diving board, tiptoeing to the end, then sitting on my butt and backing off, the height and the risk much too scary for me.

Until Zander held my hand and jumped with me.

"Take the leap, Zoe," he says, repeating the words he said when I was five, and I can almost see the memory playing in his eyes as well. "Take the leap and live unplanned for a week with me."

And because he's right—he's always been the one to push me out of my comfort zone—I nod.

Even though I'm terrified, I nod.

And when he smiles his giant, boyish smile with my acceptance and starts to drive out of the rest area. I think I made a good decision.

A great decision, even.

THIRTEEN
FEARLESS
-ZOE-

"You're killing me with this playlist, you know," Zander says, and I smile.

Payback is a bitch, I suppose.

"We had a deal."

"A deal I'm regretting."

"Can't handle a little pop princess?"

"A little, yes. An entire road trip?" He looks to the roof of my Jeep and shakes his head before looking back at the road. "You're lucky I like you, pip," he says, and then silence takes over the car as my heart flip-flops just a bit.

The next song in my playlist comes on, and I sigh.

"God, I love this song," I say, sitting back in the seat and kicking my feet up on the dash, my red Converse resting there.

I try not to think about the fact that in any other circumstance, I would lose my mind over someone putting dirty shoes on the dash.

But with Zee . . .

"You don't say," he says with a laugh. "I would think there is not a single song on *your* playlist that you don't love." I reach over and smack him in the arm.

"Shut up. I just love this one a little more. I have since I was a kid."

That boyish smile takes over his face, and even with his sunglasses covering his eyes, I can still see the fine lines starting to form in the corners.

It's strange, watching a face you've memorized since you were five change and grow old.

"Yeah? Why this one?" he asks, and because he seems genuinely interested, I answer.

"I don't know. It's just . . . When I was younger, I'd listen to it. It's pretty, you know? Childish, but it's the kind of thing little girls think love is about." I laugh and shake my head. "It's silly. The idea that someone is so crazy for you they want to drop everything and dance in the parking lot or kiss in the rain. I was raised on *The Notebook* and fairy tales and Taylor Swift. It's hard not to idealize dumb things, I guess."

He gives a noncommittal sound, and I listen to the lyrics as we drive before realizing he's slowing the car, moving it to the side of the road toward an exit. I look at the map on the display of my car, trying to see if he knows something I don't, when the GPS rebels.

"We don't get off here, Zee. We've got ten more miles on this highway."

"Detour," is all he says before pulling into an abandoned parking lot, the streetlight flicking on in the approaching dusk. He puts the car in park, taps the screen of my phone until he restarts the song we were listening to, and rolls all the windows down.

"What are you—" I start, but then he's turning the sound to full volume and stepping out.

I watch as he walks around the front of the SUV, frozen in place as he opens my door, leans over to undo my seat belt, and gives me his hand.

I take it, of course.

I think I'd follow him to Hell if I got to hold his hand when I did it.

He tugs until I step out, and he walks me back five or so steps before pulling me in, his arms around my waist, my hands instinctively moving around his neck.

"What are we doing?" I whisper, familiar music playing as I dance in the headlights in a parking lot with Zander Davidson.

"We're dancing in a parking lot, Zoe."

I let that be.

I don't dare question it.

Because right now, I'm doing something I daydreamed about, and I'm doing it because I mentioned in passing that I thought it was romantic as a kid.

So I let it be, and I let him sway me, forcing my brain not to overthink this for once.

Eventually, he breaks the silence between us.

"Wanting a man to dance with you in a parking lot because he's so fucking in love with you he can't wait to get you home and into his arms isn't childish. Thinking you're too manly to pull over and give your girl that? That's childish."

Again, I don't respond. I let my fingers touch the longish hair at the base of his neck, combing through it and letting my mind pretend this is us.

That this is normal.

The song changes, "Lover" coming on next, and I try not to lean into the idea that it's the universe speaking to me, telling me we could be more.

One of Zee's hands moves from my waist until it's resting on my cheek, tipping my face up to look at him.

His lips are centimeters from my own and finally, I can't resist asking him, to question what's happening in some way.

"What are you doing to me?" I whisper against his lips.

"Whatever it takes to convince you to be mine," he says, and my heart stops.

"Zee, I've been yours for as long as I can remember," I confess because it's the truth, and in this moment, I only have the truth as an option.

There has never been a moment where deep in my soul, this wasn't what I wanted.

Where *Zander* wasn't what I wanted.

That desire has changed with age, moved from just wanting the cute boy who was my best friend's older brother so we could be sisters to something more. To wanting the man who goes to the diner on Sunday mornings because he knows his mom is struggling with being alone.

The man who took on the peewee team because he knew those boys needed a role model.

The man who will always take on an extra shift to cover for someone else because he thinks their families are more important than him living the bachelor life.

The man who once again proves we're always on the same wavelength.

"No, that's not true. That was rainbows and butterflies and the world is magical Zoe. I had that one, but I never got to keep her. That one never had time to be mine. She is right person, wrong time Zoe." My breath stops. "I'm winning *right now* Zoe. The one with the perpetually broken heart—the one who thinks this would be hard. The one who has social constructs in her mind of who she should be and who I should be, and who we should and shouldn't be together. I'm winning the Zoe who thinks she has to do it all, even if none of it makes her happy."

And there it is.

He sees it.

He sees that he always had a version of me, but he doesn't have the version of me I am right now.

"What if she's too scared? What if she's too far gone to be won?" I ask, my voice low.

"Well, I've got a week to try, don't I?" he asks, and then it happens.

Alexander Michael Davidson dips his head down as he dances with me in a parking lot on a whim, and he presses his soft lips to mine.

The air in my lungs seizes, but my body knows what to do.

My hands move to his head, pulling him in closer, forcing him to kiss me deeper, leaning into this.

Because every molecule of this, of kissing Zander, feels so right.

Right enough that I'm able to block out the reality of where we are right now, to block out the version of me that would question this.

His hand moves up my head, tugging at the ponytail and tossing it into the parking lot before his fingers are in my hair, holding me there as he deepens the kiss.

His tongue taps at my lips, begging for entrance, and I have no choice but to give him that, parting my lips and touching my tongue to his.

And then the kiss changes.

It moves from a sweet first kiss that has my inner fifteen-year-old squealing to something so much more.

Something that has heat flooding into the veins of my thirty-year-old body.

A tiny moan comes from me, and Zander groans, his hand on my waist pulling me in closer.

We're no longer swaying.

We're no longer dancing.

My hands are on his neck, clinging to him as he devours me, as heat rolls through me, tingling in my spine and pooling in my core.

Holy fuck, I want this man.

I don't think I've ever wanted a man more than I want him right now, on the side of the road, groping me.

Then a car honks, stopping our side-of-the-road make-out session, and it breaks the magic.

Not fully, but enough for Zander to break to kiss, to move his lips away from me, and to press his forehead to mine.

His breathing is heavy, mirroring my own as he stares at me, that boyish smile on his lips.

God, I want to kiss him again.

I smile back, but then it starts to fade as reality enters my mind.

He sees it, of course.

He sees everything.

He jokes that Tony's the good detective, that he's in the field for a reason and Zee is just there because of dumb luck, but no one has ever been able to read me the way he does.

"Give this a chance," he says, his voice low. And then, like he can't resist, he dips his head down once more, and there's another peck of his lips to mine.

"It won't work," I whisper, my mind winning the battle again, doubt creeping in.

"How do you know?" he asks,

"Because you're you." I don't even know what I mean by that.

"I'm yours, Zoe. Have been for a while," he says, and my mind reels for a moment.

Zander is mine.

Insert ten-year-old Zoe doing literal cartwheels.

But reality hits once again.

We can't do this.

If we do this and it fails, not a single part of me will be able to face him again. To face this man I built childhood fairy tales on.

If I let those fairy tales I locked in a childish dreamscape into my reality, there's the opportunity for disappointment.

Grave fucking disappointment.

And what happens if you give your dreams a chance and it turns out they're trash? Or unrealistic? Or impossible?

Your reality shatters.

I wonder for a split second if I spent these past years of safety and security remembering the possibility, the joy, and the exuberance of *potential* with Zander.

I wonder if I never let myself have it because if it failed, it would ruin a part of me.

"It's not that easy," I whisper.

"Why not?" he asks.

I refuse to tell him that.

To tell him about my little girl dreams and how crushing them by testing them in the real world would destroy me in a way I'd never recover from.

"Because . . . Because if something happens, it impacts our families."

Safe.

A safe answer.

"You're my best friend's brother. My dad's employee. Our parents have been best friends for decades. Our families are so intertwined, and we'd fuck that up."

He stares at me, and I wonder for a moment how much he can see through me.

And then that thought washes away when he smiles.

"Pretend."

"Pretend?"

His smile grows like he's coming to some kind of understanding.

"Yeah. Pretend. Pretend that it's just us. Pretend that we're together, and it's easy. Pretend there are no complications, no job interview."

My mind works over reasons I need to say no.

It runs through a million situations and circumstances and ways it could go terribly, terribly wrong.

"Even when we were kids, you were one of my favorite people on Earth, Zoe. When you're home, even though shit was tense sometimes, I fuckin' love spending time with you. We laugh. We chat. We talk. It's always been that way. Pretend it's just a little bit more. That's it."

He's right.

I've always liked spending time with Zander.

I've always loved to be around him, to hear his thoughts, to balance on my mental scale how different his mind works from mine.

And even now, even though as a kid I was irrecoverably in love with the boy version of him, even though I turned him down—we always gravitate to each other when we're in the same room.

Always.

Christmas.

Birthdays.

Barbecues.

God, weddings.

We laughed and talked through Luna and Tony's entire wedding, making fun of everyone around us, making wide eyes at each other during the vows.

He's just one of my favorite people.

It's why I said yes, I guess, to this whole thing.

And maybe he's right.

Maybe that's what I need—to be spontaneous, to say yes. To play pretend.

So as the song quiets, changing into another, I move to my tiptoes, press my lips to Zander's one more time, feeling the full body flush it brings me, and nod.

"Yeah. Okay," I say. "I'll play pretend."

And the smile he gives me makes it all fucking worth any turmoil that will probably come later.

FOURTEEN
THE VERY FIRST NIGHT
-ZOE-

"Zander, this place is way too nice," I say later that night as he parks in front of a cute, historic bed-and-breakfast.

"Nope." He shakes his head and stares straight ahead.

"What?"

"Nope, I'm not dealing with this shit." I glare at him.

I should have known this would be an issue with Zander.

He's a pain, but he's a gentleman.

I should have thought this out better. Made a game plan to make sure this trip was fair and even.

"How much did it cost?" I ask.

"Nope." He pops the "p" and still doesn't look my way.

"What?" I repeat.

"Nope, I'm not telling you that." It's like he's rehearsed this conversion already in his head.

"Well then, how am I going to spl—"

"Hell no."

I blink at him, and he glares at me before turning the car off and walking out.

We drove far into Virginia, taking minimal highways and stopping at anything that looked interesting until we looped back to the coast, landing here in a little beach town in North Carolina.

Interesting included a petting zoo of mini pigs where Zee took my picture holding a tiny, pink, squealing piglet and then promptly told me, "there is no universe where your neurotically clean ass could have one."

And I mean, fair enough.

Plus, I don't think any apartments in the city will allow for that, I'd thought to myself quietly.

I quickly threw that thought and any other regarding apartment shopping or job hunting or starting anew in the city away.

Pretend, Zee had said.

I can do that.

Even if a part of me worried that might destroy me, pretending with Zander. Giving my heart the possibility and then tearing it away before I can even fully enjoy it.

I'm still lost in that thought when my door opens, jolting me back into the now.

"Come on," he says, his hand out to me.

I don't take it.

"Why won't you tell me how much this costs?"

"Because then you're going to try and pay for it." I roll my eyes.

"Why won't you let me pay for half?"

He sighs and closes his eyes, taking a deep breath and counting to five.

I've seen his father do this exact move a million times over the years in regard to some crazy shit his mother is asking of him, and some strange, far-off part of me smiles.

"This is my vacation. I'm just dragging you along with me."

"Zander—"

"Please. It's been a long fucking day. I didn't sleep last night. I'm good, but I'm man enough to admit I'm tired and cranky, and if I have to argue with you, I might say something I regret."

I stare at him, impressed.

Most men would keep going, keep pushing.

Most men I know would never be so hyperaware of their own emotions, so detached from some social idea of masculinity, that they would *never* admit that kind of thing.

But this is Zander Davidson.

And Zander Davidson was raised by Janet Davidson.

It tracks, to be honest.

So instead of arguing back (my own go-to), I nod, grab his hand, and let him help me out of the Jeep.

He doesn't let go once I'm on solid footing.

Instead, he closes the door, steps in front of me, and backs me into the car, his body on mine.

"I like that," he says, his voice low.

"Wha-what?" I ask, my heart racing in a way I think he can probably see through my shirt.

"Like that. How you think about it, let it go. How we work through shit."

"I didn't—"

"I don't mind how you fight me on every fucking thing. Not at all. Makes my cock hard, babe, you fighting me. But I like how when you know it's important to me, you stop. You think about it, think about if it's worth it to you, and make a decision that will benefit both of us."

I did do that, didn't I?

"Zander—"

His hand moves, brushing my hair back, hair that's still wild from the ponytail I haven't put back in.

"I like a lot of things about you, Zoe. I'm sure I'll find more, too. But I want you to know right now, that? That I might like most of all."

Before I can respond, he leans in, pressing his lips to mine, and any hesitation, nerves, or second-guessing melts away when his lips touch mine.

Because Zander Davidson is kissing me again.

My arms wrap around his neck, and I move to my tiptoes as they do, leaning into his kiss.

When he finally breaks it, we're both breathing heavily as he presses his forehead to mine.

"Fuck. Pretending with you is gonna be a fuck of a lot of fun, pip," he says, and even though he smiles, even though I know what he means, even though that's all I can handle right now, a tiny sliver of me I don't want to acknowledge is disappointed with his words.

We walk into the room at the adorable B&B and instantly, I know something is wrong.

"There's only one bed," I say, looking around. I'm holding my purse, and Zee has my two bags along with his tiny little backpack that probably only has underwear and deodorant in it.

"Yeah, well, you played up the adorable couple thing so well, I'm not sure what you expected."

I glare at him because it was *him* who tricked that woman—I barely even said a word.

He's talking about how, when we walked into the building, the cutest older woman greeted us and treated us like an adorable married couple, gushing over how perfect we looked together.

I, of course, had no idea how to react, smiling awkwardly, but Zander put his arm around my waist, pulling me close and pressing a kiss to my hair.

God, god, *god.*

It would be so easy.

He walks into the room unfazed, placing my bags that he insisted on carrying in gently on the bed before tossing his own backpack to the floor without care.

"I mean . . . I don't . . . how . . ." My anxiety starts to build as I look around.

"We'll share, Zo," Zee says, and my eyes go wide. I feel it. I move over to the cute antique chair in the corner, placing my purse there before walking back to the center of the room, where I begin pacing.

"We can't share a bed, Zander."

"We can actually do whatever the hell we want, Zoe," he says, and when I look at him, he's smiling. "This isn't a family vacation where the boys get the bunks and the girls share the pull-out."

He, of course, is referencing the many family vacations we've taken over the years: heading up to the cabins in the Poconos for a week in the summer. Fishing and swimming in the lake and s'mores around a fire were pretty much just a given when we were all together.

And he's right.

The boys always got the bunks or cots (the Davidsons always brought their not-quite-adopted but sort of adopted kid, Tony, with them as well, making the "boy" count odd with Zee, his younger brother Ace, and Tony) while Luna and I got to share the big pull-out couch.

We loved it.

Those trips have always been some of my favorite childhood memories.

"But . . ." He turns to me, and the words dry up in my mouth.

I don't know what to say.

Especially when I see the look in his eyes, like there is no universe where he'll be giving in, where he'll be cracking under the pressure I'm presenting him.

Like there's nothing I can say to convince him that sharing a bed is a bad, bad idea.

"I don't like sleeping with people. I like my space," I say, trying to give him any reason why he can't sleep with me. He steps closer, and the breaths become harder to pull into my lungs.

For a moment, I wonder how bad of an idea it *actually* would be for Zee to sleep in the same bed as me.

A terrible idea, Zoe. Terrible. The worst idea ever, possibly, common sense says.

"I get hot." He takes another step closer to me and all I can think about is the way it felt with his lips on mine. "And I move around a lot."

My voice cracks with my words.

My brain moves to how I don't think I'll ever recover from that, from knowing how damn perfect it is to kiss this man.

I can't handle another kiss where the world quiets and seems to make sense for just a moment.

When my heart gets a chance to speak instead of logic.

"One bed, Zo. I'm not sleeping on the floor."

"I'll sleep on the floor," I offer quickly, taking a step back, trying to put space between us.

He steps forward, closing the gap I widened.

It's strange, the inner turmoil I'm feeling.

Part of me wants to keep my feet planted in place, to let him come closer.

Part of me wants to say, *Yeah, let's do this. Let's sleep in the same bed and forget about reality.*

Part of me wants to say, *Let's do things* other *than sleep in that big comfy bed.*

But the logical side, the side that was built from expectations I need to meet and common sense and reality, tells me it would be the absolute worst idea on the planet if I sleep in the same bed as Zander Davidson.

"The fuck you will," he says, and as I step back once more, my body hits the wall. "You'll sleep in that bed next to me. I'll give you your space."

His voice is low and smooth, and it makes me not want space.

Not when it's space from Zander.

God, get it the fuck together, Zoe.

"Seriously, it's fine. You didn't sleep last night. I did. You should get a good night's sleep tonight."

"And I will. Next to you."

Now with my back to the wall, his hands move to either side of my face, and he's smiling that stupid, handsome smile that I love more than I've ever let myself admit.

"Zander—"

"You agreed to pretend."

My heart stops beating.

"Zander—"

"Pretend, pip," he whispers, breath hitting my lips.

And that's what does it.

What has me staring at him.

What has me nodding.

Pip.

The name he's been calling me for as long as I can remember, the way it comes off his lips the same something like *baby* would. The way I'm dying to close the gap, to let him kiss me, to remind myself how good his lips felt on mine.

It's all pretend, after all, right?

When his lips tip up in a smile, when he leans forward, not to press his lips to mine but instead to my forehead, I can't help but wonder if that was a terrible choice.

If mentally agreeing to pretend won't be my downfall.

FIFTEEN
I THINK HE KNOWS
-ZOE-

Hours later, I'm counting Zander's breaths.

Clearly, I'm insane, lying in a bed next to my best friend's brother, him over the sheets, me under them as if the thin cotton would stop my body from recognizing his if it touched me, and I'm counting the man's breaths.

That's not normal, right?

To lie in bed wide awake after barely a few hours of shitty car sleep and not be able to pass out because you're counting the breaths a man is taking?

But what if it's a man who, when he was a kid, your childhood self was convinced would be the one for you? A man who is somehow slowly doing every perfect, sweet move effortlessly, like he has an instruction manual to my soul?

A man who, when he kissed me, my mind went blissfully blank.

I think about that first kiss. The way his lips moved against mine as our bodies were locked together, standing in a parking lot in the middle of nowhere. How the song changed and my brain barely registered it.

How his tongue touched mine, and my body erupted in chills. How heat took over me.

How I wouldn't have been upset if it went further.

How, if we were somewhere else, I think it *would have* gone further.

What would he have done? I can't help but wonder . . .

I've heard stories, whispers of his prowess in bed—old flings gabbing at the bar, forgetting his sister owned Luna's. It was back before he started being more selective, started avoiding dating in town.

Would he have taken me into the car?

My mind starts to create the entire scenario in intimate detail, my own hand inexplicably moving down my body as it does.

Zander's asleep, I tell myself. *Maybe this will help me feel less pulled to him.*

Yes, that's it. Let me just get this out of my system and we'll be good. God, I can't even remember the last time I gave myself an orgasm, much less a man did.

That has to be the reason my body is so on edge after a single kiss.

With that small permission, I fall completely into my fantasy.

We'd get into the car in a flurry—before we opened the door, he would pin me to the side, letting me feel how hard he was. He'd grind into me, and I'd moan his name.

Fuck, Zee. I need you, I'd say, and he'd moan into my neck, a hand on my hip pulling me closer before grinding into me, hitting right where I need him while I'm on my tippy toes.

Then he'd kiss my neck once more before moving, opening the door, and pressing the seat down before helping me, nearly throwing me inside.

He'd lay me down, lying on top of me despite the cramped quarters, and he'd *kiss me*, tasting me, moving to my neck, licking there, biting there. A hand would move to my sweatpants, creeping under the waistband and panties, moving down until a single finger touched my clit, dipping into my wet.

Fuuuuuck, he'd moan. *You're fucking soaked, baby. Is that for me?* His voice would be low and gravelly, full of need and want, and it would make me buck my hips, trying to get more. He'd laugh, teasing me like he always does, but this time in a different way. A different kind of tease.

His finger would move down painfully slowly until he hit my entrance, and I'd moan loud as it slipped inside.

I let a tiny breath out as my own hand does just that, pausing to make sure my bed partner is still asleep.

This is so fucking stupid.

So fucking risky.

But fuck, if it doesn't make me a little bit wetter, doesn't make it just a bit better, the fear of him catching me.

Maybe next time, I'll make a fantasy of what would happen if he caught me like this, fingering myself in bed next to him.

I shake my head *no.* This is a one-time thing. Just enough to take the edge off.

That's my issue, obviously. It's so clear now. I don't like Zander beyond a childhood crush. I just . . . I just need an orgasm.

My mind falls back into my daydream.

He'd fuck me with just one finger, kissing me the whole time, but as soon as my hands started to fumble with his jeans, he'd stop.

He'd stop and smile that smile that melts me before moving to sit up and working at his pants. He'd keep his eyes on me as he undoes the button, the fly. As he pushed both his jeans and his underwear down enough to free himself, he'd take himself in hand, stroking quickly and hard, once, twice, three times.

A tiny, not quite silent mewl comes from my throat as my fingers work myself in real life, my body stilling again to count his breaths.

Shit.

But he's still asleep and not even moving.

Back in my daydream, Zee helps me push my sweats down, helps me take one leg out, not even caring that the other is wrapped around my ankle still before he grabs my waist, flipping us so I'm straddling him.

Yeah? he'd ask as he positioned the head of his cock at my wet entrance. I'd nod, and he'd groan before slowly, so painfully, torturously slowly, lowering me down onto him.

We'd both moan as he filled me, and fuck if I don't know down to my goddamn soul that he would fill me so damn perfectly.

Fuck, you feel good, he'd say into my neck, hands on my hips helping me move. My fingers move faster, not nearly as good as I imagine *he* would be, but an okay substitute.

One I'm used to, at the very least.

He'd move me faster over him as he got closer, helping me to grind down, the palm of my own hand rubbing on my clit to try and recreate what's happening in my mind, dragging me closer and closer to bliss.

Utter fucking bliss.

And as my fantasy finishes, as imaginary Zee wraps an arm around my waist and holds me down, filling me and groaning into my neck, I come too, trembling just the slightest bit.

But that isn't what has my entire body freezing in panic.

It's the way I moan out his name quietly as I do.

I lie there, my fingers inside me, afraid to move for what feels like an eternity.

Counting his breaths.

Trying to dissect them to make sure they don't sound different, that they haven't changed, that he's still asleep.

When I think I'm safe, I quickly roll out of the bed to pee before lying back down and falling asleep quickly.

But I refuse to acknowledge the fact that my plan didn't work.

How that orgasm, no matter how intense, just barely took the edge off the need my body feels.

Shit.

SIXTEEN
...READY FOR IT?
-ZANDER-

I lie there for what might be hours.

My body is exhausted from driving through the night, from the mental gymnastics I've been putting myself through.

From replaying that kiss in my mind.

I'm exhausted from formulating plans on how to make her see she's mine, that she's always been mine, that we were meant to be together from the start.

I need sleep.

If not because I need my body to work in the morning, then because I need my *mind* to, the mind that needs to figure out how to win Zoe over.

To make "pretending" something that lasts forever.

But my mind.

It won't stop.

Because nearly an hour ago, Zoe moaned my name while her hand worked her clit next to me, and I pretended to sleep through the whole thing.

And now I know.

I know Zoe wants me as badly as I want her, and not in some little-girl way.

Not in a *kisses in parking lots and I want to be my best friend's sister-in-law* way.

The *woman version* of Zoe wants me.

And the only thing my mind is capable of thinking is, *Baby, let the games begin.*

SEVENTEEN
OURS
-ZOE-

I'm groggy when I feel it.

One, two, three.

The squeeze of my hand.

"Wha—?" I say, opening one eye.

Zander's on his side facing me, and the room is dark.

"What?"

"It's midnight," he says in a whisper.

I blink.

I think I'm dreaming this.

That's the only thing that makes sense.

The only reason I can feel his skin on mine, the only reason I "woke" with his hand on mine.

"Can I ask you a question?" he asks, his voice low.

"Mmmm," I murmur to dream Zander, my eyes drifting shut. There's a smile in his voice when he speaks next.

"What are you scared of, Zoe?"

Because it's a dream, I give him the truth.

"That I'll live such a safe life that when I'm old, nothing sticks out."

Silence.

I open my eyes and stare at Dream Zander. His hand moves, brushing my hair back, and now his smile is sad.

Can dream people be sad?

"Okay. Go back to sleep, pip."

And because in my dreamland, I guess I do whatever Zander tells me to, my eyes close and I fall back asleep.

When I wake, Zander is wrapped around me, holding me in place with a leg hitched over my hip.

I slept through the night.

Once I was out, I didn't wake up a single time—not to pee, not for water, not because I was overly warm.

I always wake up *at least* once.

It's always driven all of my exes insane, my quiet tiptoeing in and out of bed each night, sometimes waking them as I do.

But not last night.

Not with Zee, apparently.

I slept from the moment my mind stopped its incessant wondering until just now.

A now where his entire body is draped around me, warm, bare skin against my thin tee shirt since he slept in just a pair of loose shorts.

I try and decode my surroundings without waking Zander.

Where is the top sheet? I think.

I wiggle my toes, feeling the cotton bunched up there.

That explains that, I suppose. I do have to wonder who did it, though.

Was it me, too warm and wanting fewer layers? Or was it Zander, wanting less of a barrier?

But there's no time.

No time at all to over think or try and decode what any of this means.

Because the arm on my waist just tightened.

And scruff is on my neck.

And lips are pressing at the skin beneath my jaw.

And a thumb is swiping the bare skin on my belly where my tee rode up.

And his voice is low and growly when he speaks.

"Morning, pip."

And since my own mind is groggy and I'm clearly not thinking straight, I think I would do nearly anything on this planet to hear that every single morning.

I am so completely fucked.

EIGHTEEN
PEACE
-ZOE-

I demand caffeine when we finally roll out of bed and get dressed.

I'm determined that will help with my undying desire to stay in that big comfy bed with my best friend's brother for an extended amount of time.

He asked me to pretend.

He asked me to pretend after he kissed me, and I agreed.

But I also need to remember that when this trip ends, so does pretending.

I need to protect my peace for future Zoe. The future Zoe whose life is already in confused shambles and will have to live with the knowledge of what it's like to kiss Zander and how good it feels to wake up in his arms.

I contemplate a shower, but the room we're staying in smells like Zander, and he keeps walking around with no shirt on, and the messy bed keeps looking at me, and each time I see it, I think of all the ways we could use it.

So I need out of this room.

Clearly, the lack of caffeine is what's getting to me, what's muddling my thoughts—I need caffeine for a clear mind.

Because all my coffee-deprived self can think of is Zander and the possibilities *pretending* could hold.

I refuse to even let myself start to think about the conversation from yesterday while we watched the sunrise.

Of when he asked me why we never became a thing.

Of his response of, *But I did.*

God, what does that mean? Does it mean he pictured us together? That he pictured it in another lifetime and that chance is gone? That he pictured it and *still* pictures it?

I shake my head.

I can't go there.

If I let my mind go there, I don't think I'd ever want to leave.

And if I never leave, it will be opening a complex web of issues that are so far out of my control.

Like this new job I might have.

And how I'd be living in the city if I got it, and how Zander would stay in Springbrook Hills.

And distance—long or short or somewhere in between—rarely ends well.

And the fact that, if we were to break up, we'd fuck everything up with our families. Families that have been friends since before I was even born.

I can't be the catalyst for a decades-long friendship ending.

So, I force Zander to take me to breakfast, to a little diner he found in town. He, of course, wouldn't let me help look for a place since my phone is still exclusively to be used for music in the car.

I hate to admit how freeing it's been.

Not planning my every move.

Not filling the silence in my brain by doom scrolling on social media.

Not researching restaurants before I go so I know what to order before I even walk in the door.

And I refuse to admit that Zander gave me this.

This peace.

And what it means that he knew I needed it.
Instead, I just force him to caffeinate me.

NINETEEN
PAPER RINGS
-ZANDER-

"Do you remember whenever I'd sleep over at your house on a Saturday, your dad would wake everyone up at the ass crack of dawn and take us to the diner?" Zoe asks, looking around the tiny diner in North Carolina. It's made in an old rail car, the entire place long and narrow. We're sitting in one of the only booth seats, with only one seat on each side.

"He still does it, except it's just my mom now. Sometimes I show up and go with them."

"You wake up at the ass crack of dawn and go to the diner with your parents on a Sunday morning?" she asks, looking confused. "You hate mornings."

I smile because I love that she knows that.

And I love that she knows that my parents like to go to the diner on Sunday mornings.

I love that she knows that I am not a morning person.

I love that we won't have to spend years learning the little things because she's always known me, we've always been around each other.

"Yeah, but my mom's secretly struggling with having no one at home. Some mornings, Lune and Tony go, and when Ace is in town, he goes. We all make an effort. But most weeks, it's just Mom and Pop. She misses having us all around, even if Lune and I still live in town. Going from a house of five to just two . . . Dad says she gets emotional about it." Zoe's face goes soft.

"So on Sunday mornings, you wake up at the ass crack of dawn and go to the diner with your parents." I don't respond, suddenly feeling awkward about it. "Because your mom has an empty nest."

I shrug, thankful the waitress brings us our drinks and interrupts her deep dive.

"You're a good son, you know that, Zander Davison?" I laugh.

"I'm sure my parents would disagree."

Silence takes over as I reach for the sweeteners, pretending to surveil the options.

This trip is supposed to be about Zoe, not me.

Not talking about myself or the shit I do.

"Zee, why are you still in Springbrook Hills?" The question catches me off guard, my fingers fumbling with a white packet.

"What?"

"Why are you still there?" I stop playing with the sugars and look at her. Her eyes are serious and inquisitive, like she's genuinely trying to break down the facts in front of her to find an answer. "Hunter left, but he came back because of Hannah. Luna never left because of Tony. Tony stayed because he's *Tony,* and he's always had Springbrook Hills written in his DNA. Tanner stayed because Ben left, and he felt like he had no choice. Kate came back because of her parents." Her voice trails off.

"And you?"

"Me?"

"Why are you still in town?"

"I asked you first," she says. I smile, and she does as well. "You could have left, gone somewhere more exciting. A city with actual people to protect. Found some girl who didn't grow up idolizing

Mags at the Center or having your dad as their brother's peewee coach."

"Well, now Dean and I are the peewee coaches."

"Exactly. Another example. Why'd you take that over? Because your dad couldn't do it?" I stir the sugar and some cream into my coffee, refusing to tell her she's right.

Not wanting to acknowledge the truth.

The truth that could so very much scare her.

Because I knew you'd always have to come back there, and if I was there and you were tied to that town, we might one day work it out.

"I don't know. I guess I just grew up there, and it felt . . . good. I fit there, you know? Maybe I'm like Tony. Maybe the town's just in my DNA. Can't escape it."

I don't tell her I almost left more times than I can count.

That I had offers for cities. Jersey City and Hoboken both had large agencies desperate for good body guard, and as a man trained by the well respected Joe Thomas, I would have been me in a minute.

But I stayed.

I definitely don't tell her that anytime I got wind that she might be leaving, anytime she had some job interview out of town, I'd start looking again, ready to put roots somewhere new.

To finally get out of a town where I see her at every corner.

The woman who was both always and never mine.

"Yeah," she says, and when I look at her, I see it.

She might not be able to admit it, but she feels that pull too.

"Is it your parents?" I ask.

"What?"

"Your parents. Is that what kept you in town? Or close, at least?"

A sick, twisted part hopes for what I know won't happen, at least not yet.

A part of me hopes that she'll say it's not her parents. That it's me that kept her tethered to the small town she grew up in when she had big, grand dreams.

There's a sigh, and then she speaks, stirring the tiny spoon in her white ceramic mug.

It clinks on the sides rhythmically, like she's using it as a metronome to keep her calm.

"Maybe. I guess." She looks at me and smiles, but it's not necessarily happy. "Probably. I'm an only child, you know?"

"Doesn't mean you have to stay where your parents are rooted." She pauses, furrowing her brow.

"Doesn't it?"

"You do what makes you happy, Zoe. I guarantee that's all your parents want." She tips her head from left to right, mentally weighing her response. Zoe probably has a pros and cons list in her mind for every moment of every day.

"I mean, yes. You're right. If you asked my parents, that's definitely what they would say, but the reality is—" I shake my head and cut her off.

"Your parents' happiness is not your responsibility."

"I never said—"

"You didn't have to. I know you better than I know me, Zo. I can see it."

"You have Luna and Ace. You won't understand—" I stop her again.

She's spewing the toxic shit that lives in her mind, and while it's good to know, good to have a better understanding of how her mind works and how the pressures she's put on herself functions, this shit ends with me.

"You being an only child does not mean it's now your job to fulfill any thoughts or dreams or ideals your parents had about their lives."

"That's not fair—"

"You're right. It wouldn't be fair for you to live a life that doesn't bring you joy because you think it's what your parents want of you." She scrunches her nose and shakes her head, refusing to give in.

"I'm not—"

"You wanted to be an interior designer."

Silence.

Finally, something that stops her dead in her tracks.

"It wasn't safe enough. You felt like your dad wasn't happy with that decision. You switched majors. Let me ask you this—how many moments in your career have you felt fulfilled, Zoe? How many times have you looked at what you're doing and felt like you made the right choice for *you*? That you were satisfied with what you were doing every day?"

Silence.

"My dad wanted me to work for the Colemans like he did. He used to say I was built for it, it would be solid and consistent, and I could make good money there. I didn't want that."

"But you have siblings, Zander," she argues.

"What does that even matter?"

"It means your sister owns her own business, and you work for the town, and Ace is in a damn *rock band*. If you never live up to a single of your parents' expectations or hopes and dreams, there are other people to pick up the slack." I stare at her, and my heart hurts.

She really believes that.

"I, on the other hand, am the only one to make my parents feel like they did well."

"Your parents' life fulfillment is not hinging on your career choices," I say, my words lower now.

"But isn't it?" she asks, her eyes moving to the table where she spilled some sugar, her fingers drawing lines in it.

"It's not, Zoe. And I guarantee your parents would be pissed as fuck to find out you've been living in misery to try and impress them."

"Stop. I'm not living in misery."

"You aren't happy, though."

"I am." I sigh and roll my eyes.

She's so fucking stubborn.

"Fine. Then, you're not as happy as you could be." She stares at me. "If you close your eyes, if you could redo life and ensure that whatever field or path you chose succeeded in a way that your parents would never shut up about how great you are, what would you do?"

White teeth bite into a pink lip.

I want to bite that lip.

Not the time, Davidson.

It's definitely not the time when her eyes move to me and for the first time since we left, I see honesty there.

"Something creative."

"Not marketing?" She sighs.

"Probably not. I mean, maybe if I was in some art department or something, but creative work doesn't pay the way management does in the corporate world. And it's not stable. It's so closely linked to sales, and if you don't get them, you're out of a job."

"Stability doesn't always equate to happiness or fulfillment, Zoe."

She doesn't answer, her finger continuing to play in that sugar, and I instinctively know there's no more to say.

She needs to steep on it.

"I want you to take one thing from this week," I say. It's a lie, of course. There are many things I want Zoe to take from this trip, including me.

Including being mine.

But if she doesn't, if that's just not in the cards for us, but then she leaves with a new perspective that pulls her to happiness, I'll be satisfied.

"I want you to think about where your life has been and where it's heading and what would make you happy. When you die, do you want your legacy to be marketing? Your parents won't be here forever, Zoe. What happens when you spend your life living for them, and then they're gone? Who will you live for then?" She blinks at me.

"You don't have to respond. Just think about that."

I think she might speak, argue, or something, but she doesn't.

Instead, she nods.

"Okay, Zee," she says, and I'm calling that a win.

As I'm staring off, lost in thought, thinking about all the ways I'd like to give Zoe a future that would fulfill her, something soft hits me in the face, and Zoe giggles. When I look over, she's smiling, a straw still to her lips.

"Remember the time you tried to blow the straw wrapper at Luna and it went over the back of the bench and hit Mr. Johnson? And when he stood up, you blamed it on Ace?"

When we were kids, Mr. Johnson was the town's cliché, grumpy old man that all of the kids were just a little scared of.

"Ace started crying, and I got in so much trouble," I say with a smile, grabbing the paper she blew at me and twisting it around.

"You deserved it. You pointed right at him and said, *He did it!* so loud, everyone's head turned toward us." Her head goes back with a laugh, and just like then, everyone in the vicinity's head turns toward us.

Not a single person is immune to the sound of Zoe laughing, moths to a flame. Everyone wants to catch a glimpse at the pure beauty of it.

While she laughs, I reach out to her hand, pulling it across the table and manipulating the straw wrapper onto her ring finger.

God, it looks good there.

Feels better.

Her head tips back down, the smile still on her face but transforming a bit as she looks at her finger.

I haven't let go of her hand.

"Gorgeous," I whisper, staring at her.

And I don't mean the wrapper.

I mean *her*.

I mean this.

I mean us.

"I'll keep it forever," she says with smile and a girly shrug of one shoulder. Before I can say anything else, the waitress brings over our plates, and we eat, continuing to reminisce over Sundays at the diner with my family.

We ignore conversations about paper rings and potentially unhappy futures.

And it feels so easy, I almost forget I haven't even started my mission to win her and get this every day yet, not really.

TWENTY
GOLD RUSH
-ZOE-

The little beach town we landed in is absolutely freaking adorable.

Everywhere we walk, people wave or tip their chins at us as if we're not tourists but locals taking a normal Sunday morning stroll after a late breakfast at the diner.

When we walked out of the restaurant (where Zee and I got into an argument about who would pay—he won), he asked if I wanted to walk down to the water and wander around the docks.

How could I resist such an offer?

And as we strolled that way, I fussed with my hands.

How is this supposed to work? This *pretending* thing?

Do I give into every way I want to *pretend* with Zander, ignoring how that will most likely destroy me when I'm forced back into reality?

Do I reach out when our hands brush, linking our fingers?

Do I lean into him a bit, the way my body can't help but want to?

But as always, Zander takes any confusion and overthinking from me, making a decision for both of us.

His hand moves out, grabbing my own, twining his fingers with mine.

I look at him, hoping to see something on his face, an explanation or a smile or a reminder to pretend.

None of it's there.

Instead, he's looking forward like this is so normal, like this is just *us*.

And without a word or a pause or anything, he pulls our twined hands up to his lips, pressing a light kiss on my knuckles before lowering them again.

His feet never miss a step.

He just keeps strolling.

My heart beats like crazy, and I wonder if he can feel it in my palm, if he knows how such a tiny, insignificant move impacts me.

And I know deep down in my soul that if this were us—if we were an *us* and we were walking around a tiny coastal town fully in love—this would be normal. Tiny. *Insignificant.* He'd do that, twine our fingers and kiss the knuckle of my ring finger just because.

Or he'd do it when we're wandering out of the Springbrook Hills Diner on a lazy Sunday after having breakfast with his parents.

Or when we're standing on the sidelines at our kid's peewee game, my fingers cold in the fall air. He'd take them between his hands, puffing warm air over them while keeping his eyes on the field.

Stop, Zoe. Stop with the girlish daydreams. Daydreams get you nowhere. Daydreams and living with your head in the clouds gets you in positions where you question every choice you've ever made.

The last time I let myself fall into stupid daydreams and ignore danger signs and red flags, I had to call up Zander to save me.

I don't live in daydreams anymore. I live in reality. Sound, safe, predictable reality where I have already thought of all of the outcomes of any given decision I make in order to avoid being hurt.

Except for last week when you remembered just how fucked your life is because you've been living too safe.

I shake my head, trying to forget that, to live in pretend.

A few minutes later, I feel it.

One, two, three squeezes of Zee's callused hand on mine.

I tip my chin to look at him and he's smiling at me.

"Want ice cream?" Zee says, eyes moving to a sign that says, *Marjorie's Old-Fashioned Ice Cream.*

"It's not even 11," I say, looking at my watch, the watch I am thankful I wore since Zander has my phone.

"And?"

"That's not a normal time to eat ice cream." Our steps slow as we approach the store, all the lights on.

"Looks like they open at 10:30."

"We just had breakfast," I argue, even though I'm already eyeing the case through the large glass windows.

"You want ice cream," he says, shaking his head and leading me toward the door. I slow my steps, feeling the need to argue.

I don't know why.

I *always* want ice cream.

"I didn't even answer."

"You always want ice cream, Zoe. Even in the dead of winter." I don't respond, instead furrowing my brows. "Your birthday's in February, and every year you'd force all of us to eat a freaking ice cream cake, ten-degree weather be damned."

He's not wrong.

I did do that for ten years straight.

"I don't do that anymore," I say, giving him a look.

"Why, because someone told you it was a pain and that it was too cold for ice cream?" He asks it as a joke but then stops right outside the building.

"I was kidding, you know," he says, his voice turning to concern.

I don't respond.

I don't know why, to be honest.

Why is this happening?

I know how to change the subject.

I know how to bend the truth.

I know how to phrase things to protect hurt feelings.

I could have just laughed and moved on, but . . .

"Fuck. I was dead-on, wasn't I?"

Again, I don't respond.

I don't tell him that I overheard my mom on the phone with my aunt one year, sighing that it was a pain to go three towns over to get an ice cream cake in February.

He moves, pinning me to the wall right before the ice cream shop. He's looking down, and his eyes are fierce before his hand moves, grabbing my chin and tipping it up.

"No more of that. No more changing shit to make life easy for other people.

"No more doing things that don't bring you immense, all-consuming joy, Zoe. Not while I'm here." I lick my lips, unsure of how to answer.

But I don't have to overthink it for long because, in a moment, his head is dipping down, and Zee's lips are on mine once again.

And once again, it alters something in me.

The breath in my lungs seizes, my body melts just a hint, and I loop my arms around his neck as one hand moves from where he was holding my chin, sliding up into my hair, his other hand going to my hip.

We kiss like that for an eternity, nothing more, but surely nothing less.

And it brings me immense, all-consuming joy.

Finally, Zander breaks the kiss, his forehead moving to mine and a smile crossing his lips. "Okay. Now let's get you some ice cream, pip."

The ice cream shop is tiny, with just a few two-top tables and a giant glass case with a variety of options inside. On the back wall is a huge chalkboard menu, dozens of flavors written in meticulous, neat handwriting.

I stand, staring up at the selections, when Zander walks up behind me, a single tan arm looping my belly and pulling me back against him.

"You two are just too cute!" the older woman behind the counter says, watching us standing before the case.

I should push him away.

I should step away.

I should do anything.

Instead, I lean back into him, and his arm tightens.

It feels too freaking good to fight.

So, I don't.

"Saw you two outside canoodling, too stinking cute. Not from around here, right?" she asks, and Zee shakes his head from behind me.

"No, ma'am. We're from Jersey."

"New Jersey! What's the occasion?" she asks, wiping down a counter but smiling at us.

"None, just decided to go on a road trip, escape some of the cold up North."

I know his face is split with his handsome smile.

"Can't blame you. The few times I've been up North, nearly froze my behind off. Never again, I say." I smile at her, eyeing the toppings chart.

Zee steps forward, making me move with him until I can look down through the glass case at the ice cream options.

But that hand on my belly stays.

"Whatcha thinkin', pip?" he asks, his voice low in my ear.

I take in all of my options, reading each tiny little sign and biting my lip.

Then I look up at the sign and read the size options.

Then back down at the ice cream.

Then back up at the toppings, trying to decide what I want.

I really want to get the biggest thing they have, to get every chocolate ice cream flavor I can fit in there and try a scoop of each.

Would I finish that, especially knowing we ate breakfast barely an hour ago?

No way.

Would it be amazing?

Definitely.

But I also know Zander is going to be paying, just like he insisted he do for breakfast, and I don't want the man to foot a twenty-dollar ice cream I'll only eat a third of.

"A small, half chocolate Reese's and half coffee coconut."

"A small?"

"With whipped cream," I say impulsively, seeing the sign that says, *Fresh whipped cream with real cream!*

I cannot say no to whipped cream, ever.

His chuckle vibrates on my back, and I refuse to address how that vibration travels south.

"You two know what you're getting?" the woman asks, smiling wide at us.

I blush a bit at how close we're standing, how intimate, but Zee tightens his hand on my belly, somehow knowing my thoughts and refusing to let me go.

This *man*.

"She'll get a small with chocolate Reese's and coffee coconut with extra whipped cream, and I'll have the large chocolate taster." My brow furrows when he orders the specialty item, which is every single chocolate ice cream in a big tasting bowl.

"On it!" she says and grabs a scoop to start dishing out our order.

My head turns to Zee.

"Why wouldn't you get strawberry? Or they have cherry?" I ask, tipping my chin toward the pinkish flavor.

"Because you got a small."

"What?" I say, craning my neck to look behind me at him. His lips press my temple.

"You got a small, so you only get two flavors."

"I don't—"

"You overthought what it would look like to get a large so you could try a bunch, which is what you want. Probably knew I'd pay so didn't want to be a burden there, either."

"Zander—"

"And you think it's criminal to have fruit in ice cream."

I can't stop myself from speaking, even though I should be arguing with him.

"Well, if I wanted one of the healthy food groups, I'd have ordered Italian ice. Ice cream and fruit don't belong together unless it's a topping, like a cherry, or a banana spli—" I stop myself and shut my mouth, realizing I'm rambling.

Zander's head tips back with a laugh, the sound filling the ice cream shop before it simmers, and he presses his lips to my temple.

"Exactly. You hate fruit ice cream. You're gonna try all of mine."

So he got what he knew I'd like.

"How do you know what kind of ice cream I like?" I ask, looking back at the case, not wanting to look at his face.

I'm afraid of what I'll see there.

His lips are still in my hair when he answers quietly.

"I've spent my entire life categorizing your likes and dislikes, waiting for the moment you'd let me in."

Ice cream lands on the counter, the older woman smiling at us with hearts in her eyes.

"You two remind me of my George and me when we were young. Always together, couldn't keep our hands off each other." I feel my face turn red at her words, and Zee tips his head back in a laugh again.

"Haven't seen love like that in years. Wish my grandkids would settle, but these days it's all online dates and booty calls." My eyes go wide and Zander snorts a laugh in his throat behind me.

"No one wants to find their person and settle, you know? But life doesn't wait. It keeps moving, even if you stop."

I sit with that.

Life keeps moving, even if you stop.

For the first time, I wonder if that's what I did all those years ago —did I stop moving, expecting life to stop with me?

"Anyway, ignore an old woman reminiscing. I'm just saying, don't let that one go, young man," she says, tipping her head to Zander.

"Honestly, I'm still working on convincing her she's meant to be mine."

My entire body stills, blood rushing and making me overheated.

He's just saying that.

We're playing pretend.

"Oh, the look she has? You've had her for a while. Keep on working at it, though," she says as if I'm not right here. "And even when she argues, you keep pushing, you hear me?"

"Yes, ma'am," Zee says. I turn my head to glare at him, expecting him to be smiling at her. But he's not looking at the woman.

He's looking at me.

And not for the first time, I can't help but wonder what his plan is in all of this.

TWENTY-ONE
DELICATE
-ZOE-

We eat way too much ice cream (the chocolate ganache was *to die for*) before saying goodbye to Marjorie, the owner, and then wandering around the quaint town. We stop in a third shop, at some place where Zee buys me a tee shirt for the town's local peewee team because it makes me smile, and he buys something ("A gift for Luna," he says when he's checking out) before we walk down to the water, spending nearly the entire afternoon walking and talking, enjoying the not-absolutely-freezing weather.

But as we're walking back toward the bed-and-breakfast, Zander stops.

"What?"

"Fuck it," he says under his breath.

"What?" I repeat, confused, but then he's tugging me into some small alleyway between brick buildings.

And then I'm pinned to the wall, Zander's hand on either side of my face.

"What are you doing?" I say, my voice low and quiet.

I don't know why I'm asking.

I can read it all over his face.

But it's Zander, so he tells me.

"I'm going to kiss you, Zoe," he says. "I'm going to kiss you, and it's going to be real, but you can pretend it's all part of the game. I'm going to kiss you because I can't stop thinking about it, and you're driving me fucking insane."

"Zander—"

"Say no and I won't," he whispers, his lips brushing mine as he does.

I don't say no.

I don't say anything at all.

I don't think I could stop him even if the logical side of me were in control right now, the side that knows this is a bad idea, the side that knows the possibility of getting hurt isn't small.

Instead, I lean in.

"Fuck," he murmurs before his lips are fully on mine. "*Fuck,*" he groans against my lips.

Then he steps closer until I'm fully pressed against his body, and he's kissing me now like I'm some lifeline to sanity.

Like if he stops, the world stops spinning.

His tongue touches mine and *I* groan.

This is not sweet.

This is not gentle.

This is not a girl kissing the boy she's loved for as long as she can remember.

This is a man kissing a woman that he needs wholly.

When I move to my toes, his hands leave my face, trailing down my body to my hips and then to my ass, lifting me up until I wrap my legs around him.

"Fuck, this ass," he murmurs in my neck, but I can't think about that.

I'm stuck on the way his hips press into me more to hold me in place and the way I can feel his hard cock at my center, right through my leggings.

And because I'm so far gone from reality, from doing the right thing, so far into *pretend* zone, I grind my hips against his.

"Jesus, fuck," he murmurs, kissing down my neck, his tongue tasting. My hand is on his head, keeping him there, my hips moving continuously, and I think for a moment I could come like this.

Fully clothed, Zander's lips on my neck, in a random alleyway pinned against a warm brick wall in goddamn North Carolina, I could come.

"Let's stay another night here," he murmurs against my skin, breaking my chain of thought.

"What? Why?" I'm nearly panting, needy.

His tongue runs from where my shoulder meets my neck and up, up until his teeth bite my ear lobe. His breathing is heavy, reflecting my own, when he speaks again.

"Because I'm not getting into that Jeep without tasting your pussy, Zoe."

My breathing absolutely stops this time.

Not a single breath enters my lungs.

But one leaves without my permission when I say, "Okay."

TWENTY-TWO
AUGUST
-ZOE-

After Zee helps me off the wall, he grabs my hand and we walk back to the room in silence.

My hands are shaking.

Every molecule on my body feels like it's on fire, like I can feel every single centimeter of my skin and each one is on hyperdrive.

My clothes are too tight.

My breathing feels weird.

And Zander Davidson just told me he wants to eat my pussy.

What fucking twilight zone am I living in?

Because last I remember, I was just his little sister's best friend that he liked to sit with during family events to laugh at everyone around us.

And now we're sharing a hotel room.

And a bed.

And potentially a whole lot more.

Zander locks the door behind him, and I keep walking in, putting my bag on the little desk in the corner, digging through it like I'm searching for something.

Anything.

I'm looking for *anything* to distract my mind, my hands.

Except, of course, my purse is clean and organized, and I'm pretty sure Zee knows that about me, so it must look stupid, me digging through my bag, unzipping little bags and peeking in like I'm missing a teeny tiny earring back or a lip gloss.

And then I feel it.

Warmth behind me and then a broad chest lining up against my back.

Zander's tall. Really fucking tall. And I'm not short at 5'9", but he still towers over me.

And when his back lines against mine, when his hands move down my sides to the front of my hips and he rests his thumbs in the waistband of my leggings, my entire body stops moving.

His chin rests on my shoulder before he speaks.

"What are you doing, Zoe?"

His words are barely a whisper, and I feel them on my back more than I even really hear them, the vibration moving from his chest through my thin tee and straight to my clit that's starting to throb.

"Looking for . . ." My thoughts trail off as one of those thumbs starts to brush the soft skin of my belly, back and forth, making me lose my train of thought.

How can I even try to think of excuses when his thumb is on sensitive skin?

"You're looking for nothing, pip," he says, pressing his lips beneath my ear. "You're nervous because you know I'm not leaving this room until I make you come."

My body freezes, and a rush of heat hits my core.

There is no universe where my panties make it out of this room alive.

"Zander—"

His hands press, pulling me back into him, and even through his thick jeans I can feel it.

Zander Davidson is hard.

He's hard *because of me.*

Again, what universe am I living in?

"Stop. Stop with the excuses. Stop with the denials. This is something. Always has been. The universe decided this week was our time, and here we are. I don't know much about the universe except that it's never steered me wrong because it's always directed me to you."

My heart stops beating.

The words this man is saying . . .

If I let them, they could change everything.

He turns me, pressing my ass into the desk and his body to mine.

"Don't. Don't question it. Don't overthink this. Pretend with me for now. Pretend that this is easy, that there is no family shit to worry about, no job to stress about."

He stares at me, big blue eyes I've known my whole life.

Eyes that are now staring at me like I'm the world. Like I'm *his* world.

Like I'm everything.

I don't think I've ever been *everything* to a man, in a fairy tale or otherwise.

His hand moves up my back to the nape of my neck, and he tugs on my ponytail until the tie comes out then scrubs at my scalp to relieve the tension.

"Fuckin' hate these."

"What?"

"Stupid ponytails. Your hair should be down. Gorgeous. The kind of hair a man dreams about wrapping around his fist."

My soul leaves my body.

"What do you say, Zo?" I can't even remember what he asked. My mind is stuck on *hair a man dreams about wrapping around his fist.*

"What?" I ask, still lost to the world.

"What do you say? You gonna pretend with me?"

I wait for long, long minutes.

It could be an hour.

An eternity.

But it's probably just a few seconds where every option runs through my mind and I quickly calculate outcomes and weigh risks and rewards.

But if the reward is Zander Davidson . . .

"Okay," I say.

"Okay?"

"Yeah."

He smiles his most handsome smile, the one I fell in love with years ago without even knowing it, and then he moves, lips pressing to mine, and everything changes.

This kiss is *hot*. It's unlike any other kiss I've shared with any other man. My entire body becomes flames, my hand moving up to run through his hair that's always just a bit too long, always styled with what I can assume is his hands and water and nothing more.

Hair I've been secretly dreaming about running my hands through for *years*.

Then his hands are on my ass, squeezing and pulling me closer until I can feel his hard cock once again on my belly, the thought alone making me spasm.

"Fuck," I murmur under my breath.

His thumbs move to the waistband of my leggings and without even second-guessing, I help him, my hands working moving as I continue to kiss him, as we work together to peel them down to where I can kick them off.

Then his hands are running up the backs of my bare thighs, moving to cup my ass exposed by my thong, and then he *groans*.

The sound moves through my body, sending wetness between my thighs.

And it makes me brave.

I decide that I want to feel him, too—I want mine.

If he gets to feel my skin, I should get to touch his too.

Breathing heavily against Zee's lips, I move my hands up his front until he gets the hint, until he helps me take off his shirt, revealing a broad chest with a light sprinkling of hair that I've been daydreaming about for longer than I'd like to admit.

He's everything I could ever ask for—not chiseled, not perfection. A wide chest with a flat belly, but it's soft—not perfect.

Zander enjoys life. Any form of working out comes in just living everyday, not by spending hours at a gym.

Unlike me, who spends my regimented morning hour on the treadmill, forever fighting the pooch of my belly because some crazy voice in my head tells me once it's gone, everything will be fixed.

My hands run up his bare chest. I revel in it, and goddammit, I know he knows how much I like this.

How much I like *him*.

I know because he smiles at me as I do before dipping down again to take my mouth, his hands working quickly under my tee to undo my bra and then slide everything up and over my head.

And finally, *finally*, he pulls me into him, bare skin against bare skin, and *fuck fuck fuck*.

It's everything and more.

His chest hair tickles my tight nipples in a way that has me sighing, and one of his big, calloused hands scrapes up my back until it's in my hair at the base, the other moving down as he bends, curving his arm around my ass and moving to lift me.

Instinctively, my legs wrap around his and *shit*. I thought having his jean-covered cock against me in pants was nice, but in just panties? *Fuck*.

I moan, grinding on him without hesitance because I need this.

I need more.

I need him.

"Taking our time, baby," he says into my ear, his hand on my nearly bare ass pressing me in deeper. "We're taking our time. We're in no rush, and I've been dreaming about this too long to speed through."

His words have me moaning again.

Not the fact that we have time to explore, to do everything my mind is thinking, but because he, too, has been thinking about this.

For years.

Wasted years, my mind can't help but think.

I force myself to shake that thought out because I don't think any other past version of myself would have let this happen.

Would have let it get this far.

Would let it get *further*.

And the current version of me *definitely* plans to take this further.

He starts to move as he holds me, walking me toward the bed, but I can't keep my hands off him. They run down his back, up his chest, my nails scraping at his neck, my lips pressing anywhere they can reach. It's like my body wants to ensure he's real, wants to categorize every moment while it can.

"Sit here," he says, placing me on the edge of the bed. His shirt is off but his pants are still on, and I'm in just a tiny pair of panties.

This is normally when all of my anxieties roll in.

When I start to worry if I live up to whatever image the man I'm about to sleep with had in his mind. Is my belly too soft? Are my boobs too small?

A whole slew of worries and concerns usually infiltrate my mind.

But as I stare at *Zander fucking Davidson*, I can't help but let that all go.

I've known this man my entire life.

He's seen me in bathing suits as recently as last summer at Autumn and Steve's pool party.

He knows what I look like.

And he wanted this any way.

Wanted this and *demanded* it, even.

But even if I didn't have all of that, if I didn't have that comfort, I still think I'd feel this ease.

The way he is staring at me is like he's a man who's been starving, and I'm the only meal in a hundred-mile radius.

The breath stops in my lungs as I watch him take me in, his pupils dilating, and, through it, my confidence and comfort raises.

I lean back in the bed, resting my weight on my hands and putting my breasts on display for him. My tongue dips out to lick my lips unconsciously as I watch his hands slowly, so fucking slowly, move to the fly of his jeans, undoing the button and lowering the zipper like he can't even be bothered.

Like he's utterly distracted by the woman in front of him.

The look in his eyes fuels me, my desire, my passion, my confidence, and I move a hand.

I am not like this.

I am not straightforward.

I am not one to put on a show.

But for him?

For Zander?

Nothing sounds more exciting.

His pants start to fall to the ground as I move one hand to my tit, fingers pinching my nipple. A low moan falls from my lips, and I watch Zander's jaw loosen just the tiniest fraction, his mouth opening a bit.

His response fuels me, my hand moving to my other tit and repeating the action, my back arching just a bit into my hand.

"Jesus, Zoe," he murmurs, watching me.

But he doesn't get closer, doesn't close the gap.

He doesn't stop staring.

He does, however, fuel me, his gaze making me feel braver.

I move a bit until my back is to the headboard, supporting myself, and he just keep watching me, taking a small step closer to the bed, maintaining our distance.

"What are you gonna do, baby?" he asks, his voice low.

"I don't know," I whisper. But both hands move, pinching and twisting my nipples, the sensation spiking straight to my clit as it does, my breath catching in my chest as I moan.

"That's a good start," he says with a groan, and I watch as his hand adjusts his hard cock through his underwear.

The move corresponds directly with my clit, already throbbing near painfully.

Even though I got myself off just last night, it wasn't enough.

Something tells me that being with Zander will be a life-changing, soul-shattering experience.

That I'll never be the same.

Fine by me, I can't help but think.

One hand trails down my body, gently brushing the skin that sits above my panty line, the very tip of my finger dipping beneath the lace.

Zander's breathing gets heavier, and that just urges me on.

The fact that boring old me is turning on this dream of a man? I'm feeling invincible.

My body begs me to move farther.

Without my permission, my hand dips, my middle finger circling my clit gently. So, so gently.

But I'm so on edge, turned on just by a kiss, by the idea of more, by the idea of being fucked by Zander, that it sends my body up in flames, engulfing me completely.

My head tips back, my hair falling with it, and I moan to the ceiling.

"Fuck, Zoe," Zander murmurs. "Eyes on me, baby. Eyes on me when you touch yourself. From here on out, I control all of that. You agreed to be mine, and that means your pleasure? It's mine."

His words make me *moan,* and I'm fully shocked by how wet that makes me, the way his words make my pussy clench.

I'm usually not one to give up control.

I like things my way, and I like them predictable.

But Zander . . .

My thoughts are cut off when his thumbs hook in his boxers then pushes them down.

His hard cock bobs in front of me, thick and long, and my mouth *waters.*

When I finally am able to break my gaze, I look back at him, and he's smiling, a small quirk on the edges of his lips.

He knows what he's doing to me.

Then he grabs himself, pumping slowly once, twice.

And again, I moan.

I've never seen anything hotter than a naked Zee standing in front of me, jacking his cock while staring at me touching myself.

The idea is one that I'll file away for eternity, using long after this ends to make myself come.

I move a finger, dipping into myself, and mewl as pleasure bolts through me.

"Are you wet, baby?" he says, and I moan. "Tell me, Zoe. Tell me how wet you are."

"I'm so wet," I say, my voice breathy. "It's so tight. God."

His hand moves again, stroking himself harder as I moan.

"You know, last night, I wasn't sleeping."

I freeze.

I should act stupid, act like I have no idea what he's talking about.

But what's the point?

It would be a lie.

And aren't we past that? If we're going to pretend, might as well jump in fully.

Instead, I stay silent, pulling the finger out and then pushing it back in.

Instead, I let my mind drift to the idea of Zander listening to me fingering myself right next to him in bed.

He smiles.

"You were so quiet, I wasn't sure. But then I heard it: your fingers pumping. All I could think about was slapping your hand aside, moving down your body, and eating your sweet pussy."

My breathing is impossible to control right now, heavy and harsh, and he knows it.

He's smiling.

I watch as his thumb moves, rubbing over the wide head of his cock, his expression changing just a bit, and I categorize that for whenever I might need to know what makes Zee's face go a bit wild.

"You don't have to be quiet now, Zoe. You don't have to hide from me." I can't fill my lungs, my legs widening farther as I slip a second finger in, moaning at the stretch.

"Fuckin' beautiful," he murmurs, not for my ears, but a reminder to himself.

I want him to see.

I want him to see what I was doing that night, thinking of him inside me.

My other hand moves to my panties, pulling aside the stretchy fabric until I'm exposed to him, his eyes zeroing in on where two fingers are now disappearing as I fuck myself.

My bottom lip feels full as my mouth opens, my chest heaves, and my eyes lock on Zander.

His eyes are on my fingers.

I clench around said fingers, and he groans, deep.

"Jesus, pip. Look at that. Fucking *look* at that. The way you take your fingers, the way you're so soaked. Were you this wet last night? Is that what I was missing?" I bite my lip and nod, even though no, I wasn't this wet.

This wet is because Zander is looking at me like he's never seen anything hotter in this entire universe.

"Need to taste that," he says, the words said low like he's talking to himself. Then he moves, kicking off his clothes from around his feet. He walks over to me, his cock bobbing, and my tongue comes out to lick my lips as I subconsciously think about licking that dot of precum, and he smiles.

It's a good smile.

Feral.

Animalistic.

But I can't focus on it as he settles in the bed next to where I am. I stare, slightly confused because he feels a mile away and his skin isn't on mine.

That is, until he speaks.

"Panties off, climb on," he says. I blink at him, my fingers paused deep inside me.

"What?"

"Take off your panties and climb on my face, Zoe."

"I don't—"

"I don't give a shit. I'm telling you right fucking now, you need to move, take those panties off, grab onto this *headboard,* and ride my face until you find it."

Oh god, oh god!

This is not happening.

This is *not* happening.

Zander Davidson did not just tell me to ride his face.

"Keep hesitating and I'll get mad, baby."

I blink at him.

And fuck, an unhinged part of me wonders what it would be like for Zander to *get mad* in bed.

It's not like I've never done this—I have, of course. But on my terms.

Everything is always on *my terms.*

Except for when it comes to Zander apparently.

A part of me I don't have control of shocks me when I move slowly to my knees before facing him and lowering my panties, carefully kicking them to the floor.

He turns to get a full look at me.

"A goddamn fucking *dream,* Zoe. Holy fuck." A hand moves, running from my knee up my inner thigh, up, up, up, until the side of a thick finger meets my center. My hips try to move, to get more before he looks in my eyes. "Still."

I oblige, my body freezing at his command.

"Good girl," he whispers, and my pussy clenches at the words.

The side of a rough finger glides, brushing my wet entrance, my swollen clit, then back down, repeating the process, sliding my wet down my leg and back up.

"Zander," I whisper.

"Widen for me, Zo."

I do, moving my knees to give him more room to play between my legs. I moan as he uses that room, sliding a single finger over me again, featherlight.

He passes over my entrance, through my wet, over my clit, back to my entrance, and repeats the same, torturous cycle over.

He never enters me.

He almost does, the very tip of a finger moving in before going back to brush over my clit, playing with me.

Teasing me.

For a fucking *eternity*.

"Look at you, being so good, not even moving." I can't. I'm frozen in a battle of pleasure and obedience, dying for more and intuitively knowing that doing as he asks will get me what I want.

"You want more, baby?" he asks low and gravelly.

I nod.

I don't trust my voice, don't trust the words that could come out of my mouth.

"Alright. Now you climb on, baby. You hold onto that headboard, but you ride my fucking face." I open my mouth to argue, but his wet hand moves to my chin, pinching it between a pointer and thumb and pulling it to look at him.

"You ride my face, Zoe. You do not hold back. You ride it until you come on my mouth, and then you move down and take my cock." My eyes widen. "I was tested last month; nothing came up. I'll use a condom if we have to, but I really wanna fuck you bare, baby."

I lick my lips.

Why do I want that too?

I've never done that, ever.

"I—" I clear my throat. "I'm on the pill. I had my yearly recently, all good." He smiles a boyish smile and looks at me.

"Then I get you bare."

What is he doing to me?

Then his hand moves, slapping the side of my ass before urging me forward.

The slap reverberates to my clit.

"Get the fuck on my face, Zoe."

And then I do without argument because it turns out I might like to be in control in the real world, but when I'm playing pretend, I like being bossed around.

I straddle Zander's face, my fingers curling around the headboard, and I slowly lower onto his face. His rough hands move to my hips, holding me where he wants me, and then it happens.

His tongue runs along my pussy, and my head tips back as I groan, loud. His hands tighten with the sound, pulling me closer to his face as he begins.

And fuck, he *begins.*

His hands pull me down, then he starts to move, showing *me* how to move until I'm grinding as he eats me.

One of his hands lets go as I moan, my legs still holding me up a bit, until a thick finger enters my pussy.

My head tips back, my hands losing grip on the headboard as I grind on him willingly now, already close to the edge.

His finger moves as he sucks my clit, swiping my G-spot, and I moan his name.

That has him growling into me, the vibrations traveling up my body and pulling another feral noise from me.

"Fuck, I'm so close," I moan, and the hand on my hip tugs, trying to get me to put my full body weight on to him. "I can't—" I start but then his hand leaves, slapping my ass hard before tugging me down with more force.

And I have no choice but to abide, to completely sit on his face as I find it, as I come saying his name with his mouth on my clit and his fingers in my pussy, continuously swiping as I slowly come back down to Earth.

I move back to putting weight on my knees, his mouth leaving me.

"Alright, baby, remember what I told you?" he says.

I get his cock now.

And, to be honest, that sounds amazing.

It really does.

But . . .

I move, turning, swapping my position until my legs are back to being on either side of his head but I'm facing his cock.

And then I lean down, my ass in the air, my pussy over his face, and, to my delight, his hands on either side of my ass.

"Zoe—" he starts with a warning, but I don't listen.

Because then I have my mouth on the tip of his cock, my tongue swirling, and he's groaning my name in a much different way.

"*Fuck*," he says. It's then he proves to be a good sport, even when I don't listen to him.

Because then two fingers are in my pussy, his mouth latched to my already oversensitive clit, and I moan as I start to take him farther into my mouth, bobbing my head as I do.

Zander moans against my cunt, bringing me back to the edge near instantly.

But this isn't for me—it's his turn.

I need to give him this.

I take him deeper, opening my throat as I moan and feeling the head of his cock slide in as he bucks his hips.

I can't even tell anymore who is urging who on, whose moves are taking the other closer because I'm rabid. I'm deep-throating this man as he moans into my pussy until I'm teetering on the edge. His free hand digs into my hip in a way I know will leave fingerprints in the form of tiny bruises.

And then, right when I'm about to come again, he slaps my ass, unlatches, and moves us. He shakes his head when I mewl in protest, a smile on his wet lips as he moves me until I'm on my back with my head on the pillow, Zander hovering over me.

"Now, normally, you be a bad girl and don't listen to what I tell you to do, I'll fuck you, come on your back, and make you wait until I'm ready for you again."

My pussy convulses.

I am so totally fucked in the head.

There is no rational world where that should be hot.

"But this being the first time I get you, I wanna watch your face when I fill you." His hand moves to my pussy, the entirety of it rubbing from my entrance to my clit, and I moan, bucking my hips. He smiles a devious look.

"I wanna watch you come on my cock, then I wanna feel that shit take me over the edge."

"Zander," I breathe.

"That's it, baby. And when you come, you say my fucking name."

"I—"

"I've been thinking of this for *years*, of coming in this pussy. But in every daydream, every dirty fantasy, I come to the thought of you moaning my name." His thumb slides into my pussy, and I moan, clamping on him. "You gonna give me that?" he asks.

"Yes, Zander."

"Fuck yeah," he says through gritted teeth, then his thumb is gone, and I moan at the loss, but it doesn't last.

Because then he's entering, his thick cock almost too big, pulling at tight muscles. He fills me completely, my back arching off the bed as he does.

"That's it, baby." He looks down, watching where he's disappearing in me, and groans, a sound that reverberates through me.

"Zander," I whimper, trying to get a handle on all the emotions and feelings, on my breathing, trying to relax until he fits perfectly.

"God, better than I thought, Zo. So much better. You were made for me, a perfect fit." He moans as he pulls out, slamming back in. "*Fuckkk.*"

He repeats the move, leaning forward, his eyes locked on mine, his breathing heavy as it hits my lips. "Fuck, Zoe. Goddammit," he says in a curse like he's mad at me for this being so good.

So perfect.

I agree.

I understand.

I'm thinking the same damn thing.

There's no way this should feel so good, so perfect. So life-altering.

But I guess that's reason enough.

It's just . . . Zander.

He slams into me again, and it starts to build as he hits the ache in my belly. With each thrust, I start to clamp down on him, my body begging for him to stay, and he feels it.

"That's it, baby. Fuck. Need you to come on my cock, Zoe. Come on me and take me with you."

"Zander," I moan.

"Fuck yes."

We're both right there, both holding out because it feels like once this happens, once we share this, something will change.

I have no idea why, in my head, it's different if I come on his face, but having his eyes on mine, his breaths twining with mine, it feels important.

"Now, Zoe," he whispers, and that's it.

I come from his cock alone, moaning his name before he slams into me one last time, throbbing as he comes, collapsing on top of me and breathing into my neck.

"That wasn't pretend, Zo," he whispers, and I close my eyes.

Because he's not wrong.

TWENTY-THREE
STATE OF GRACE
-ZANDER-

We order shitty pizza to be delivered to the bed-and-breakfast (I run downstairs to grab it in a pair of sweats, and the owner winks at me as I do), and we eat in the big bed, despite Zoe's protest.

"We can't eat in bed, Zander," she said.

"We actually can," I said. *"We're full-blown adults, Zoe."* I smiled at her, and I saw it there—the way she was fighting the tipping of her own lips.

"But it's . . . That's not normal."

"Told you. We're not living safe and by the book this week." My eyes traveled to where the white sheet was pooling at her waist, giving me a glimpse of the bare skin of her hip beneath my tee.

I decided at that moment, I needed that forever. That look she was giving me, half annoyed, half turned on, I needed to figure out how to keep it.

But I thought it was a win when she rolled her eyes and grabbed a slice.

And now we're recovering from round two, my fingers running through her hair as her head lays on my chest, my other hand holding hers.

My eyes are on the clock, waiting for it to change.

For midnight.

Because every midnight is a new day I get to start with Zoe, a new day I get to work toward convincing her she's meant to be mine.

In the silence, the time change is loud, and the feel of her hand in mine as I squeeze it once, twice, three times is already becoming a comfort.

"Hmm," she murmurs like I've already trained her that when I do that, it means something.

Fuck, I like that.

I also like the way her hum vibrates against my chest, the intimacy of being with her like this, no matter how simple.

"It's midnight," I whisper, continuing to move her hair from her face. She washed it at some point after pizza but before round two, her straight hair washing out with it and leaving her with those wild curls I love. "Can I ask you a question?"

"What is this?" she asks, moving and looking up at me. "What's this midnight question thing?"

"I want to start every single day on this trip learning something about you. I want to know all of your midnight secrets."

She stares, leaning into me, and I wonder if she'll figure it out at this moment: what I'm doing. What I've *been* doing.

"Okay. Fine," she says.

"What?"

"I said fine. Ask your question."

I thought she'd argue.

I thought, at the least, she'd have a question of her own.

But instead, I just move and ask mine.

"What kind of house do you want?"

"What kind of house?" She looks at me so very confused, and shit, it's adorable.

I fucking love this woman.

I just need her to realize it once and for all.

"Yeah. A house? A condo? A giant mansion?" She smiles and shakes her head.

"Is there any rhyme or reason to these questions?" I shake my head in the negative.

I will never tell her that this entire trip, from the questions to the stops to the random shit we're doing, is all based on things her ten-year-old self put into a box.

I won't tell her I'm trying to make all her fairy-tale ideas come to life so we can live in the real world together.

"Not at all."

"You're weird, you know that?"

"You like it, though," I say with a smile, like we're kids teasing each other.

But still, I don't expect her reply.

"Yeah, I guess I do, don't I?"

A fucking step in the right direction, I tell myself, trying to fight the smile.

"A house," she says eventually. "Not a big one, but big enough so everyone has some room to breathe. But not too much, you know? I want us to bump into each other a lot. I don't want my kids getting into *too* much trouble."

"Mmm," I say, my fingers playing with her hair, stopping in tangled curls I love so fucking much and giving her the time she needs to expand.

"My house was too big growing up." Her voice is low and far off. "My parents wanted to give me whatever I wanted, but it was too big for three people. I could hide and not see them for days if I wanted."

"But my house?"

"Your house was tight, but perfect. You couldn't get away with too much shit there. You also couldn't stew on your emotions and avoid Luna if you were mad at her. Your mom would catch wind and make you guys talk it out. I liked that."

"That she made us talk it out? Or that we had each other?"

"All of it, I guess. I know my mom was done after me, but I

always wished I had a sibling. A brother or a sister to yell at and fight with."

"I get that," I say, because I do. I agree, even. "The house was annoying when you wanted to be sneaky, but I never felt alone."

"Yeah," she says in a whisper, and I know that means she felt alone sometimes.

I wonder if she still does—feel alone when she's off in the city, living the life she crafted to make other people proud.

Never again, I tell myself. *Never again will she feel lonely.*

TWENTY-FOUR
LONG LIVE
-ZOE-

We get back on the road the next morning, and it feels bittersweet.

In that little town, it felt like we were living in a sweet little bubble, as if we could act on everything I once thought was so far out of reach.

And now that we're leaving, the doubt and confusion are creeping back in.

I want to go back.

I want to go back and live in that simple bubble.

And I'm scared to death by how much I want that.

It's as I'm staring out the window, letting that feeling take over, when his hand reaches over and grabs mine.

One, two, three.

It's quickly becoming a comfort to me—grounding, in a way.

Isn't it funny how a simple gesture can mean so much in just three days?

"We'll go back sometime," he says under his breath, and I smile.

But I don't ask how he knew what I was thinking.

It's just Zander.

It's just us.

We've made it to South Carolina when he notices them.

It's my own mistake, really. I pull down the visor to check my face for food after we get back in the car after a junk food stop, and there they are.

"What are those?" he asks, tipping his chin to the visor where two pieces of paper are pinned.

"Nothing," I say, slamming the visor shut without even checking my face.

"It was something," Zee says, leaning over and flipping the visor down again. I move my hand to it, trying to stop him.

"Zander—"

And then he has them.

Two rectangular pieces of paper, delicate and yellowed with age but so goddamn dear to my heart.

"Are these . . . ?"

"They're tickets," I say quickly. "Now give them back before something happens to them."

"Hey, I remember this," he says with a smile, looking at the top one.

Taylor Swift: Fearless Tour
Madison Square Garden
August 27, 2009

Luna and I were fifteen.

Tony was nineteen; Zee was eighteen.

And they were forced to take us to a concert for a country-pop star against their will.

Please don't look at the second ticket, I think to myself.

Please, please, please.

But I've never had good luck.

So, when he sees my dad's handwriting on the top ticket that reads *Zoe's ticket,* his hand moves to look at the bottom one.

Zee's ticket.

My dad has been cautious and careful with me my whole life—his only child, his little girl.

Despite hours and hours of pleading for him to just drop Luna and me off at the venue in New York, I knew even then there was no chance.

I thought my mom would take us.

But when Luna and I were pleading to see our favorite musician in concert, Mr. Davidson was over to watch some game on our big-screen TV.

"Make the boys take them," he'd said. "That way, we don't have to watch some girl race around and scream about boys."

"You think the boys are old enough for that? To handle the girls?" my dad asked. I was sure the answer would be *hell no, I was just kidding.*

But Mr. Davidson had shrugged, staring at the TV, his mind only half in the conversation, I'd thought.

But my entire *heart* was invested.

"They're mature. Got phones. And Zee knows if anything ever happens to his sister, I'll hang him by his toes. So, yeah. They should be good."

My dad shrugged, murmured an *okay,* and three months later, he was handing over four tickets to his best friend's son.

"I labeled each of them, boys. Girls go in the middle, you two on the ends. Don't want any strangers next to them, do you understand?"

The boys nodded, taking the slips of paper from him and stuffing them in a pocket.

I remember how, on the drive there, Zander was fielding texts from his bitchy high-school girlfriend, Marie, who wanted to spend her last weekend at home before going to college with her boyfriend, but instead, he was taking his little sister to a concert.

I remember Luna murmuring that her mom hated that girlfriend.

I remember Tony telling Zee that when he went away to school, it was only going to get worse.

I remember hoping that when I was old enough to date Zander, he wouldn't be dating some bitchy woman.

I remember how, the way my dad wrote on the tickets, it was Tony, Luna, me, and then Zander.

I remember fighting the urge to sit through the whole concert, to ignore my idol on stage so that I could sit next to Zander the entire time. The urge to *accidentally* brush my elbow against his, to make a joke about how Luna was losing her mind, just to make him smile.

And I remember what happened about one-third of the concert in.

When she started to play "You Belong With Me," Zander looked down and smiled at me.

He leaned down, because he was always tall and I hadn't had my final growth spurt yet, and joked, "Is this song about Marie?" loud enough for me to hear.

And I remember smiling big and feeling confident and saying, "Only if that means I get to be Taylor." I meant it but regretted it instantly.

It wasn't cool to wish you were the singer in a song about a boy who has a shitty girlfriend and the singer wishes he were with her instead.

It revealed way too much.

But I remember the way his head tipped back and he laughed in a crowd of one hundred thousand people screaming along to a song, and I still could hear him.

I could hear that laugh anywhere.

And most of all, I remember how his hand tugged on my ponytail and he said, "Sure thing, pip."

And even though that night was the first time I saw my idol in concert, the first time my dad let me get a hint of being a big kid, going somewhere without a grown-up present, even though it was a bonding experience for my best friend and me, I still remember that moment most of all.

Sure thing, pip.

It was the first time I'd been upgraded from pipsqueak to pip.

"It's not a big deal," I say, reaching for the tickets.

I need them back.

I need them safe.

It sounds insane, but the idea of something happening to them has my blood rushing, panic flowing in my veins.

"You kept them?" he says, ignoring me and staring at them. He turns his body just a bit so I can't take them from his hands.

"Give them back," I say, not answering. "It's not a big deal, just something silly."

"Then why do you want them back?" he asks with a teasing smile.

"I just do, okay?" I say, grabbing onto the corner. He tugs just a bit and I panic, letting go.

"No, no! Don't rip them!" My eyes go wide with terror.

"I thought they were no big deal," Zander says, looking at me, trying to decode me. He's always been good at that, pulling out the true meaning and intentions of what I say.

I stare at him, trying to decide how to answer without revealing everything.

"*Pretend.*" His word runs through my mind.

Does that include being honest about dumb shit I find embarrassing? Dumb shit that has the potential to give everything away?

I look into his eyes and know the answer.

"I lied. They're important to me. Now give them back." And when his eyes go warm and he hands them back, watching me carefully pin them back up, I know I made the right decision.

"I think about that night a lot, you know," he says.

There's no smile on his lips, just honesty in his eyes.

"Your dad pulled me aside before we left and threatened to kill me if anything happened to you. Said he'd make it look like an accident."

My eyes go wide.

"No, he did not."

"Swear to God. I'm sure now that he was joking, but I was eighteen and your dad looked like he meant it and I don't know. It scared the shit out of me," he says with a laugh. "I also remember that night Marie was so pissed off at me, bitching because she was leaving for school the next day and wanted to spend the night together. She said I was playing favorites of her versus my sister."

"That girl had issues," I blurt without filtering my thoughts. My hand covers my mouth, and my eyes go wide.

But he laughs again the way he did that night.

Magic.

I don't think I've ever heard a laugh like his, one that both brings me joy and calms my soul.

"She did," he says.

Silence fills the car as I stare at those tickets, a cacophony of memories and thoughts coming to mind.

Then he breaks the silence.

"That's the concert you're going to tell your kids about, isn't it?" I turn to him and smile, then I nod.

"I mean, yeah." He smiles again, but it's smaller. More tender.

"We'll tell *our kids about it.*" My belly flips and flops, a strange mix of excitement and warmth and absolute panic.

"Zander—" I say, the words a warning.

"No. Live in the fantasy of this, Zo."

And then, because I'm still wrapped in the warmth of his laugh, I sigh then nod.

And the smile I get that time makes it worth whatever inevitable pain I'll deal with when this all has to end.

TWENTY-FIVE
OUR SONG
-ZANDER-

"Can you take that stupid thing out?" I ask hours after the ticket conversation as we approach our next destination. Zoe's feet are on the dash, her elbow out the window of her Jeep and her head back, silly pink cat eyeglasses on her face.

She looks at ease.

She looks relaxed.

Except for that stupid fucking ponytail.

"What?" Her hand moves to the dial to turn her music down to hear me.

I hate to admit it, but some of this shit isn't half bad.

The old stuff—the stuff I was forced to listen to when Zoe and Luna were young? That drives me up a wall. But the newer stuff, the stuff with a folky twist to it, I can hang with.

At the very least, it's great road trip music, perfect for driving with the windows down through old country roads as we avoid any major highway.

I've realized that as soon as we hit a highway, Zoe rolls her window up, bottling up her sunshine and smiles, the overthinking and dissecting coming back in her eyes.

So, for now, I'm staying on the backroads.

"Your hair tie. It's giving me a headache just looking at it."

"Uh, no," she says with a laugh.

"Take it out, Zoe." She looks at me confused, like what I'm saying doesn't make sense to her.

"Zander, I will not be doing that."

"Why?"

"Because then my hair looks a mess, and it whips everywhere."

"What's your excuse when you're just walking around town?"

She blinks at my profile, and I glance over quickly before putting my eyes back on the road.

"What?"

"Every time you're around town, you have your hair in that damn ponytail, slicked all the way back like you used a damn glue stick."

"I mean, I kind of do. I have this wax—"

"Exactly. Why?"

She doesn't get it.

She doesn't understand my question or why I'm asking. That much is clear when I look over and she's furrowing her brow, fully confused. "When you were a kid, you wore your hair wild. All over. Your mom would chase you around with a comb, trying to pin it back with little barrettes."

"I was like, ten, Zee."

"Okay?"

"Now I'm an adult. I need to look put together. And I don't always have it in a ponytail," she says like she won some argument.

"You're right. Sometimes you fry the crap out of it and straighten it."

"What do you know about straightening hair?"

"I have a sister and a mom. I grew up with you. Know that those straightener shits get hot enough to leave giant burn marks and stink up a house."

"Jesus—" She rolls her eyes, looking to the roof of the car like I'm exhausting her.

"Why, Zoe?"

My gut tells me that just like every change she made in her life to fit some mold, there's a reason for this, too.

I think she'll play it off or keep up the game.

But she surprises me with an honest answer I don't have to drag out of her.

"Because people like me better this way," she says with a sigh.

"What's with you and making people like you? You're Zoe, the girl who told me to fuck off and leave you alone when you were twelve."

She did, too. We were camping, and she was sitting at the campfire, and I kept giving her shit for how delicate she was with her marshmallows, barely toasting the sides and starting over when it caught fire.

"I was so grounded for that." I shrug and smile.

"I deserved it. I was bugging you, and you told me to stop multiple times politely. I didn't."

There's silence as we both get lost in the memory of our shared childhood.

I like this most, I think.

Having this history, these memories we share.

"What happened to her?" I can hear her sigh even over the wind from the open windows.

"She grew up, Zee." I shake my head.

"No, she disappeared."

I know when, too.

I know the exact night she changed, the exact night that girl disappeared.

We stop at a red light, and I reach over, grabbing the thick scrunchie and tugging until it starts to slip from her hair.

"Zander!"

When it's free, her curls fall wild, if a little dented where the hair tie was.

I made sure that after she washed her hair, she had no time to use the arsenal of hair tools she brought to fry her hair back to her preferred state.

"Zander, give that back!"

I look at her and smile, loving this version of Zoe.

This is my *version.*

What does she always say? Zoe's Version?

This is Zoe, Zander's Version.

I like her best of all.

"No," I say, then I drive as the light turns green.

"Zander!" I glance over, and her hair is wild in the wind, flicking left and right, a full-on tornado of curls.

God, she's so damn beautiful.

And she doesn't even know it.

"No," I say, and then when we hit the speed limit, I toss the scrunchie out of the window.

"What the fuck?"

"You look gorgeous with your hair down and natural. I like it that way."

"Well, I don't!" she shouts, reaching for her purse.

"You grab another, I'm tossing that one out the window, too." Her head turns to me, and I just know if we weren't in the car, her hands would be on her hips.

"Zander."

"Zoe."

"I can't even see the road, my hair is so crazy!"

I look over at the Zoe tornado and she's right.

She definitely can't see through her dark curls flying all around.

Fair enough. *I can help with that,* I think, reaching back behind us, my hand moving a bit until I find it.

"Here," I say, handing her a Springbrook Hills Bulldogs hat that says *coach* on the back.

She glares at me.

"If your only concern is that you can't see, here's a fix."

"Zander."

"Why don't you wear your hair crazy anymore, Zo?"

Again, I think she'll ignore me, not answer.

And then she does.

She might not realize it, might still be in her head overthinking every single interaction, convincing herself this is temporary, but she's opening up to me.

Slowly but surely, she's letting me in.

And there's no way in hell I'm leaving without a fight.

"Because it doesn't look professional. It doesn't tell people I'm someone to trust with their business or that I have my shit under control. It looks . . . chaotic."

"Chaotic is beautiful."

"Not when you're trying to convince people you're the right fit for a job. Or when you want people to think you know what you're doing or are trying to convince people you can handle yourself."

A lifetime of Zoe trying to convince people of things.

A lifetime of Zoe thinking she doesn't meet those expectations she's set for herself naturally, that she needs to change to fit some mold.

"Says who?" She sighs, clearly annoyed, and snaps out her answer.

"As soon as I started straightening my hair, my parents stopped bugging me about my plans for the future. People started taking me seriously. Men started asking me out."

"Even more reason to wear it naturally," I say under my breath.

Her hand moves out and slaps me, but there's a smile there.

"Shut up."

"You know that could have just been you—your confidence, your own vision of yourself. Chances are, you thought changing your hair changed something about you, and people felt that. Not the other way around."

She stays quiet with my words, playing with the brim of the hat while she thinks.

I let her.

And then she does what I hoped.

She moves her hand to her hair, gathering it and pulling it through the hole in the back before settling it on her head.

"How do I look?" she asks with a soft smile, tipping her head my way, her shoulder lifting as she does.

Shy, but beautiful.

"Fucking gorgeous," I say, a pang of something I won't look at too closely hitting me in my chest at seeing her in my hat, her face split with a smile.

She rolls her eyes, her hand moving to crank the music again before she goes back to sitting in the passenger seat, watching the scenery change.

I reach out, grab her hand, and place it on my thigh, my thumb brushing over her soft skin as I drive one-handed.

"You sit with me, your hair's wild, okay?" I feel her gaze burning on me. She's waiting for me to look at her so she can try and read my face, but I don't.

I give her this, this moment to think about what I'm saying.

"When we're together, you're not the version of you you made for other people. You're the version of you who danced crazy in my living room, the one who got grounded for telling me to fuck off when I was bugging you. You're that Zoe when you're with me, okay?"

Silence.

It lasts through the end of the song that's playing, but my thumb continues the brush over the back of her hand, and as I do, I wonder if I went too far.

Too obvious.

Where we are is precarious, close both to paradise and utter ruin.

But then she speaks.

"Okay, Zee."

And with those two works, I feel like I won something big.

I might have won the old Zoe back, too.

TWENTY-SIX
GIRL AT HOME
-ZANDER-

Zoe's in the shower at the little hotel I found in Georgia while I lie in the bed, waiting for our takeout to arrive, thinking about that night.

This isn't new—I think about that night often.

The look on her face.

The fear in my gut.

The words she said.

The way I figured that was my sign to move on.

And how she was always just a little bit different after, and I could only guess why.

Because the night Zoe changed was the only time I took a shot at her, and I've regretted it for almost fifteen years.

One summer night when Zoe was 19 and I was 23.

"Zander," the voice says when I answer my phone.

I know who it is, the contact giving me her name, but even if I didn't, even if the number were blocked, I'd know who it was based on that voice alone.

"Zoe?" I ask, my gut dropping. "What's up?"

Her breath sounds shaky when she speaks again.

"Can you . . . uh, can you pick me up?"

Not shaky—scared. Or hurt. Or both, maybe.

"Zoe, what is going on?"

"Can you pick me up, Zander?" The words are a bit firmer but still shake. "If not, I—"

"I'll get you, babe, but where are you? Are you okay?"

There's a beat of silence before she speaks, the words a whisper.

"I didn't think . . . I didn't think he'd try."

Acid burns.

He.

He'd try.

Try what?

Who?

Who made her sound this scared?

"Zoe, are you okay?" I ask, standing from where I was sitting on the couch in the apartment Tony and I rent, moving to grab my keys and wallet.

"I'm not hurt," she says, her voice cracking. "Maybe this was—"

"Where are you?"

I don't miss how she doesn't say she's okay, just that she's not hurt.

Fuck fuck fuck.

"Where are you, baby?" I repeat, my voice lower, calmer, as I walk toward my truck.

We can't both be freaking out.

One of us needs to be calm.

And with that hint of calm control, she relaxes just a bit, something I can feel even through the phone line as she gives me her location. I slam the car door, start my truck, and begin to drive in her direction.

"On my way," I say, putting her on speaker and placing the phone in the cupholder.

"Okay, I'll just—"

"You'll stay on the line, Zo. You're not going anywhere."

The way she sounds, I need to keep her on the damn line.

"You don't have—"

"I do and I will. Your voice? Zoe, it's shaking. You've got me worried. I'm not letting you go until I see your face." The panic of that truth, of the conclusions my mind is making, has my own stomach churning.

"Zander—"

"Stay on the line or I'm calling your father," I threaten.

Something tells me . . .

"Please don't." Her voice is low and scared.

Instantly, I regret threatening her like that.

"Fuck, Zoe, I—"

"Please, Zander. You're the only person I wanted to call. Please. I just . . . I don't need them all to know." I only wait for a beat to pass before I answer.

"That's fine, pip. No worries. I'm on my way. Stay on the line, okay?"

"Okay, Zee," she says, and the way her voice shakes has my foot hitting the gas heavier.

———

When I get to her, Zoe is standing outside an apartment complex, her arms wrapped around herself, and I have an absolutely terrible feeling about all of this.

It's not right.

Something happened.

I don't think I've ever seen sweet, carefree Zoe like this: wrapped into herself, fear on her face, voice shaking.

I park at the curb, and she tries to get in my car instantly, but instead, I kill the engine, hop out, and walk out to her.

"What's going on, Zoe?"

"Zander, I—"

"What's going on? What's got you shaken up?" There's no real reason for her to be on this side of town.

None of this is adding up to anything even slightly good.

My entire life, I've felt responsible for Zoe Thomas, for keeping my sister's best friend safe, keeping her whole and happy. The girl who would come downstairs at two in the morning and chat with me about everything and anything. The girl who would sneak me all of her burnt marshmallows because she knew I liked them that way and my mom would limit us to three each.

The girl I've watched go from the best friend of my little sister to a gorgeous woman with goals and dreams.

And something happened to knock that light from her eyes.

"Nothing, can we—"

"Why are you here?"

"I just—" She reaches for the door handle again, desperate to get in and get away, but my hands go to her shoulders, and I hold her in place and force her to look at me.

"Tell me, Zoe. What's going on? Why were you here?" I tip my head to the rundown apartment building just outside of town.

I know Zoe's friends. None of them live over here.

There's no logical reason for her to be here.

She sighs and looks at the sky, her dark curls tumbling down her back.

"I was with my boyfriend."

"Your boyfriend." The words twist a knife in my gut, something I absolutely will not be digging into more than I have to.

"*Ex*-boyfriend," she says with a huff. "Now, can we go?"

"Recent ex, I assume?"

I don't like that.

I don't like that at all.

And not just because the idea of Zoe having a boyfriend or a recent *ex-boyfriend* makes fire run in my veins.

"Yes, Zee, can you just give me the third degree in the car? I'm cold."

Something isn't right.

Something is so wrong, and I just know it has to do with some man and Zoe.

My fucking Zoe.

"No."

"No?" Her brow furrows, and it's sweet, but the edges of my vision are going red. I just *know.*

"No. Did he touch you?"

Silence.

"Zoe, did he touch you?"

More silence as panic fills me.

Dread.

Someone touched Zoe. Did he . . .

"We just had an argument."

"An argument." She nods, reaching for the handle. I don't unlock it, instead moving in front of the door so she has to step back from the vehicle and face me. "And then what?"

"And then I left, Zander. That's it." Her arms cross on her chest, her annoyed tough girl facade firmly in place.

"What did you fight about?"

"Nothing." The word comes so quickly, I know it's a lie.

"Jesus, Zoe. I'm about to lose my fuckin' mind if you don't tell me everything." Her jaw goes tight before she answers.

But she answers.

"We fought about me going out, okay?"

No, not okay, but we'll get there, I suppose.

"You going out?"

"Last night, I went out dancing with Luna. She posted a video online and he saw it. He was annoyed and told me I shouldn't do that anymore. I told him I would be doing whatever I wanted."

I fight the smile.

I really want this smile.

She's so damn headstrong, some kid telling her not to do something will probably urge it on more.

Tell me you don't know Zoe without telling me *you don't know Zoe.*

"What made you leave?"

Silence.

That's not good.

That's really not good.

Fuck fuck fuck.

"Did he say something?" She sighs.

"It's not a big deal, Zander." She refuses to answer, but the fact that she neither confirms nor denies it tells me so much.

"Not buying that, pip." She's not going to tell me, that much is obvious.

Fine. I'll go find him myself and ask.

"What apartment is he?" I ask, rolling my shoulders back and taking a step away from my car, toward Zoe, toward the apartments.

"Zander—"

"Tell me what happened or I'm knocking on every door in this complex until I find him."

"No, seriously, it's not a big—"

She's not going to give in.

Not without a bigger threat looming over her.

"Tell me or I'll call your dad."

Silence.

That's what she was avoiding, right?

I'm not sure why, but I know in my gut it's true.

"Zander, it's not a big deal, really. I just want to get out of here."

"What *happened?* What made you run out without even worrying about your coat? What made you call me and not your dad? Tell me what happened and we can figure it out together." She bites her lip, a finger grabbing one of her messy curls and twirling it, a nervous tick she's had for as long as I can remember.

Long moments pass before she speaks, and I wonder for a moment if it would have been better if she stuck to her guns, kept avoiding the question, and just forced me to take her home.

"He pushed me into a wall. I left right after, but I left my purse in his place, so all I have is my phone. I'm fine, but I—"

Something in me snaps.

"Where is he?" Her eyes go wide, as if she instinctively knows what that means.

I'm going to have some fucking words with him.

"Zander, no."

"Where the *fuck* is he, Zoe?"

"Zander." She's got that look on her face, her indignant tough girl coming out, the nervous one going back into hiding.

I need to be rational with this version of her. I can't run on anger and the need to protect her.

"How are you planning to get your bag?" I ask, my voice low and even.

Almost normal.

Almost.

"What?"

"Your bag. It's got your wallet? Your ID?" White teeth come out to bite a pink lip.

"I figured I'd call him in a day or two after we both cooled down."

"You were planning to go meet up with a man who *put his hands on a woman?*" My heart is racing. "With who?"

"I didn't think I'd need to go with someone. It really wasn't—"

I want to pin her against my car, to talk some sense into her.

I want to yell at her for being so careless with her safety.

But she's shaken.

She'd been through enough.

And I have to wonder, if she's been dating this guy for six months like I've heard Luna mention to my mom, how long has this kind of shit been going on?

So instead, I take a deep breath before cutting her off.

"Come on, pip. Which apartment?"

"Zander—" I step closer to her until we're barely a few inches apart, her head tipping back to look at me as I stare down at her.

I keep my hands to myself.

Even if I want to hold her head in my hands, even if I want to touch her to reassure myself she's okay.

"I'm trying to be nice, trying not to freak you out, but I'm *raging, Zoe*. I will not allow you to be in this prick's presence ever again, to get your bag or otherwise. I'm going to let him know that. You tell me where to find him, make this easy, I'll go in with you, help you get your shit, and we'll be gone. If not, I'm knocking on every door, and each wrong one will make that rage boil. That shit will build, so when he fuckin' opens that door finally, I might lose my shit, baby. I really don't want to lose my shit, especially not when you're already shaking. So please, do us both a favor and tell me *which fucking apartment* is his."

She stands there, eyes wide, and fuck, I think I went too far.

But then she speaks.

"We'll just go up and get my bag?" she asks, and a small smile comes to my lips, a smile of relief.

"Yeah, pip. That's it."

She stares at me like she doesn't quite believe me.

I don't believe me either.

But she turns and leads the way.

I pound on the door Zoe points out, watching her eyes go wide instantly, a hint of betrayal running through them.

She can get over that some other day.

"Jesus, calm down!" a deep voice says from inside. Feet hit the floor, the sound getting louder as he steps closer before it opens.

"Look, I'm over your shit—" he says, opening the door, then his words stop when he sees me standing there.

Clearly, he doesn't expect me.

"Who are—" he starts, but I push the door open, moving forward and into the shitty apartment.

"You the fuckwad who put his hands on her?" I ask, tipping my head to Zoe.

"Zander—"

"Get your bag, pip," I say, keeping my eyes on the man.

"Who the fuck are you?" he asks, a tough guy attitude on.

But he's barely taller than Zoe and scrawny as fuck.

I'm not the type to enjoy a workout, but I do it just enough to keep up at work, and I come from good, broad genes.

I loom over the man.

And I realize then that he's just that—a fucking *man.*

Twenty-seven, twenty-eight, edging in on thirty.

Way too fucking old for Zoe.

"Are you the man who pushed Zoe?"

"Who the *fuck* are you?" he repeats.

I step forward, and the coward steps back. My hand moves, pressing him in the chest until he stumbles back, hitting the wall.

"Answer my fucking question. Are you the piece of shit who pushed a nineteen-year-old girl?" His eyes go wide.

"Nineteen? She said she was twenty-six." I don't look at Zoe.

I know if I do, her blue eyes will be wide, her mouth will be open, and her face will be pale as can be.

My finger moves into his chest, stabbing there. "You look at her and tell me she's twenty-six."

Silence.

"Look at her and tell me that looks like a twenty-six-year-old woman." His eyes begrudgingly look over at my boss' daughter, but he stays silent.

"You can't."

"Man, what the fuck—"

"You're a sick fuck. Why'd you fight with her, huh?" I ask, my stomach churning because without asking, I know.

I know why shit escalated.

Know why Zoe didn't want to stay in this apartment.

I know why she called me and not her father.

"Look, man—"

I step forward until I'm in his face. Fury is running through my veins, anger, and aggression, and something I cannot look at too closely or it might implode.

"Why did you push her? Put your hands on a fucking *girl*. A teenager." I feel her move, feel her argument starting, and I put my hand out to the side, not moving my head even a fraction of an inch.

"Stay, Zoe."

She stops moving.

I can't see it, but I do feel it.

"She was here all the time, being a fucking tease—"

Tick, tick, boom.

My hand moves to his throat and I lift.

His legs kick, his hands coming to where mine are, but I continue to lift him just enough so he's on my height.

"Learn this now. No woman owes you shit. She comes over every day for a fuckin' year, you feed her, you pay her bills? She owes you *nothing*. Nod if you understand me."

He nods, his face going pink.

"Now, don't know how much my girl told you, but I live close. Real fuckin' close. And I'm going to keep my eyes on you. At all times, buddy. You even sneeze on a woman and don't say sorry, I'll be back here, paying you another visit. And I won't leave you with just a cough that lasts a few days."

There's silence as he starts to kick his feet.

"Nod if you *fucking* understand."

He nods again.

I should put him down.

"Stick to women your own fucking age, you piece of scum," I say. I can't put him down.

His face is turning blue now, fingers digging into my hands, but all I can think is how scared she looked when I pulled up.

How terrified her voice was when I answered.

But then I feel her hand on my back.

"Zander," she says, low and soft.

I let him down.

He gasps in air, sliding to the floor.

My vision is still tinged in red, and I just know that tonight when I let my mind travel, let it think about the *what-ifs* of what could have happened, that red will return.

"You got your shit, pip?" I ask.

"Yeah, honey," she whispers.

"Let's go," I say, putting a hand on her waist.

But not before I spit on the piece of shit who thought he was entitled to anything from Zoe.

We're in the car when I feel like I've calmed enough to let a breath get to the bottom of my lungs. Only then do I feel safe enough to speak to Zoe.

"Why wouldn't you want your dad to know?" I ask.

I don't ask how long she'd been with him, how she met him, or if her crew knows about the older man-child.

I just ask a question that doesn't make much sense to me.

Because *why call me?*

She sighs, and I can't help but think she'd been waiting for this question. Dreading it.

"He'd get himself in trouble," she says of her father.

She's not wrong.

Her hand on my arm, her soft voice—that was the only thing that stopped me.

But a father?

Knowing his only daughter was put in a position like that?

He'd definitely get himself in the kind of trouble she's thinking of.

"But I can get myself in trouble?" I ask with a laugh, though none of this is funny.

"No, it's not that. I just . . . I don't know. It was just you who I thought to call." She shrugs as she says it, her fingers playing with a frayed edge on the strap of her bag.

Something about that settles in my gut, feeling so fucking good as it does.

I like that.

That I'm the first person she thought of to call.

"I also don't want them to think of me like that."

That makes me pause. It also takes a bit of the shine away.

"Like what?"

"I don't know . . . just . . . whatever. It doesn't matter." I look at her, watching her face in the dim lights of the car as I slow at a stoplight.

"What?"

There's a pause, one where I think she won't tell me. Where she'll brush it off again.

"I want to be easy. I don't want to cause people any kind of issues. I don't want my dad to think I am irresponsible or that I put myself in that kind of position on purpose. I knew better. Fuck, I so knew better. He taught me better, and I . . ." She sighs, and the light goes green, forcing me to look at the road and start driving again. "My mom would worry, too."

"Isn't that the job of parents? To teach you, to worry about you?" When I glance over, she's looking out the window away from me.

"I don't want to be a disappointment." The words are almost inaudible.

"You are so far from that, Zoe. You know that, right?" She sighs heavily, the kind I know means it's been weighing on her for some time.

"I'm an only child. There is no one to pick up the slack. You won't get it. You three . . ." There's a light, self-deprecating laugh in her voice. "There's three of you. Less pressure to live up to expectations."

"Are you saying I get to be a loser because Ace is going to be a rockstar?"

"Ace is so *not* going to be a rockstar," she says, and I can almost hear the eye roll. But she hadn't seen him and the look he got in his eyes when he told Dad he was going on tour with Hometown Heroes this summer. "But no. Of course not. You're . . . you. You're everything your dad would have ever wanted."

"And you're not? God, Zo, your dad never shuts up about you. Goes on for hours about his princess. And your mom? That woman lives for you."

"My mom is a stay-at-home mom with only one child. She has nothing else to live for besides maybe waiting for grandbabies."

"I don't think you're giving your mom enough credit."

"You're right. She also lives to feed my dad." I can't help but laugh because that much, at the very least, is true. But still . . .

"I don't get it, Zoe. What are you saying? That you're not good enough?"

"Nothing. I'm saying nothing." I don't speak because she's saying *something*, even if she doesn't realize it. And I've known Zoe her whole life. She likes to stew on things, and if you don't interrupt her, if you don't try to guide her . . .

Two or three blocks later, she turns to where I'm sitting in the driver's seat. "Did you ever feel like you needed to grow up?" My brow furrows in confusion.

"What?"

"Like . . . like you still have all of your little kid ideas. Like you look at things and see fantasy. Fairy tales. Every idea you have, you can only see the good outcomes." There's a pause while she stares at me, but she's not looking at me. Instead, she's lost in her mind. "But that's not real life, you know?"

"I don't—"

"I don't want my parents to keep looking at me and thinking, *There's Zoe, never using her common sense. Never living in the real world. I wonder when she'll start acting like an adult.*"

"I don't think they ever think that, Zoe." A bitter laugh falls from her lips.

"Trust me, they do."

"Why do you think that?"

"Well, they tell me."

"They tell you?" A hint of anger runs through me at the thought that anyone, much less her parents, has been telling Zoe she needs to be anything but herself.

"It's not in a mean way. It's just . . . subtle. Like my mom will ask if I'm ever going to settle down, or my dad will ask if I *really* want to stick with interior design as my major instead of something more stable." I think I'm starting to understand.

And truly, I see both sides. I don't think her parents are being malicious about it, but she's right—they don't have any other children to focus on. So all of their focus is on making her successful.

But maybe their version of success isn't what Zoe wants.

"Your parents adore you, Zoe. They just want you happy."

"I know. But I'm . . ." She pauses like she's trying to explain something to me that she doesn't think I'll understand. "Okay, so, it's just me. There's a lot for me to prove. My parents don't have other kids to brag about, so I need to make sure that all the risks and sacrifices they made for me were worth it." She looks out the window. "And I'm not trying to open a business or working to be a rockstar. So, my version of brag-worthy has to be based in reality."

"We're not . . . That's not fair, Zoe," I say because I know she's thinking that she's somehow less than Luna or me or Ace.

"I know that. I do, really. But I'm the only child. And I *want* them to be able to brag about me. Right now, I'm just a girl going to community college who has a major that has a low chance of being able to be applied to a job in the real world. I have no idea what I want to do." I shake my head.

"You're nineteen. You don't have to know everything right now."

"I know. But in a way, I feel like I do. And then my dad has spent my entire life telling me not to get myself into a situation like I *just* got myself into. He would be so damn disappointed if I did."

"He wouldn't, Zoe. He might barge into that guy's place and beat the shit out of him, but he wouldn't blame you. You're nineteen. It's normal."

I'm sure as fuck not happy about it, but it's normal.

"I should have known better. I should have left. I shouldn't have been there in the first place."

I want to agree, but not because she did something wrong.

Because she should have been with me.

Woah, where did that come from?

"No one would hold it against you, Zo."

She turns to me, her eyes nervous.

"Do you promise not to tell anyone?"

"What?"

"I don't want anyone to know this happened. Do you promise not to tell anyone?" Her eyes are earnest, pleading. Begging, almost.

"Zoe, I—"

"I'm serious, Zander. Don't make me regret calling you."

And I want that.

I want to be the person she calls if she's in trouble. The one she trusts.

So I sigh, and then I nod.

"Thanks, Zee," she says, relief flooding her.

And I drive, deciding then and there that it's going to be my job to make sure Zoe gets to live a life that makes *her* happy—not everyone else proud.

Because Zoe has been mine for so fucking long, I don't even remember when it happened.

And I think it's time to let her know that.

———

"Where's your dad?" I ask not much later as we pull up to her house, noting there are no lights on and no cars outside.

"Date night with Mom," she says, eyes locked on her house as well.

I watch as her hand moves to the door, but I lock it before she can open it, stepping out and moving around the car to open her door myself.

"What a gentleman," she says as a joke, a small smile on her lips. I hold out my hand, and she takes it, using it to hop out of my car before moving toward her house.

But I don't let go. Instead, I hold her there.

I also don't comment on the joke, my face serious.

I *feel* serious.

I want her to know without a shadow of a doubt that what I'm about to say, what I'm about to do, is serious. That it means something to me.

"I'm glad you called me, Zoe. Glad I'm the person you think of to call."

Her eyes are wide when I move, pulling her closer to me, my arm wrapping her waist.

And for the first time, Zoe Thomas is in my arms in a way that is not purely platonic.

She's in my arms, and my hand is in her hair, holding her close.

Hair that is crazy soft and smells like damn strawberries.

Then she tips her head up to mine, and I see it on her face.

She feels it.

The pull.

The demand that I hold her close, to make her mine.

To kiss her.

My head dips down as hers tips up, my lips not on hers, but we're breathing the same damn air.

Finally.

Fucking finally.

It's like a part of me that has been hers from the beginning is dancing in excitement, in joy.

A part I refused to ever acknowledge.

But then she says it.

The words are breathy, whispered.

"Zander, you have a girl." My gut drops because she's not wrong. There's a girl I've been dating casually for a few weeks. Nothing serious, but still . . . there's a girl.

I should step back.

I should let her go.

But my hand stays in her hair.

I keep staring at her, reading her eyes, letting her read mine.

"Zoe, you say the word and she's gone. Say the word and I'm yours," I whisper, and I mean it.

In the moment, I can't even think of the girl I've been casually dating's name.

Long moments pass as her breaths cross my lips, as I plead with her to just say fucking *yes.*

To end this game we've been playing our whole lives once and for all.

"You should go home, Zee," she says, and with her words, my hand loosens in her hair. "Thank you. For helping me."

And I left.

Because the poor girl had already been traumatized enough without her best friend's older brother trying something on her.

But I never tried again, be it because of my bruised ego or shitty timing, I'll never know.

But I do know that after that, Zoe was different. She was refined, dressed more muted. That's when she started wearing those stupid ponytails and frying her hair until it was pin-straight every single day.

That's when she started dating stupid men, men who were safe, men who her dad liked well enough, men her mom would have over for one of her extravagant dinners.

But never men that, when she brought them to family events, lit her entire face up. Never men who, when they pulled her in close, her eyes smiled like he was telling her an inside joke without words.

Not like how she does with me.

And because of that, I know I won't be making the same mistake twice.

TWENTY-SEVEN
I'M ONLY ME WHEN I'M WITH YOU
-ZANDER-

The next day, it rained all morning, which, for a road trip, is shitty, but, for what I have planned tonight, is great because that means the clouds will be gone by then, leaving clear skies.

It also means it wasn't hard to convince Zoe to lie in bed for the majority of the day.

Wins all around.

For the majority of yesterday, she had gone further into herself, clearly overthinking what had happened the night before, trying to figure out how it could fit into her chaotic, unbearably suffocating life plan.

I let her have that. Because no matter what, this is right. This is good. It might not fit into her perfect picture of what her life *should* be and what *others* want her life to look like, but it's right.

Because really, I'm coming to understand that's Zoe's problem.

She has absolutely no vision for how *she* wants her life to look, how *she* wants her life to go, other than how she wants others to perceive her.

Every move she's made in both her professional and personal life has been with her parents in mind. How they would see that move, whether it would make them proud, whether it would be *impressive* enough.

Except, she doesn't see how her parents just want her healthy and happy.

So I gave Zoe the car ride yesterday, letting her be quiet and introspective, and then I reminded her that night and all day today what it's like to be together.

For us to be together.

Because it's fucking perfect.

We can lie in bed and laugh all day about dumb, insignificant things, spend hours reminiscing on our shared pasts.

She moans my name and has my cock hard in just a fraction of a second.

It's perfect.

And now we're setting out to the next step in my plan to show Zoe just how good we are together.

"It's getting dark. Should we find a hotel or something?" Zoe asks, staring out at the darkening sky as we drive.

"Nope," I say with a smile.

"No?"

"Nope."

"Do you have a hotel in mind already?" she asks, looking at me confused.

"We're not staying in a hotel tonight, Zoe."

When I glance over at her, I laugh at the look of nerves, shock, and just a hint of irritation.

"Zander—" I stop her before she gets too frustrated.

"Do you trust me?" I ask.

"That's not the point. I like a hot shower."

"And you'll get one tomorrow. I think I'd actually like to join you in that." She shakes her head and rolls her eyes, but I don't miss the touch of red that hits her cheeks. "Fuck, you wanna do that?"

"I would be more than happy to do that *tonight*," she says, a hint of irritation and something hotter simmering in her words.

I almost rethink my plan for a split second.

I almost turn around, pull into the nearest hotel, and drag her inside.

But I have a plan.

We have daydreams to live out, after all.

"Not tonight."

"Where are we going?"

"Don't worry about it, Zoe." She lets out an irritated huff that has me fighting a smile.

"I can't stand you."

"That's not even close to the truth," I say, letting that smile out but continuing to take her to our destination,

A few minutes pass when she sighs. I look over at her and see she's biting her lip, playing with the frayed edge of her shirt.

"What's wrong?" I ask.

"I don't like this." The words come through gritted teeth. She's clearly uncomfortable, and something is off.

"You don't like what?" My heart drops, wondering if she means this as in *us.*

God, when did I get so soft? When did my every moment of contentment boil down to Zoe Thomas?

Probably a long fucking time ago, I think to myself. *So long I can't even pinpoint it.*

"I don't like not knowing." I glance over and stare at her.

"What?"

"I don't like not knowing," she says. The words are terse, annoyed, like she doesn't want to admit them.

"I don't understand."

"*I don't like not knowing!*" Her voice gets higher, and I feel my eyes widen. I want to ask more, but instead, I wait. Wait for her to expand. And she does because she's Zoe and I know her better than she thinks I do. "I don't like not knowing what the plan is. I don't like . . . spontaneity. It gives me anxiety."

I keep my eyes on the road, mulling that over.

"That must be new."

Her head turns to me.

"What?"

"That must be new. Or at least, I've never known you to be like that." We hit a bump, and her hand goes to the handle of the Jeep, grabbing on. "When we were younger, it was Luna who was cautious. Luna was the one who wanted things explained before we jumped in and wanted to go over the pros and cons. You were always first to go on an adventure."

"Yeah, well, I grew up."

I hate that.

I hate that she thinks that's what she had to do in order to be an "adult," to lose all spontaneity and turn her life into predictability.

"And became what?"

"An adult, Zander. Some of us do that, you know? Grow up? We can't all live in some kind of fantasy land of flirting and playing cops and robbers."

It's meant to hit somewhere that hurts. She didn't say that without intention. She wants me to be offended, to stop the conversation before it gets too deep.

Before she's forced to reveal things she holds too tight.

And maybe it would have if I didn't know it was a defense mechanism.

"There aren't many robbers in Springbrook Hills, Zo. You'd know that best of all." She rolls her eyes and shakes her head, and *god, she's so fucking pretty.*

"You know what I mean."

I do.

But it's so much more than that.

Silence fills the space as I wait for her to expand, but this time, she doesn't, instead staring out the window, biting her lip as I drive.

"Why did you change?" I ask eventually, my voice quiet.

My expectations are low. I don't think she'll give me an answer.

So really, I'm not surprised when she asks me another question in response.

"When did I change? Because I think you're missing the difference between *changing* and growing up," she says, and the question is like a challenge.

And I think, for some reason, if I answer it right, I'll get an honest answer.

If I answer it wrong, I'll be losing some kind of test.

"After that night. That night I picked you up. That was the day you changed."

A long minute passes and although I can feel her eyes on me, trying to read me, I don't look at her.

I wait until she speaks.

"How did you notice that?" I smile and shake my head because she still just doesn't get it.

"I notice everything about you, Zoe."

She doesn't respond.

I don't think she knows how, to be honest.

So this time, I do her a favor and I fill in the silence.

"That night, we were in the car, and you told me you didn't want me to tell anyone because they would think you were irresponsible, that you'd be a disappointment. I tried to explain how fucking wacked that was, but you ignored me. You were so wrapped up in supercharged emotions—"

"I wasn't wrapped in emotions, Zander. I was coming to an understanding. I was realizing that everything my parents feared was actually *valid*. That night, I decided that living with my head in the clouds was leading me in a bad direction, just like my dad always told me it would."

"That's not—" I start, but she's on a roll now and keeps talking.

"I thought I liked that guy, even though my gut said it was a bad idea. I knew he was too old. I probably knew he was a piece of shit. That's why I didn't even let him meet Luna. I thought he liked me. It wasn't even a big deal. But then . . . well . . . you know."

"Oh, I fuckin' know," I say, remembering that night, my voice low.

Even now, ten years later, my blood heats with the memory.

"After that, I was more careful. Now everything is planned, no surprises. I think things out. I think . . . No, I know. It's for the better. It's safer."

"Safe is boring."

"Safe is *safe*." I shake my head in disappointment.

I don't know if I'm disappointed *in* her or *for* her.

"You sound like your fuckin' father."

"Is that a bad thing?"

"Not if your job is to keep people safe and to foresee every outcome. But if you're a young woman with a life of excitement out there to live? No. If you're a woman living so safe, she's making herself miserable? No, it's not a good thing." She thinks about that, and I let her, resisting the urge to speak and fill in the silence for another few minutes. I let her stew on it, give her the opportunity to speak first.

But she doesn't.

She just keeps staring out the window, ignoring me.

So I ask what I've been wondering for a week.

"So if you think everything out, what happened last week?"

Her body freezes.

Ding ding ding. Target hit.

"What?"

"What happened last week? You quit your job and dumped that boring stockbroker—"

"He wasn't boring."

I'd met the man briefly at Luna and Tony's wedding.

He looked exactly like what you would expect: a well-tailored suit, refused to eat anything that looked processed or out of his hyper-specific diet, and had hair combed perfectly with gel or hairspray or who the fuck knows.

He looked like a salesman.

I remember wondering if that's how he won Zoe over—if he got her by selling himself instead of stocks or companies. Just a tiny shift in language and Zoe was sold to the safe, boring man of her reality.

"He was as interesting as watching grass grow."

"Just because he wasn't your type of person, doesn't make him boring, Zee."

"Was he your type of person?" I ask impulsively, and I almost regret it.

Almost.

But then she scrunches her nose and tips her head from the left and to the right, and I know the answer before she even says it.

"I guess not." She sighs, and I'm actually a bit shocked she answered honestly. "Okay, yeah, he was a little boring." She looks at me with a tiny smile. "He organized his socks by colors."

I scoff out a noise, head tipping back with a laugh, and then listen to her giggle along.

The most gorgeous fucking sound known to man.

I'll die on that hill.

"So, I guess you don't organize your socks by colors, huh?"

"Only if by that you mean I buy all the same color socks and throw them in one bin."

"You don't pair your socks?" she says, aghast, like I committed some terrible sin.

"They're all black, and they're all the same height. So, no." Her eyes are wide like that's absolutely insane.

I shake my head, letting that settle for a minute as we drive before I try again.

"What changed last week, Zoe?" I ask.

I think she'll ignore me.

I think she won't tell me, or at least won't tell me the truth.

But then she starts.

"It's silly, really." When I look over, her fingers are playing with that frayed edge of her shirt again. "So silly."

"Nothing is silly if it matters to you, Zoe."

It's silent before she picks up again.

"When Luna and I were kids, we had this box of wishes. Your mom made us make it once and it became a time capsule, almost. It was . . . It was special. I thought Luna lost it, or it was stuck at your parents or whatever, but she found it and we were going through it last week when I was over there." She sighs, looking out the window, avoiding my gaze.

I reach out, grab her hand, and strum my thumb across the back of hers, the skin warm and soft.

"So, I found this little paper where we put everything we wanted out of our lives. Like jobs and where we wanted to live—the whole nine."

The MASH card

"Okay, and?"

"And my life was so different than what I had once envisioned. You're right. I've been playing it safe. So I lost my mind, and I quit my job the next day, and I dumped Jeffrey and, you know what? I felt okay about it."

She sounds kind of surprised by that.

"And now you have a new job interview coming up, right? Is it more aligned with what you want to do? Design?" I ask, tipping my chin to the magazines that have stayed in the passenger seat, becoming more and more worn with repeat reads.

I could manage that: a commute if she landed her dream job, something that makes her happy.

I'd drive the hour to her every day, leaving early to beat traffic and get to work on time. Or we could find a place halfway . . .

My mind goes off on workarounds for a woman I'm not completely sure will even agree to be mine once we return to the real world.

My gut twists, and I feel sick at that thought, one I've refused to inspect too closely since this trip started.

Zoe huffs out a half laugh and shakes her head.

"I don't have any experience in the field of design. Not enough that I could apply for a job and land it. No, this job is pretty much the same, just a different corporation."

"A corporation," I repeat. She said the word with malice and disgust, making it stand out.

"No, I didn't mean that. It came out weird." She shakes her head again, trying to find her footing that I've clearly made shake.

I know she *absolutely* meant it like that, regardless of how it came out.

"I just mean, it's a big company. Pay would be about the same, but my title, if I land the job, would be better. More impressive." I nod.

The title would be impressive.

That's the only perk she can think of for this job.

"Did you like your old job?" I ask, and I see it before she even opens her mouth.

No.

She was miserable.

In fact, I saw it over the years when she was commuting from Springbrook Hills and working from home and then when she was home for holidays or long weekends after she left to live in the city.

She was miserable in that job. Probably in that field.

"I didn't hate it. I wasn't fond of the people I worked with, that's for sure." Her voice is like she's reading a speech she's prepared, something she repeats regularly.

For herself or for others, though?

"But the job—you liked it?" I ask.

She tips her head to the left and then the right, like she's weighing her response, the pros and cons of either one.

"Yes and no. When I started, I had more creativity. I worked on the campaigns I was assigned to, designed them, and thought up the concepts. It was like design. But as I climbed the ladder, it was more just being responsible for keeping the people *doing* the designing on track."

"So why not go to a more hands-on position?"

She breathes in deeply.

"They don't make as much. Definitely not enough to afford to live in the city and not enough to help my parents out if they ever need it when they retire. And I want them to be proud of me. Executive assistant doesn't sound nearly as brag worthy as *VP of Marketing*."

I blink.

"You know your parents don't give a shit about that kind of stuff."

"They do. You should hear them when I get a promotion." I shake my head and scoff.

"Because they're *proud* of you, Zoe."

There's a pause, and I think she's deciding if she wants to tell me something.

When she starts, I know she decided in the affirmative.

"Did you know when I first went to school, I was an interior design major?" she asks, and once again, her face is looking out the window.

Avoiding my eyes.

"Of course, I know that, Zo." *I know everything I can about you.* "You changed a year in." *Not long after that night.*

"That whole year, my dad kept telling me it wasn't a marketable skill. That there was no security in that kind of job. That I should move to something more flexible, more able to adapt to different options."

My gut sinks, and her hands move back to her shirt. "Over the summer, when I was home, I told him I was thinking of going into marketing. I wasn't sold on it, but I was weighing my options. You'd think I told him I was going to be a doctor. The relief that took over . . . I don't know. He seemed proud."

My gut sinks for her.

It also sinks for her father, who, I know to my core, does not feel she ever wasn't impressive or brag worthy or whatever fucked-up shit she thinks.

I was new when she was in college, but I remember even before I worked for Mr. Thomas, he'd come to my house and have a beer with my dad.

No matter what Zoe was doing, he was proud of her.

My Zoe, off at school learning how to make spaces beautiful. She's gonna go design some celebrity's house or something, I'm sure. No idea what half the shit she says means, but she loves it. And she's gonna be great at it.

"So you changed your major?" I ask.

"I mean, not right away. But the first semester of my sophomore year, I took a class on art history. It was a gen ed. I almost failed it, I was so shit at it. I figured it was a sign, you know?"

"Why? Because you weren't amazing at telling which dead artist made what sculpture?" I ask, annoyed.

Irritated at the school for making her take some stupid class that made her question herself.

Mad at her father for not making her feel like her chosen field was a good choice.

And mad at Zoe for deviating from what she wanted.

Just mad all around, really.

She laughs, and at least there's that. The laugh doesn't sound stifled or nervous or sad. Her hand moves to the driver's side, slapping me playfully.

"Stop it. It was more than that. It was just not for me."

"You've been staring at those magazines since I picked them up for you."

"My pickings are slim, Zee. You took my phone."

"You've got your music."

"Thank God for small blessings," she says with an eye roll.

"Look, you want me to take back control of the radio, I'd be more than happy to give the *Taylor Slaylor* playlist a rest."

"No!" she says quickly, and fuck, she's cute.

I want this always.

Zoe and me arguing about dumb shit, driving around. Killing time together.

"You haven't been reading that book you brought," I say of the self-help book that she'd hidden in the back seat behind bags.

She bites her lip.

"I mean, you're right. I should—" She reaches back.

"You grab that book, I'm tossing it out the fuckin' window."

"Zander!"

"I'm not playing games, Zoe. This trip is not for the version of you that you think everyone wants to see. It's for the version of you that needs some fresh air, the version you hide away."

"There's only one version of me, Zander," she says, her voice quiet now.

I look over at her and shake my head, sad.

"No, Zoe. That's just not true. There's this version—the one that's so tightly wound you can't even figure out what to do next without consulting a self-help book. The version that is so crazily curated to fit some kind of standard only you are holding yourself to."

"That's not true. Work sets me to these standards. Dates do. Society does as a whole. It's not enough to just be good anymore, Zander. You've got to be the best at what you do and then keep working to be better. I might live a regimented life that's boring, but it's because I want to succeed."

"No," I say, shaking my head. "It's not because you want to succeed. It's because you think if you don't hit those imaginary tiers, if you don't hit that level of 'success' people around you—Zoe, people who love the real you and always *have*—will be disappointed. You've lived for ten years walking on eggshells that are other people's vision of what you should be."

There's no response, and when I look at her, she's staring at me with a blank face.

I'm not sure if it's blank because she's shocked or because she can't handle what I'm saying, but I keep going.

"The real version of you is so far buried beneath other's expectations, I thought there was a chance she was gone forever, Zoe. But then you questioned it all and threw away what you knew, and I got a glimpse of her. That Zoe? That Zoe is the one I fell for when I was 23, and I begged her to let me give us a chance. That one has been coming out little by little again, shining just a bit in the sun. I fucking *miss* that Zoe. That Zoe? That Zoe I would sit up at two AM and have ridiculous conversations with. That Zoe would point out stars and make her own constellations. That Zoe sat in a photo booth with me and giggled like she didn't care who heard her snort-laugh." I can see her eyes go wide from the corner of my vision, and I smile.

"But that Zoe started to fade that night when I picked you up. I watched for over a year, watched her disappear." Finally, I look at her, and her eyes are on me.

Softer now.

Not nearly as shocked or hurt or whatever other feeling she's feeling.

"I'm making it my job to bring her back, pip," I say, and then I look forward, turning her music up and letting her stew in her thoughts while I drive.

TWENTY-EIGHT
UNTOUCHABLE
-ZANDER-

"Do you remember when we were kids and your mom and Mags would set up all those blankets in the backyard on the solstice or when there would be a full moon or something like that?" Zoe asks twenty minutes after I leave her to stew.

I wonder, not for the first time, how she always seems to be on the same page as I.

Because those are some of the best nights of my childhood.

My mom and her hippie sister Mags would spend the day getting ready, doing God only knows what, and making the backyard a literal fairy dreamland. They'd lay out snacks and tons of blankets, and we could invite a few friends over to join in on the chaos. Then we'd lie out under the stars and find patterns or wish on the moon or wait for some kind of meteor shower.

I'm like my dad in that I don't necessarily put too much thought or faith into it, but even if it never once brought me love or wealth or health or what-the-hell-ever (which my mom heavily argues that those nights definitely brought *all* of those things to us), it did give me memories that bring me joy.

"Yeah. Those were a blast. Sometimes your sister and I do them in Tony's backyard now."

"Doesn't surprise me," I say, reaching over to grab her hand, squeezing it three times, and placing it on my thigh.

I can't stop thinking about it.

How I like this best.

Reminiscing about our shared childhood, remembering just how much history there is between us, her hand on my thigh as we drive, my thumb brushing over her soft skin.

"What did you used to wish for?" she asks as we continue to drive, the sky darkening further.

"What?"

"Your mom always made us make a wish, even if it wasn't that kind of star show. What did you wish for?"

I smile.

I won't tell her that when I was a teen, I wished for a chick with a fat ass to fall in love with me so I could slap it anytime I wanted.

She doesn't need to know that *that* wish most definitely came true —it just took fifteen years for her to admit it

So instead, I go with the easy answer.

"I wanted to be a football coach."

"And you are," she says, her voice holding a smile.

"Yeah, not exactly the kind I thought I'd be when I was fifteen, but I can't complain. Those kids are fuckin' awesome."

"Your mom always said you have to be super cautious of what exactly you put into the universe. You can't be broad."

"That explains that," I say, not telling her that it also explains a lot of other wishes I've made in this lifetime.

A few more minutes pass, and I wonder what she's thinking.

Is her own mind stuck on the wishes that did or didn't come true?

Or is she still thinking about what I told her earlier?

About old Zoe and new Zoe.

"National park?" she says as we pass a sign, entering our final destination.

"Trust the process, Zoe."

"It's not a process; it's a car ride."

I shake my head with a smile because I both can't stand her and absolutely adore her.

"Jesus, pip. We gotta work on bringing fun Zoe back. This one's too uptight."

Silence falls over the car as it bounces on dirt roads. I look over at her, and in the dim light, her hands are crossed over her chest and she's looking out the window.

Fuck.

"What?" I ask. "What did I say?"

"Nothing."

It's never *nothing* with women.

If I learned a single solitary thing from my mother and my sister and from the sage, battle-tested advice of my father, it's that it's literally *never* nothing.

Especially not when it looks like that.

"Zoe, what is it?" I turn into the spot I reserved for the night, a tiny plot of open, grassy field next to a parking area.

"It's nothing, Zander, really. It's dumb."

"It's not, and if you don't tell me, I'm gonna get into a mood of my own."

Silence, and I think she might ignore me.

Or she might give me some kind of attitude back.

But instead, she surprises me.

"You don't like this version of me."

"What?"

"You said we have to work on bringing the fun Zoe back." I blink at her. "This version of me isn't *fun Zoe.*"

Fuck.

I did say that.

I didn't *mean* that, but I said it.

Goddammit, I need to stop fucking this up.

I need to stop forgetting that she's delicate.

Opening the door, I hop out and slam it shut, then I jog in the warm air until I reach her door. Opening it, I put a hand out, begging her to take it.

Please take my hand.

She stares at it before rolling her eyes, unbuckling, and taking it.

I pull her into my arms, one going around her waist and the other running up her back, burying itself into her curls at the nape of her neck, and pushing her face into my chest.

My head dips until my mouth is at her ear.

"Zoe, I like every fucking version of you: the princess who used to chase me around with a wand and try to turn me into a toad, the version that sang karaoke in my living room like she didn't care who was watching, the version that wrote in diaries about how big of a crush she had on me then left them under my little sister's bed."

She tries to pull her head back, to escape—from embarrassment or to yell at me, I don't know—but I hold her head in place, continuing. "I love the version that keeps a ticket from a concert we went to fifteen years ago. I love the version that wants everyone to see her value, and I fucking love the version who jumped into her car to go on a random road trip with me. I love the version that doesn't want me to get crumbs in her damn Jeep, and I love the version that gave in when I told her I needed food. I love the version that remembers crazy things we did as kids because that means we have memories together since the beginning."

Her head tries to move, her voice starting to protest with my name, but I press it in more.

"You keep pretending, Zoe. You keep living in this road trip ideal world where this is all fun, and we can figure out the details later, but know that I'm not pretending. This is us. This is me and you, and I'm not turning back." Finally, I let go of her head, and it instantly moves back to look at me.

Her eyes are glassy, but beneath that, there is a universe of questions and emotions and thoughts.

Some great.

So fucking great that I just know there's a chance.

Some are not so great—some things I'm just gonna have to deal with eventually.

Ledges I'm going to have to talk her off of.

That's fine.

I'll spend my life talking Zoe off ledges if she lets me.

"Zander—" she starts, but I don't let her. My hand moves to her chin, tipping it up, and with my lips to hers, I move her back, pressing her into her car and aligning my body with hers.

And then I kiss her.

And I remind her of who we are.

And I let her soul remember that and force it to forget the complications and potential disappointments.

Because none of that—not a single, tiny molecule of it—matters if I have this woman as my own.

"Come on. Let's go look at the stars," I say and watch her eyes go wide and her mouth opens just a bit.

Fuck.

I can't think of a thing in this life I wouldn't do to get that look from her again and again.

"What are you talking about?" She looks around, trying to piece things together.

"The sky is dark out here. We did this with everyone as kids. Now we can do it with just us." She blinks, and god, she is so damn cute.

"But we don't have anything." I can almost hear her panic building over not being prepared for any and every occasion she might have.

"You already have, like, fifteen giant blankets in the trunk. At our last stop, I bought a cooler filled with food and snacks."

"Where was I?" she asks, brows furrowed.

I can't resist.

I press my lips to the spot between them, like my kiss can fix whatever is ailing her.

"Spending an hour in the bathroom. Off flirting with old men. Overthinking." She stares at me, blinking before she shakes her head and speaks in an awestruck voice.

"Who the hell are you?"

"I think your Type A planning is rubbing off on me," I say with a smile. "Let's just hope some of my coolness is rubbing off on you."

"Excuse me?!"

"You could really use some." I grab her hand and lead her to the back of the SUV to grab our stuff. "Come on. Let's go stare at the stars."

TWENTY-NINE
GORGEOUS
-ZOE-

"Can I ask you a question?" he says, and without even looking at the clock, and I know it's midnight.

Zander's midnight questions.

"Only if I can ask one back," I say. He smiles like he knew that was coming, like he knew he would only get so long where he could be the main question asker.

I've been planning this for 24 hours, what I'd ask tonight, knowing I could probably get a question of my own.

"Deal," he says with a smile.

He had to know this was coming.

"If you could live anywhere and jobs or money weren't an issue, where would you live?" he asks, and it's an easy answer.

I love my hometown.

"Springbrook Hills." He smiles in the light of the stars, moving a curl from my face, and I keep going. "Living in the city made me realize I hate people." His head tips back with a deep laugh.

"You? The woman who can talk to a stranger for hours about their life story?"

"Okay, maybe it's not that I hate people. I hate . . ." I roll to my back on the plaid blanket, staring at the dark sky and the bright stars. "I hate how many people there are. And how I know none of them."

Zander rolls with me until he's on his side next to me again.

"You were spoiled at home. No one's a stranger for long in the Hills."

"No. And it feels like everyone's a stranger in the city. Even at work, in the office. Don't get me wrong, I had coworkers I was friendly with there, but it's not the same. I'd say hi and bye, and we'd share niceties. We'd go to get drinks and talk about work. But I couldn't tell you if they have sisters or brothers or anything important. I miss that when I'm not home: knowing everyone and having everyone know me." I sigh.

"I know it sounds stupid and like I'm just boring and from a small town, but—"

"You're talking to the man who never left that small town. And Zoe, everything you just said? It's why I never left. I love Springbrook Hills. I love the community. I love knowing when I have kids, they'll have aunts and uncles they aren't related to by blood. Love knowing they'll spend summers at the Center and they'll have Dean as their guidance counselor. Nothing wrong with loving a small town."

I sigh.

It feels strange admitting this. Most people want to flee a small town and jump to a big city. In a way, I feel like a failure, missing it when I'm in the city so many dream about.

Let's move on.

"Okay, my turn," I say with a smile, turning to Zee. He wedges a hand between me and the ground, lifting me with a strong arm until I'm on top of him.

"Hit me," he says, his smile wide as he tucks a curl behind my ear, but not before staring at it with something so freaking close to adoration.

Maybe I'll keep my curls, stop straightening them twice a week.

If it keeps him looking at me like that, I would do almost anything.

And with my mind still warm with his look, I ask my question.

"Why were you so mad the night Hunter got engaged?"

I remember it so well, Hometown Heroes playing on the little stage in his sister's bar, Hunter calling up Hannah to ask her to marry him with the help of the kids from the Center, a whole spectacle.

And the entire time, he kept glancing at me in the dim bar, his jaw tight.

He lasted thirty minutes before he walked out the back.

I still don't know why I followed him.

"Zee, what's wrong?" I asked, the cold ripping through my light jacket.

"Go back inside, Zoe," he said through gritted teeth, like he was holding back words and only his teeth were keeping them from spilling out.

"Is everything okay?" He looked terrible. Angry. Pained, even.

"Go inside, Zoe. It's cold."

"Zander, I—"

"Get the fuck inside." He turned to me, and I saw so many things in his eyes, the one light out behind Luna's shining down on him and masking the majority of them. "It's cold. You're going to get sick."

"Cold doesn't make you sick." He scoffed out a laugh and shook his head at me.

"You know, it's so fucking funny to me how every other moment in the past, what, Zoe? Ten years? You've done everything in your power not to be alone with me. Now you're so fucking eager to follow me out, to dissect all of my emotions that, to be honest, aren't your fucking business."

That hit.

Because he wasn't wrong.

When I was nineteen, I called him in a panic and needed his help. I called him not because I had no one else to call, no one else to help me, but because at that moment, he was the only person I could think of.

It took me almost a year to figure that out, to decode that the reason I was avoiding Sundays at the diner and going to see my dad at work was because of Zander Davidson.

The boy I'd always loved.

The boy I turned down.

And I'd done it only partially because the timing was wrong. And it was—it was so fucking wrong then. He had a girl, not a serious one, but one all the same, and I knew in my heart of hearts that if I had said yes, if I'd accepted, I'd wonder for the rest of my life if he'd ever give that offer to someone else.

Say the word and she's gone, Zoe.

My heart would know it was for me and me alone, but my common sense? She'd never fully believe it.

Even if he did dump that girl anyway that following week.

But I'd turned him down partially because I knew how easy it would be to lose myself in Zander Davidson. To risk it all—my future, my past, my heart. To put the relationship our parents have at risk for what? A teenage crush?

But my biggest regret isn't even saying no the night he saved me.

It was giving him a tight smile and a nod when he told me to leave out behind his sister's bar, not saying a damn word and turning around.

Because I know now that if I had even tried, he would have fought for me.

He would have fought for this.

But I turned around like the coward I was.

The coward I am, really, still playing pretend.

When he doesn't answer me after a while, both of us lost in my own memories, I repeat the question.

Something about the stars, about this night, gives me courage I didn't think I had three, four days ago.

"Why were you so mad that night?" He sighs, and I try to move, to give him room, but that arm wraps my waist tighter, holding me in place.

"You know, my question was a softball. You couldn't give me one back?" he asks with his easy smile, the one that he uses to play everything off.

I think that for the first time since we went on this trip, if I gave him an out, he'd avoid answering and act like it never happened.

"I didn't ask questions for three nights. Seems fair to me," I say, my voice low, my hand moving hair from his forehead.

This feels important.

I need his answer.

He shakes his head and smiles. "Swear to God, tomorrow night, I'm giving you a hard one."

Silence fills the air as we lie in some national park in Georgia, the stars our only witnesses.

I almost interrupt, almost tell him he doesn't have to tell me, but then he speaks.

"I was standing there, trying to be happy for them. I wanted that, to be happy for them. They both went through shit, both deserved it, to find each other and have each other. But I was standing there, and Tony and Luna were fucking canoodling and happy, and all I could think was *that should be us.*"

My heart stops.

The world stops.

The entire fucking universe.

"It should have been us, you know? All along. That should have been me and you, getting engaged in front of everyone, the couple everyone knew would make it from the start."

"But we never—" I try and argue for a second time since this trip started.

"We did, Zo. Whether or not you admit it, whether it was formal or if the world recognized it, we did. We *always did. Always were.*"

"I don't—"

"Don't play dumb. You're a smart woman. Don't treat me like I'm stupid, either." I can feel my heart racing, but the craziest part is how I can feel his through his thin shirt as well.

"Zander—"

"Why did none of the men you dated ever work?" he asks, and with that, I try to move, to roll off him, to get space, but he holds me close. "Those men who, on paper, were perfect. Were safe. Made you smile just enough. You looked good with them. Looked happy enough. You've settled for a safe, okay life so far. Why not settle down, get married? You want to please your parents so bad, why not give your mom the wedding she wants? The grandbabies?" I bite my lip.

He's right.

I never did.

And I won't admit this, but most of my relationships have ended as soon as they brought up a future.

Marriage.

Kids.

That's when it stopped working for me.

When the distraction became too real.

"There was always something—some string, some tether that kept us together. You felt it, always knew it was there. It stopped you, held you back, wouldn't let you give everything to the men who would die to win you."

"I don't—" He cuts me off again.

"Why haven't you left town, Zo?"

"I did. I lived in the city."

"For three months. And as soon as things got too real, got too permanent, you cut ties and ran home. Why?"

"I don't—"

"I'll tell you why I haven't left," he says, his voice firm, and I'm scared of what he's going to say.

We talked about this early, both skirting around loving our hometown, but there's more.

There's always more when it comes to Zander.

And I just know this conversation is going to change something in me.

Or cement something in me.

"Zander—" I start, trying to stop him.

I'm *scared*.

"You. You're why I've stayed here. Not intentionally, but when I look at it? Yeah. It tracks. You tied me to this town the same way I did to you. It wasn't your parents, not your friends. We were both waiting for the moment when it was right. I think we ignored seventeen thousand signs along the way, but here the fuck we are, Zoe. Where we were always gonna end up one day."

I stare at him.

I don't know what to say.

But I do know I don't want to argue.

What does it mean that I don't want to argue?

"All good, Zoe," he says, his voice so low. "All good. We'll tackle this when we're back home. Live in the fairy tale for now. Okay?"

And right then, I let the little girl who always trusted Zander Davidson with both my safety and my heart take the reins.

"Okay, Zander."

THIRTY
GLITCH
-ZOE-

We sleep under the stars that night, cuddled under blankets and waking slowly with the sunrise.

And while he packed well for a junk-food dinner, grabbing pre-made sandwiches and chips and drinks, his breakfast game was a bit more lackluster.

Still, I didn't complain when I had a soda as my morning caffeine (it helped that Zee promised to stop at a coffee shop as soon as we were on the road) and chips as breakfast.

Because I got to do it in Zander's arms, the man still groggy as we watched the sunrise together.

Of course, it wouldn't be me if we didn't hit a bump as we packed up and started for the car. Zander is dipping his hand into a bag of Cheetos with one hand, the bag and my keys dangling in the other.

I stop walking altogether.

"You can't get in like that," I say, my eyes wide as I stare at Zander's fingers.

They are absolutely *coated* in orange cheese powder.

He laughs like I said something funny, then he stops when he sees my face.

"What?"

"You can't get into my Jeep like that, Zander."

"Zoe—"

"If you get cheese goo all over my Jeep, God help me, I'll call your mother and tell her it wasn't the dog who ate all of her cookies that she baked for the high school football team but you and Tony when you came home drunk off your asses."

"You wouldn't." A small smile starts to spread on his face.

"I won't if you clean your hands."

"How the hell am I supposed to clean my hands, Zo?"

I give him a sigh that screams *men*.

Though, to be fair, I think that's the kind of sigh only women can interpret correctly.

"Follow me," I say, walking to the back of my SUV, opening the back tailgate, and digging through my emergency bag before handing him a package of wipes.

"You have wipes? In a Jeep?"

"I have wipes in my emergency kit."

"Wipes are for emergencies?"

"When it comes to Cheeto fingers in my car, yes." His smile grows, and I want to be annoyed, but there's this bubbling effervescence that has been with me all morning that I can't escape.

"What else do you have in there?"

I sigh, moving things around.

"Granola bars, flares, a heat blanket, a travel sewing kit, dry shampoo—" I toss the wipes back in their spot as Zander takes over the riffling, moving me out of the way.

"Is that . . . ," he says, digging through my stuff.

No no no no.

I tug on his shoulder, trying to get him away before he can see—

"Jesus, it is. A vibrator is an emergency?" His smile is filling his entire face now, and I can feel a burn taking over mine.

"I'm going to kill your sister," I mutter under my breath, and then, in a mix of elation and confusion and horror, Zander throws the pink vibrator onto the grass.

"Oh my fucking god, is that my sister's vibrator?"

"Zander!"

"Zoe, I just touched my sister's fucking vibrator. I'm sure as fuck throwing that shit as far as humanly possible. Give me those wipes again. And that hand sanitizer. And maybe a flame thrower to burn off my top layer of skin."

I can't help but laugh, moving over to the small bullet vibrator and picking it up, wiping it with a wipe I had in my hand.

"This is not your sister's," I say, and Zee still stares at the tiny toy, confused.

"Whose is it?"

"It's mine, I guess."

"Yours?" I give him a tight smile because, actually, it probably would have been less embarrassing to just say it was Luna's.

"Why is there a vibrator in your trunk?" I sigh.

"Because I was with Luna last time I was restocking my emergency kit, and she threw it in the cart. She said orgasms were emergencies. I was at my parents' and, well, didn't want to *bring it inside*, so I just . . . left it in my trunk."

"Huh," he says with a smile, and I want to run and hide, to ignore this is happening.

But then I'm pinned to the Jeep, Zander in my face, breathing against my lips.

"Let's make a deal."

"A deal?" I parrot, my breathing heavy.

Why is my breathing heavy?

It's the look in Zee's eyes.

The one that says he's about to give me a challenge, and he knows I can't turn down a challenge.

"Use this while I drive."

"What?" I ask, my voice shaky.

He presses his hips into me and *fuck*.

He's hard.

Last night, we didn't do anything, just stayed up late talking and laughing and watching the stars.

Is it normal to need him this much after just a day?

And what does that mean for my chances of being able to move on and live a normal life after this?

Pretend, Zoe, I remind myself.

"I'm gonna drive. You're going to use this and make yourself come while I do."

"Zander—"

His hand grabs mine, and he wraps my fingers around the little vibrator.

"That's what I want, Zoe. Will you do it for me?" he asks, his lips under my ear.

And because I don't think I've ever been able to say no to Zander, I nod.

And the groan he lets out makes it all worth it.

When we start driving, I don't start my music.

I don't roll down my window.

I just sit there, frozen in panic.

Part of me wants to hope that Zander just forgets whatever his plan is.

That would be easy and most definitely the *safest* option.

But the other part . . .

"Turn it on, Zoe," he says a few minutes in, his voice low.

"What?"

"Turn it on," he says, tipping his chin to my hand still wrapped around the small pink vibe.

I could argue.

I could say no.

I know in my gut if I did either, he would back off.

Instantly.

Instead, I press and hold the button until it starts to buzz.

My heart skips a beat, and my pussy clenches just a bit.

"Over your sweats," he says.

"What?"

"Start over your sweats, baby." His voice is low and growly, and it sends a shot of heat through me.

"I don't—" His hand moves, leaving the steering wheel and grabbing my wrist with the buzzing toy. Then he guides it until it's over top of my loose grey sweats, the toy right over my clit.

"Oh," I say in a whisper.

"There you go," he murmurs. "Leave it right on your clit for a sec, baby." I do, and my hips move instinctively with the vibration.

"Still."

His words aren't a suggestion, but a command, and my body listens before my brain can even interpret the word.

"Good," he says, and my breathing quickens with the praise. "Leave it there."

The buzzing stays the same, but the pleasure rises, slowly and surely.

"Zander—"

"It feel good?" I don't answer as he drives, but when I look over, his jaw is tight. "Bet your pussy's already soaked, isn't it?"

Again, I'm silent, the vibrations taking away any use of my words.

"Go check." I pause. "Both hands in your sweats, vibe on your clit, finger in your pussy. Tell me how wet it is."

I should say no.

I should argue.

I should definitely not finger myself in a moving vehicle.

But safe Zoe seems to have taken a vacation, too.

And she's nowhere to be found when both of my hands dip past the loose waistband of my sweatpants, one finger headed straight for my center, the vibrator landing on my clit.

I moan.

I moan deep as I feel my wet, as the vibrator hits where I need it most, as pleasure takes over me.

"Tell me, pip."

"I'm so wet, Zander," I say in a whisper, my eyes drifting shut.

"Two fingers in, fuck yourself," he says, and when I open my eyes halfway to look at him, I see that his jaw is even tighter, his eyes locked on the road.

I do as he asks.

I slip two fingers in my wet and move them in, then out, and then in again, slowly using the other hand to circle my clit.

My head thrashes on the headrest, probably creating a rat's nest in my hair, but I don't care.

Oh *fuck*, it feels so good.

"Fuck yeah," he says through gritted teeth, making me realize I said that aloud.

In the car.

In broad daylight.

While Zander Davidson drives.

"Fuck, fuck," I say as the edge comes, as I feel the blaze start to grow.

"No," he says, then before I can register what's happening, his hand is moving mine aside.

The vibrator is being turned off.

And his hand is replacing mine.

When I look over, his eyes are still on the road.

But his fingers are now inside of me, the heel of his palm pressing against my clit.

"Oh, god, fuck," I murmur.

"That's it, Zoe."

"Oh, *fuck*."

His palm moves with the way two thick fingers are fucking me, the pleasure building wilder than before.

"You gonna come on my fingers, Zoe?"

"Yes," I whisper.

"That's it, pip. Be a good girl and come for me."

And that does it.

I'm not sure if it's the words or the way his fingers crook or the way the heel of his palm presses hard on my clit, but I moan his name, coming in a never-ending stream of explosions and lights behind my eyes.

His hand stays there, fingers planted as I come down from my high, and when my eyes start to open, to register the real world once more, I look over at him.

He's breathing heavy.

The knuckles of his hand on the wheel are nearly white.

His jaw is so tight, I worry about his teeth.

And most importantly, in the baggy shorts he's wearing, his cock is hard.

He sees me looking and smiles, shaking his head.

My own hand, still wet with myself, moves to his wrist, and I tug until it drags from my pants, and then I do something I never thought I'd ever do.

It's not me who does it, not safe, quiet Zoe who worries about what people think.

But instead, Zander's Zoe takes hold of me, and I move his wet fingers into my mouth, licking them clean as I keep my eyes locked on him.

"Fuck," he says low before taking his hand back and moving it to the wheel.

Suddenly, the car jerks, moving down a ranger trail and behind some trees.

"Back seat." The car stops, parking in a spot where it could probably be seen from the road but still hidden enough for . . .

"What?"

"Get in the back seat, Zoe, and take those sweats off."

"I don't—"

He leans forward, wrapping a hand around my neck in a way that sends a shiver down my spine and pulling my face closer to him.

"Get in the back seat. Take off your sweatpants and your panties. I'm coming back there, I'm gonna get my cock out, and you're going to ride it." My mouth opens just a bit, and he smiles as it does, moving his hand up, brushing his thumb across my bottom lip. "She likes that," he murmurs to himself.

I do.

I like that a lot.

Even though I just came, I'm empty, the edge barely taken off.

So, I smile, hand fumbling for the door and moving until I'm in the back, naked from my waist down.

Zander opens the driver's side, pushes the chair back, and hops into the back next to me, slamming the door as he does before he starts to move, tugging his shorts and boxers down just enough for his cock to bob out.

I stare at it, marveling at the precum already there.

"Come on, baby, get on," he says with a smile.

But I have other plans.

It's only fair after what I just got.

Instead, I move to where he's sitting, kneeling in the small area between his legs with the front seat still pushed all the way forward, and wrap my hands around his cock.

"Zoe—" he says, a warning in his words, but they cut off when I lean forward and run my tongue along the underside and over the head of his cock. "Jesus fuck." I smile, jacking him once, twice, keeping my eyes locked on his.

And then I wrap my lips around the head of his cock.

The feral noise that comes from his chest has my pussy clenching as if it didn't just get its own orgasm.

"She fuckin' loves this, sucking my cock," he murmurs to himself, and I moan around him. I watch as Zander's jaw drops just a hair, shallow breaths coming through his lips as he stares at me with surprise.

I think surprising Zander is my new favorite pastime.

So I do it again as I move my head down farther, working him in and then out until my lips touch the base

"That's it, take me all the way down your throat, baby. Fuck, you're so good at this, aren't you? Look how pretty you look with my cock in your mouth." His hands grab my hair, holding it back, my eyes drifting shut with unexpected pleasure. His hand tugs though, forcing them back open.

"No. Keep those pretty blue eyes open, baby. Keep them on me while you suck my cock." My eyes snap to his, half-lidded with lust, one hand in my hair, the other in a fist, gripping the edge of my seat.

"Look at you. Goddamn." I start to bob more, moaning as I do, the orgasm from earlier washing away as need rolls back in.

I need to sate it.

My hand drifts down past my belly until my fingers brush my still-sensitive clit. I moan around his cock, but my eyes stay locked on Zander's as I continue to circle it.

"Are you playing with your pretty clit while you suck me, Zoe?" I do my best to nod. "Dream woman. *Fuck*." His cock throbs in my mouth against my tongue as I move farther, letting him hit the back of my throat. "Put a finger in, baby."

Who am I to argue?

I do as he demands, sliding one finger easily into my wet and moaning again as I do. "Another," he says, and again, I obey, sliding a second finger into my pussy as I bob my head again.

"Now ride those like you're riding my cock."

And I do.

I bob my head, fucking his cock with my mouth to the same rhythm I use on my own pussy, undulating my hips to get more, to try and get everything I can.

It doesn't take long before there's another tug on my hair, fiercer this time.

"You're not coming anywhere but my cock this time, baby," he says, his hands moving to my armpits and tugging me up. I settle on the seat, a knee on either side of his him, his hands moving down to my hips as my hand guides his cock into me.

My head tips back, dark curls brushing my lower back as it does, and I moan as he fills me

"Stay like that, just like that," Zander says, and I look down at him, at where his eyes are locked, where I'm leaning back just a bit, revealing the place where my pussy meets the base of his cock.

"Jesus, the prettiest sight, seeing you filled with me. Are you full, baby?" One hand moves up my body to the side of my face, an almost sweet gesture in this filthy moment.

"God, yes. It's so good." He continues to stare as I stay seated, the hand on my face moving down and in until his thumb hovers over my clit. Finally, his eyes move to mine.

"Do not move, Zoe."

"What?"

But before he can answer, his thumb is on my clit, rubbing.

I clamp down.

"Oh, fuck," I moan, my head rolling back again. I try to move my hips, to buck, to get him to move inside of me the way I need.

His hand moves from my hip, slapping my sensitive inner thigh, and I moan again, the pain zipping straight to my clit.

"*Oh fuck,*" I moan deep.

"Do not move, Zoe. Stay still or I'm coming in this cunt and leaving you wanting. I will not let you come until we're at our next stop and I can eat this pussy for hours." I moan in pain and pleasure and panic. "Do you understand?"

"Yes, Zee," I say low.

"Good girl," he says and smiles when he feels me clamp on him. His thumb goes back to slow circles of my clit. "Now, I'm going to play with your clit, feel you wrapped around me, feel you come like this, nothing but my cock and my thumb, you understand?"

"Oh, god," I whine.

"You understand," he says with an evil smile. "And then I'm going to fuck your cunt until *I* come. If you come again, great, but I will not be worried about you." He leans forward, tongue moving along my neck before he whispers in my ear, "I'm gonna use your pussy for my pleasure, you understand me?" I nod. "Such a good fucking girl you are, aren't you?"

I will be whatever the fuck he wants me to be if he just *makes me come.*

I'm so full of him, his thumb working my clit slowly, barely even touching it, as he makes lazy circles around the swollen area.

"I'm gonna play with this now," he says, his voice low and throaty. "Do you like when I play with you, Zoe? When my fingers rub this clit because it's mine? When I tell you to be fucking still while I fill you with my cock, when I do whatever I want with this body?"

I can't answer.

All there is, is his cock buried in me, his thumb slowly circling my clit. His eyes lock on mine.

His hand moves again, slapping that sensitive area of my inner thigh, and I groan.

"Answer me, Zoe."

"Yes."

"Yes, what?"

"Yes, I like it. I fucking *love it*, Zander. Jesus."

His thumb presses a fraction harder, taking me closer but not close enough.

I want to move.

I want to move *so fucking badly*. To buck my hips, to get him deeper, to move and start riding him.

But instead, I stay leaned back, giving him the room he demands.

"That's my girl," he says, his eyes moving down to where he's inside of me, and he groans.

"You close?"

"Yes," I whisper.

"How close, baby? Tell me," he says, his words low, his thumb moving faster.

"I'm right there, Zander."

"You being good, waiting for me to let you go?" I nod.

Words don't work anymore.

Not a single one is on my mind other than *don't come until he says*.

And then he smiles, looking at my pussy, and nods.

His eyes meet mine.

His thumb presses harder.

His other hand moves to my shoulder, pressing to ensure he's as deep inside of me as he can be, knowing what I need.

"Fall, baby," he whispers, and somehow, I know I need to keep my eyes open, locked to his as I come.

And *fuck,* do I come.

My entire body erupts in flames, the pleasure taking over me, and I moan his name, my eyes begging to drop closed, but I can't stop watching the carnal way he's looking at me like I'm everything he needs, like he's never seen anything hotter, like I was made for him to destroy.

And I think that might be the case as I buck once on his cock accidentally.

His hand on my shoulder moves, slapping my inner thigh again, moving the hand from my clit and up to my throat to hold me there.

"I said still, baby."

The orgasm didn't satisfy me.

The desperate edge is gone, but not moving, having him thick and hard inside of me, the slap to my thigh, his hand on my throat . . .

I need more.

"I need more, Zander," I moan, a plea.

"You trust me to give you what you need?"

I don't answer.

Again, my mind doesn't fucking work.

"Do you trust me, Zoe? With your body? With your mind?"

There's a pause as he continues to stare, his hand tightening just a bit. "With your heart, Zoe? Do you trust me?"

This feels like a test.

Like a trial.

But I'm so far gone, my shield so demolished, I have no choice but to tell the truth.

"I trust you with my whole soul, Zander."

It's the truth.

I've trusted Zander to keep me safe since I was five and he was telling ghost stories around a campfire, letting me know when to cover my ears.

I've trusted Zander since I was twelve and told him my crazy dreams at two in the morning.

I've trusted Zander since I was nineteen, and I called him to come save me.

And I've trusted Zander since I was nearly thirty and jumping into a car with him to go on some chaotic road trip.

So I nod.

"Fuck yes," he growls through gritted teeth. "Fuck. Yes."

Then somehow, he stays inside of me as he moves, as he flips me to my back, as he gets to his knee on the small back seat, as one leg moves up over his shoulder and one falls to the floor.

And he stays in me as he drags his cock back out to the tip, staring in my eyes as he does.

"I'm gonna fuck you hard, Zoe, so hard, I might not be able to have you tonight. It's too much, you tell me, and I stop and fuck you sweet. If it's not too much, you like it, you take your fingers and you rub that clit. You make yourself come one more time on my cock, you take me with you."

I stare at him, open-mouthed.

I need him.

I need him any way I can get him.

"Okay, Zo?" he asks, and I remember I'm supposed to nod.

I nod, agreeing.

And then he slams in deep so I can feel the pull in my hips, slams in so deep, he brushed a new bundle of nerves inside of me that's never been hit before.

I moan.

I moan loud, no worries about being on the side of the road, being in broad daylight, being cramped in the tiny back seat of my Jeep.

"Fingers. Clit. Now," Zee says through gritted teeth, eyes on where he's pulling out again.

I do as he asks.

My clit is already so sensitive, as soon as I put my fingers there, I'm close, like it's just been one never-ending orgasm I can't control.

He pulls back and slams in, and my head tips back, a moan caught in my chest, but my fingers keep moving.

Two, three, four slams, and I'm on the brink.

Already.

But really, orgasms always seem to be right there when it comes to Zander.

"Get there, Zoe," he says.

I'm right there.

I'm right fucking there.

And then I look down.

Look at where my hand is, where he's disappearing in me.

And then I fall.

I scream his name, sound stopping in my ears altogether, but I don't miss the low groan of my name Zander lets out, nor do I miss the way he throbs inside me as he comes.

And I don't miss how yet another small, irrevocable part of me leaves me as he cleans me up and helps me put my sweats back on, kissing my lower belly as he does.

I'm wondering just how many pieces I'll have left for myself when this trip is over.

Eventually, we head back on the road, stopping for the promised coffee, and I can't stop smiling.

It's like a night under the stars with Zander was everything and more, taking away all of the worries of reality and giving me what I need to live in a fairy tale.

Or maybe it was the three orgasms.

It most definitely could be the three orgasms.

"Okay, so we're headed for Florida today, but tomorrow, I'm not sure what the plan is. We can go to the beach, or we can go to Disney."

"Disney?" I say, my voice squeaking a bit.

"That's what you wanted as a kid, so I put it on the roster. I just wasn't sure if you still wanted to go."

I went to Disney exactly one time when I was eight years old. My parents scraped and saved for what I imagine was years to make it happen and it was, in fact, the most magical week of my life.

But Zander . . .

There's no way in hell Zee actually *wants* to go to Disney.

The man is football and beer and working on his car.

He is not *happiest place on Earth,* and Mickey ears, and princess waves.

"No," he says, the Jeep bumping along another backroad, interrupting my train of thought. "No. I told you, we're done with that. You play that game with everyone else, but not me. Never with me, Zo."

I don't answer.

I don't argue, either.

Partially because I know there's no use.

And partly because it's been nice not basing my opinions on other people's likes or dislikes.

So instead of arguing, I nod.

"Okay," I say, fighting back the people pleaser who wants to say, *Whatever you want!* "Disney, if I get the choice."

"That's my girl," Zee says, and the shiver that runs through me with his words is visible.

He smiles the smile of a man who knows a woman's body and the effect his words have on said body.

I shake my head and roll my eyes.

"You'd really spend a day at a theme park targeted for little kids just because you told me you'd take me when I was twelve?"

He sighs and smiles like he can't believe I still don't get it before he answers.

"I'd go anywhere with you, Zo. Disney it is."

THIRTY-TWO
EVERYTHING HAS CHANGED
-ZANDER-

We make it to Florida and stop for the night at a chain hotel right outside Orlando, fucking as soon as we walk in the door then ordering take out and fucking while we wait for it.

After we eat, we fuck again because, apparently, I'm making up for lost time.

I remember once, when I was in my late twenties, I thought that maybe I just needed to have sex with Zoe once, that it would be enough to get her out of my system.

I see now that would be impossible.

A lifetime of fucking Zoe would still never be enough.

At midnight, though, I don't get a chance to ask her her question.

Instead, the little hand I'd been watching draw shapes on my chest sleepily as I daydreamed about what that one finger would look like with my ring on it moves to my bicep and squeezes.

Once, twice, three times.

I can't fight the smile when her head tips up to me, a small smile of her own on her lips.

"It's midnight," she whispers.

"Mmm."

"Can I ask you a question?"

"That's my line," I say, my hand moving her hair over her shoulder.

"Well, I'm stealing it."

So, I steal one of hers.

"Only if I get to ask one, too."

"Deal," she says, and I think she moves to try and sit up, but I hold her tighter, the arm on her waist keeping her down.

If I can have her skin on mine, I will.

I watch her eyes roll and feel her head on my chest like she knows what I'm thinking and that I'm crazy, but she doesn't argue.

"You want pets?" I ask.

"What?"

"Pets. Do you want any?" She shrugs, and I feel it against me rather than see it.

"I don't know. I don't think about it much. It's hard living in the city because I'd want a dog to have space to run around, but that's impossible in New York without a boatload of money." A tiny yawn. "And I'm too lazy to go to a dog park all the time, especially when it's cold out."

Zoe hates the cold.

Always has.

"So, you want a dog?" She nods.

"And a cat, I think. A little one. Like those squish-faced ones?"

"Got it. So a dog and a squish-faced cat." Her head moves to look at me, and in the dim light, I can see her smile.

God, it's pretty, that smile when she's not stressed about the real world or about how people will interpret her words. When she's not worried if she's living by some crazy standard she thinks other people have for her.

"Your turn," I say, my voice low when she doesn't ask.

Her body tightens.

I think she spoke on impulse and now is second-guessing herself.

"I'll use it tomorrow," she murmurs.

"Ask now."

Silence takes over, her breathing steady, and I wonder if she fell asleep, but then her little voice rings through clearly in the dark room.

"How many kids do you want?"

It's weird, but I'm proud of her.

Not because she asked her question but because this question, in particular, means that she's opening up to a future with me.

A shared future where those kids are *our* kids.

"Three," I say.

"Three?"

"Yeah. Liked my parents setup. Would want that for my kids."

Silence fills the room before she speaks sleepily.

"Yeah. Three would be good."

And long after she falls asleep, her even breaths panting on my chest, I can't stop thinking about what a little girl with her dark curls and my eyes would look like.

I wake to Zoe's lips on my neck.

"Wake up," she whispers there, her breath warm. "It's time to go."

My hand moves, wrapping her waist and pulling her down to me. I shouldn't be surprised when I realize she's fully dressed as she flops onto me with a giggle. Zoe has always been a morning person, up with the sun and ready to take on the day.

Meanwhile, I can barely open my eyes from the grogginess, but I force myself to.

To open and see her gorgeous face smiling at me, her eyes shining. *She's excited.*

Fuck. I haven't seen this version of her in *years*. The one who is blatantly excited, even if it's not necessarily cool, even if no one else is. Even if she thinks that her excitement is something others would categorize as annoying.

"Zander! We need to go!" she says with a sigh as I press my lips to her neck. Her hand stops pushing on me, instead pulling me close. "Zander," she says again, her voice going lower and much less convincing.

"What?" I ask into her neck, my tongue coming out to taste her there.

"We have to . . ." Her voice trails off as her hand moves to my hair, combing it slightly with her nails.

Goddamn.

I want to spend the day with her in this bed, continuing to make up for lost time.

But she wants to go.

We can't spend all day in bed together. Not today.

We have a lifetime to do that still.

Today is for Zoe.

"You wanna go today?" I ask, pulling back to look at her, my eyes adjusting to the morning. She bites her lips, and fuck if I don't enjoy the hesitance in her eyes. "You wanna go," I say, then I move, sitting up and pulling her into my lap. The sheet pools at my waist, and her legs in shorts wrap the naked skin of my bare back.

Not this morning, Davidson, I tell myself. *Our girl wants to do something. And it's important to her.*

But still, when my eyes move to the clock displaying it's just five minutes after seven, I groan. Loud.

"You know, you're the only person I'd get out of bed for before eight." That makes her happy, a smile spreading across her lips.

"What about my dad?" she asks. I flop back into the pillows, taking her with me as I look at the ceiling of the hotel room.

"Jesus, can we please, for the love of God, not talk about your father while you're in my bed?"

"Technically, it's a hotel bed," she says. I roll until she's under me, my body hovering over hers as I hold myself up on my hands.

"Are you ever gonna make it easy on me?"

"Would you like me if I did?" I stare at her for long moments, her smile reflected on my own lips.

"It would make life easier, but a lot less interesting," I say. I do a push-up, moving to kiss her. "And it wouldn't be you. So no. Don't make it easy on me, okay?"

"Never," she whispers, and all I can think through the rest of the day is how much I know I'm going to have to fight her when I get her back home.

Worth it.

THIRTY-THREE

MESSAGE IN A BOTTLE

-ZOE-

"This is wild," Zee says, looking around the massive gift shop. "Did you know they could put one character on so much shit and sell it so many different ways?" He turns to me, holding a bottle of what looks like hand soap up. "If you press the pump on this, it gives you foamy soap that looks like a mouse."

I smile and shake my head.

"Not sure what you expected at Disney," I say, wandering over to where they keep the ever-present ears—dozens of styles from all of the characters I grew up with and ones I learned to love as an adult.

"Oh, there's a bathroom. I'm going to go before we start getting in lines. Will you be here for a bit?"

I murmur a yes, only half listening to him, fingers moving to touch a sequin-covered ear on a headband.

I've been to Disney one other time, when I was a kid.

I knew that trip was coming for months, and at the age of just eight, I spent those months doing anything and everything I could in order to make money for souvenirs. My mom firmly informed me I could get whatever I wanted while we were here, but I needed to use my own money.

I spent the four days of our trip categorizing everything in the gift shops we wandered into, meticulously deciding what items would be the best bang for my buck. I had exactly sixty-seven dollars, and I needed to be smart with every last one.

Actually, looking back on that, it seems I might have been cautious and overthinking for longer than I thought.

On the last day, I was stuck between a pair of Minnie Mouse ears and a themed stationary set I could use when I got home.

"I don't know which to get," I had said to my mom, feeling the *panic of having to choose one or the other creep into my veins.*

"Zoe, come on. We gotta go. We have reservations," my dad said.

There are few things on this planet my father hates more than shopping, and few things he loves more than food.

"I don't know," I said, *my voice lower again.*

"Zoe Ann, be reasonable. When are you ever going to use those? At least with stationery, you can use it for school or to write letters."

My gut churned, now weighing common sense versus what I really wanted.

Those stupid fucking mouse ears.

I couldn't explain why I wanted them so badly even though we were getting on a plane for Jersey the very next morning and my mom was right—I'd never use them again.

I just wanted them.

So badly.

But then the nerves rolled in, fears that if I chose the ears, my parents would think I was a dumb kid, that I was irresponsible with money.

That they'd be disappointed if I bought something frivolous instead of the safe, useful choice.

I left with the stationary set, a set I never used because I kept saving it for something "important," not wanting to waste it.

Dropping my hands from the ears, I turn to go see what else the gift shop has—maybe a water cup or keychain I'll actually use.

But I bump right into a broad chest, strong arms moving to catch me as I stumble.

Zander.

Zander, always catching me before I fall.

But what happens if you fall in a different way? Will he catch you then?

I shake my head to get the thought out before it takes hold.

"You ready?" I ask, trying to step back, but his arms hold me tight.

"What were you looking at?"

"Nothing," I say quickly.

Too fucking quickly, because Zander can read me better than anyone ever could.

Instead of moving to leave the store like I want him to, he turns me in his arms, moving me forward as he walks us back to where the wall of ears is.

"You want a pair?"

"What? No."

"Yes, you do. Which one? The sequins? You were touching that one."

"No, Zander. They're silly. They're for kids."

"I've been in this park for barely two minutes and can promise you they are not just for kids."

"They're a waste of money."

"Nothing's a waste of my money if it makes you happy, Zoe."

My body goes warm like I just drank a big cup of hot cocoa and it's pooled in my belly, happy and comfortable.

"I'll never wear them again," I say in a whisper. "It's not practical."

"We left practical in Jersey, and I don't plan on letting you pick it back up when we get home. Which one do you want, Zoe?"

I chew on my lip for a moment, trying to ignore how his words impact me.

And what a stark contrast to what my well-meaning mother said years and years ago.

And when I answer, I think a tiny part of me I didn't realize was torn, heals.

"The mermaid ones," I say with a smile.

"Whatever you want, pip."

Later in the day, we're waiting in line for a ride when Zee's hands slip around me. He pulls me back against him, our bodies flush, his voice in my ear.

"You happy, Zo?" His voice is low and warm but sends shivers through me all the same.

"What?" I ask, my own voice low.

I'm probably hitting him in the nose with these silly ears, but I don't dare move.

"Are you happy?"

"I mean, yeah. We're in Disney. The happiest place on Earth." His arms tighten, and we take a step together as the line moves forward.

"No, I mean in general, Zoe. Are you happy? Here. With me?"

One hand moves on my hip, hooking into the belt loop, thumb moving to the soft skin above my shorts.

That thumb brushes, sending sparks flying through my veins.

"With you?" I repeat, my voice whisper quiet.

He hears it, though, of course.

I couldn't tell you how, but the man is so damned in tune with me.

Because this is just what was always supposed to happen.

You and Zee, the little voice in my head tells me.

That thumb keeps stroking, and something about it—the contact, the touch of his hand on my skin—something about it has me answering honestly.

"Yeah, Zander. I'm happy."

He steps closer despite the line not moving, pushing his body even closer to mine, and without my permission, my body leans back into him.

That thumb dips below the line of my jeans, just barely, but it happens.

"Me too," he whispers.

"What are you doing, Zee?" I whisper again, my voice shakier, my blood burning.

The man puts a single inch of his skin onto mine, and I need him instantly.

"Driving you crazy," he says. "Gotta return the favor."

"Zander—"

"I look at you and want you. In the car, in a bed, in a random alleyway, in the middle of fucking Disney World, I see you and I need your skin on mine."

My tongue dips out to lick my lips, and we step as one as the line moves forward, that teasing thumb doing a number on my blood pressure and my poor panties.

"I have no idea what you've done to me to wrap me so tight, but you'd better never stop," he whispers, the thumb dipping even lower to graze more sensitive skin.

"Never," I say without even thinking about the words I'm saying, without remembering this is pretend and complicated and how. right now, we're in a magical la-la land of romance.

And that thumb presses, my need for him growing.

"Zander, maybe we should—" I start, needing him more than I need to go on this damn ride.

"Next!" the cast member shouts, waving us forward.

Zee's hand leaves my skin, leaving it cold and lonely before he grabs my hand and tugs me forward.

"Later," he says with devious thoughts clear in his eyes.

And I never thought I would curse the happiest place on Earth so heavily, but here we are.

It seems this really is just a week of surprises.

THIRTY-FOUR
ALL TOO WELL
-ZOE-

I don't want to think too hard about why I'm in such a sour mood today.

Yesterday, we spent the entire day wandering around a theme park, riding all of the best rides and eating more junk food than any two people should eat in a 12-hour period before Zander basically had to carry me from the park and back into our hotel room because I was so exhausted.

I passed out without even having him, which, to be honest, is probably part of the reason I'm so grumpy.

But he did wake up again for his midnight question.

This one was asking what color I want the front door of my house to be.

The correct answer, of course, was red.

A red door on a white house with a big wraparound porch.

He smiled, kissed my temple, and told me to go back to sleep.

I actually think there's a chance I may have dreamed that up.

But then again, I think there's a chance I've imagined this entire trip, to be quite honest.

Still, as we make our slow trek back up to New Jersey, I'm annoyed.

This is also why I'm playing the saddest, angriest of songs on my playlist.

"Fuck Jake Gyllenhaal," I murmur, looking out the window as the ten-minute version plays and I remember every shitty boyfriend I've ever had in glorious, painstaking detail.

It fuels my angry fire.

"What?" Zee says, looking my way with a smile on his lips. I roll my eyes and shake my head.

"I said, fuck Jake Gyllenhaal." He blinks twice before looking back at the road.

"I'm sorry, *what*?" There's laughter in his voice, and I wonder if maybe I was wrong about him being my dream man over all these years because this is a serious subject, and he's brushing it off.

Even in pretend, I can't be with a man who doesn't understand the direness of how terrible Jake Gyllenhaal is.

"Fuck Jake Gyllenhaal. He didn't even show up at her birthday party." He keeps staring blankly at me like I'm crazy, alternating between the road and me. "It was her 21st."

"I'm sorry, are you . . . Are you angry at an actor you've never met because a singer you've also never met dated him?" I roll my eyes.

"Because he dated *Taylor Swift* and was a dick to her."

"Ah, yes. Taylor Swift," he says in a voice that tells me he finds this topic *hilarious* instead of *serious*.

And then he goes down a terrible path.

"But Jake Gyllenhaal is a good actor. Does that mean I can't enjoy his movies?" I glare at him, aghast.

I was definitely wrong about him being my dream man, I think.

"No, he's not even a good actor." Zee guffaws a laugh out loud, and I sigh, fighting a smile and trying to look stoically in the distance and be mad. You know, to channel the "All Too Well" vibes.

"You can't say he's not a good actor, Zo." I purse my lips and tilt my head before I disagree.

"I very much can."

"What about *Donnie Darko?*" he asks, and I tip my head to the roof of the Jeep, Zander's smile no longer a small thing but taking over his whole face.

"*Donnie Darko?!* Are you kidding me? That movie was absolute shit."

"It's one of the greats," he says, arguing his point that has zero value.

He's totally doing it to rile me up.

And it's *totally* working.

"Oh my god, shut up. You didn't even like that movie. You just thought it would make you look cool if you did." He smiles as he stares off at the road.

We both know I'm telling the truth.

"Lies."

"I'm totally right. We asked you what it was about, and you spent ten minutes not making any sense, mumbling about choices and dimensions and a big bunny. It was insanity."

"It's a great movie. I can't help that you two were too slow to pick up on the true meaning."

"What about Tony? Because he's smarter than you and me combined, and he has no idea what it's about." His lips tip up again before he answers.

"Tony is too black and white to enjoy a movie like that. I'm all grey."

"Yeah, you're as grey as Luna is, all sunshine and rainbows and good vibes."

He doesn't reply, keeping that smile as he does, mostly because he knows I'm right about this, too.

The Davidson kids are as morally gray as *Finding Nemo.*

Silence lasts for a few minutes as the song ends before Zee reaches over, grabs my hand, and brushes a rough thumb over the back of it.

"Whoever you hate, Zoe, I hate too."

And for some reason, that means more to me than most anything he's said on this whole trip.

Because finding someone who can be irrationally mad at someone just because you told them to be *and* can give you killer orgasms?

I don't know if you can legally let a man like that go without a fight.

Even if you're only fighting yourself.

THIRTY-FIVE
HOW YOU GET THE GIRL
-ZOE-

"Can you grab my wallet for me?" Zee asks an hour later, as we approach a toll in North Carolina. I'm in a better mood, the overcast skies having burnt off to sun and warmth as we drive and my playlist moving to happier songs.

"What?"

"I need cash. I have some in there."

"I can—"

"Swear to fuck, you offer to pay, I'm pulling over and spanking your ass."

I stop for a full beat, contemplating.

That could be interesting.

Zee stares at the roof.

"Jesus fuck, she likes that," he murmurs to himself. Then he looks at me. "We'll dig into that later. Right now, get me my wallet, baby."

My mind is too scrambled to argue, so I do as he asks.

"Get me two singles."

I open the leather bifold and look in, grabbing two singles and handing them over.

But then I stop, my hands frozen.

I recognize something.

I carefully pull out a folded photo strip that I instantly recognize, unfolding it and staring at it the whole time Zee deals with the toll person.

"Here, change," he says, holding his hand out to me.

I don't look.

"Zo?" he asks, then he stops.

I assume he looks at me, but I don't even move my eyes from where I'm staring.

"Where . . . Where did you get this?" I ask, looking at it.

It's from my birthday party years ago, *Zoe's Sweet 16* written in a loopy font from the personalized service.

It's a film strip.

My parents had rented one of those photo booths, and I made sure I got photos with everyone that night, including my best friend's older brother, who, now that I think of it, came home from school for the party.

He came home from school to attend my sweet sixteen.

"Your party."

"I know it was my party. It literally says it on the bottom." I look to see he's driving, eyes on the road.

"Then what are you asking?" he says.

I pause, unsure.

It's strange how he's barely looking at me, barely engaging in a conversation, almost like he's nervous that I found this.

"Why is it in your wallet?"

It's three photos.

One, we both have our tongues out.

The next, I remember Zee was tickling me, and I was laughing.

The third is cemented in my mind as the best part about the entire party that I begged my parents for months to throw me because it was what everyone else was doing.

In that third one, Zee's lips are pressed to my cheek.

Nothing scandalous, nothing inappropriate. It's the same way he'd do to Luna or how Tony would do to me as his wife's best friend.

But I remember in my sixteen-year-old head, it was everything.

I also remember rummaging everywhere the next morning in tears, looking for this damn photo.

"Zander, how do you have this? It was gone after my party." There's a smile on his lips.

"I took it from the machine."

I let time pass, waiting for him to tell me more, looking at the strip again.

It's yellowed with age, well over ten years old at this point, the center where it was folded fraying, but it's still all there.

Me and Zee.

Even then, it was Zee and me.

"Why do you still have it?" I ask, my voice low now.

"I like looking at it sometimes."

I like looking at it sometimes.

I don't know what to say.

As always, Zee does.

He reaches out, putting a hand on my thigh and squeezing.

"You were always mine, Zoe. Even then. Even before we knew it, you were mine."

An echo of my own thoughts.

I fold up the photo, slipping it back into his wallet carefully before he takes it, puts it in the console, and grabs my hand. He pulls it to his mouth, his eyes still locked to the road, and presses his lips to my fingers.

"Always mine," he says.

THIRTY-SIX
THE ARCHER
-ZOE-

"It's our last night," Zander says, tossing his bag on the bed and gently placing mine on the white duvet.

In this fantasy world, I think I could fall for Zander with that move alone, the way he takes such care of my things.

But tomorrow is reality.

Tomorrow, we're back in Springbrook Hills.

Tomorrow is my interview for a job I was tepid about before I went on this road trip, and now I'm so overly confused about it that I don't know what to do.

I know in my gut this isn't my dream job. It's not something I would love, something that would bring me utter, all-consuming joy.

And before, I was fine with that.

But now . . . I can't help but wonder what's the point of living if you're not working toward all-consuming joy in every moment?

"Yeah," I say, looking around the hotel room.

"Let's go out." He takes a few steps toward me, one arm wrapping my waist and tugging until I'm pressed to his front. His free hand moves up my side, grazing curves, as my hands move to the back of his neck, and then he brushes wild curls behind my shoulders.

I haven't done anything with my hair since we left except let it dry with some curl cream and gel I bought at a pharmacy in North Carolina.

Each time I look in the mirror, I'm a bit shocked and confused to see the curls I've kept well-managed for years, but I'd be lying if I said I didn't like the look of them, much less the ease.

I especially love the way Zander looks at them like he's excited to see my curls again. Relieved, maybe.

"Go out?"

"Yeah. We should celebrate. One last hurrah until next time."

"Next time?" I ask like a parrot, repeating his words back to him.

"You think this is gonna be our last road trip together, pip? I think every winter we'll schedule a week, run from the cold."

I stare at him completely unsure of what to say and how to respond.

I'm blown away by the openness with which he's talking about the future. *Our future.*

"All good, baby. You keep living in the fairy tale. I've got my eyes on the future for both of us."

I can't breathe.

His words take over me, and all I can think about is a future with Zander Davidson and what that might mean for me.

For us.

For our friends, for our families.

Because if we do—if we do this and it doesn't work out, it will—

"No. No more thinking about that. We're still here, a million miles from home, and I have at least one more day of you living in pretend land with me."

"Zander—" He quiets me with a kiss before stepping back and away from me, moving to where he tossed his wallet. Grabbing a credit card out, he hands it to me.

"Go. Go buy something pretty." I stare at the blue card as if it will bite me.

"Something pretty?"

"We'll go to a nice dinner. Last night of vacation and all." My gut drops with the final understanding that this trip is actually ending.

The idea that this fantasy I've dreamed of since I was little will come to an end.

Reality will set in at midnight, like I'm Cinderella and Zee is Prince Charming, and I'll go back to being the daughter with a plan and a goal, the one who has an interview tomorrow afternoon, the one who will always be Zander's little sister's best friend. The threat of ruining a lifelong friendship will again hover over us. It won't just be about a man and a woman enjoying each other's time anymore. Real life will start to creep in and ruin everything.

"But this is not the end of this," Zander says into my ear, countering my thoughts as an arm wraps my waist and pulls me into him again. "Not even close, Zoe. This trip ends, but we do not."

I should remind him that this is pretend.

I should remind him that this is the equivalent of a vacation fling.

But I don't.

I don't respond at all, and his hands go to my face in a move I have grown to love in just a few days, forcing me to look at him and pulling our faces closer.

He does this when I get too far into my head, holding my face and grounding me, reminding me to live in the now when the panic starts to take over.

"Tell yourself whatever you have to in order to keep your sanity. That's fine, baby. Tell yourself what you need to hear, but know that if this is us playing pretend, I plan to play with you for the rest of my damn life."

"Zander—"

"Later." He steps back and tries to hand me the credit card. "Go. Go buy a pretty dress. Something that I'll want to take off you as soon as I see you in it, so when you sit across from me all night, it's all I can think of."

Ideas instantly start running through my mind, and he smiles upon seeing them.

"Yeah, I know you like that," he says, then he presses his lips to mine. "Take my card, go shopping. Torture me."

"I have money, Z—"

"I know you do. I want this. I wanna spoil you." He presses the card into my hand, and involuntarily, my fingers wrap it. "Give me this. Let me spoil you, pip."

And who am I to argue with a request like that.

So I say yes.

And the smile my man gives me when I do makes it all the better.

And I don't even let my mind linger on the way it's so damn comfortable calling Zander Davidson *my man*.

THIRTY-SEVEN
DRESS
-ZOE-

"Where are you?" I ask my phone, my voice brisk and almost business-like as I walk down the small Main Street toward the boutique I scouted in the hotel room.

"What?"

"Where *are* you? And can you get the crew together quick?"

"What are you talking about?" my best friend asks.

"Luna, I'm having a mental breakdown in small town USA, on a mission to buy a dress that your brother, and I quote, will think about taking off of me through our entire dinner. I need an emergency group meeting."

Silence.

Silence hits my ears.

"I'm sorry, what?" Luna asks,

"Jesus, Luna, get your head in the game! I'm panicking!"

"Okay, okay, okay. Let's rewind, okay? Where are you?"

"I'm in Maryland."

"Okay, good," she says, coaching me like I'm a child who lost her parents. "And what are you doing right now?"

"I'm walking down a road toward a boutique."

"Great, Zo. And what are you doing there?" Her words are so patient, but I don't have *time* for patience.

"Jesus, Luna, I'm not a moron. I'm walking to go buy a dress." There's a pause.

"Okay, I'm not gonna lie, I am so totally confused. Why are you freaking out?"

"Because this is all . . . chaos."

"How's your trip? I haven't heard from you since you left. Zee's texted me a few times to provide proof of life, but you're not replying to *any* of my texts."

"He's texted you pictures?"

"Yeah. One in Disney, I guess? Another of you eating ice cream. One where it's super dark."

"Oh," I say, shocked that Zander's been documenting this trip so intensely. I sigh. "Your brother stole my phone. I haven't seen your texts."

"He what?"

"He stole my phone so I couldn't text you and call you and have a meltdown and overthink things. Oh, and so I couldn't research where we're going. He's making me go with the flow."

The words are almost sour in my mouth, even now.

This trip may have made me rethink my career and my love life, but it didn't break me from my need to plan.

"Go with the flow? You?"

"Yes, me. God, I'm not that uptight." Silence.

"Luna!"

"I mean, you're not *uptight*," she says with skepticism. "But you're definitely a planner. You like to know what's going on."

"Yeah, well, that hasn't been an option." She's quiet as I continue to walk down the street.

Talking to my best friend, though irritating, has already started to ease my panic.

"Wait, he didn't want you to call me? But you're doing all of that right now."

"He gave me my phone so I wouldn't get lost and he could find me when he needed to pick me up."

"Make sense."

"But now I'm calling you, having a meltdown, and I'm ready to overthink."

"How have you not overthought this whole time?"

"Because he told me to pretend."

"What?" I see the store but keep walking when I spot a coffee shop

right behind it.

"Pretend I'm living in a fairy tale and not allowed to think about what happens when it's over. Fuck it, I'm getting coffee first."

"Is that a good idea? More caffeine? You seem a little on edge as it is." My jaw tightens, teeth grinding as I try and take a deep breath.

The air won't hit the bottom of my lungs.

"Shut the fuck up, Luna."

"Okay, okay," she says with a laugh. "Okay, you get your coffee, I'll round up the crew, then you call from the coffee shop once you're settled, yeah?" I take another breath as I open the door, a plan and the smell of caffeine making me feel a bit more at ease already.

"I don't have all day."

"Five minutes, Zo. This is Springbrook Hills, not New York City. Valid.

"Okay. Call you in five."

Ten minutes later, I have my phone propped against a bottle of water, my headphones in, a giant iced coffee in front of me, and I'm meticulously picking at a muffin while I wait for everyone to get on to our call.

Somehow in ten minutes, my best friend wrangled nearly our entire friend group on one video call. Hannah's sitting in the messy office at the Center, while Kate and Sadie are hunkered together in

Rise and Grind, the coworking and coffee shop Sadie owns. Jordan's in her office at the Coleman Construction site, and Luna's in the bar, which isn't open for the day yet.

Now everyone is waiting on me, staring expectantly.

"So?" Sadie says. "How's Zander in bed?" Luna goes a bit green.

"Oh my fucking god, Sadie. No. No way. We are not talking about *my brother* fucking my *best friend.*"

"But if they're fucking, then they're together," Hannah says, always the logical one.

"One does not always equate to the other, Han," Kate says.

"Says you who couldn't even keep your hands off Dean long enough to get married before you had Jesse," Sadie says with a laugh. Kate glares at our friend slash her boss.

"You guys, I don't have time for this. I'm freaking out, and I'm supposed to be buying a dress."

"A dress?" Jordan asks.

"A dress to go to dinner with Zander as it's our last night." I bite my lip before taking another sip of my coffee.

"What do you mean last night?" Luna says.

"We're heading back home tomorrow. My interview is at two."

"Your interview?" Sadie asks.

"You're still going to that?" Luna asks, her face confused and a bit hurt, maybe?

"Well . . . yeah," I say.

"If you get that job, you're leaving town," Luna says. I stay silent.

"Are you guys gonna like, do long distance?" Sadie asks, confused.

My gut drops.

My gut drops because this is why I jumped into pretending.

Reality makes beautiful things look too hard.

Reality makes beautiful things feel impossible.

"It's not . . . We're not . . . ," I try to explain, but suddenly I have no words.

"You definitely are," Luna says.

"What?"

"You *definitely are*," she repeats, and with the words and the exasperation, she sounds like her mom, annoyed that her kids aren't understanding basic facts.

"No, we're not."

"But you've been fucking," Sadie says.

"Sadie!" Luna yells.

I ignore my best friend.

"We've been . . . We've been pretending."

"Pretending?" Kate asks.

"It was his idea, really. We're pretending that this is normal. That we're together."

"I think you lost us, babe," Jordan says, her voice low and soft.

I sigh, trying to figure out how to explain the last week.

"So, we got in the car and started driving and . . . Okay, so it's been great, right? We watched the sunrise on the beach, then out of nowhere, he stopped and made me dance with him in a parking lot—" Luna cuts in.

"No fucking way," she says under her breath.

I ignore her.

"And he kissed me there, and I told him it wouldn't work—"

"Zoe!" Hannah disciplines, interrupting again.

"—but he told me to play pretend. To pretend that we were something more."

"And . . ."

"And I agreed." Silence fills the line. That can't be good, especially not from these women. Someone is *always* talking. "Anyway, the second night, Zander needed sleep, obviously, so we stayed for a few nights in North Carolina, and it was so pretty. We stayed in the cutest little bed-and-breakfast run by this older couple, and they were adorable, Lune. You would have loved them."

Silence from the peanut gallery again, and I keep rambling because now I've started spilling it all and I can't fucking stop.

"And then he drove us down to Georgia and found this little

town with, like, no lights at night, and I thought it was weird, but then Zee had all this shit set up for a picnic so we could look at the stars."

"Oh my fucking god," Luna says, her voice low and shocked, but I don't have time to question that.

I don't have time to overthink it.

I need to just get it all out.

"So we went stargazing and then we slept in Georgia, and then he took me to Disney—"

"Disney?" Sadie asks, aghast and confused. "You're telling me Zander Davidson took you *to Disney World?*"

"Well . . . yeah. I told you we're doing this because when I was little, I told him he had to take me to Disney."

Again, silence.

It's starting to be a bit unsettling.

"It was just, you know. It was just part of the trip."

"Zoe . . . ," Luna starts her voice low.

"Oh, honey," Hannah says, like she can't help but feel bad.

"You guys, what?" I ask, my eyes wide and the panic creeping in again.

"Zander didn't take you to Disney because he wanted to go. He didn't take you because it was part of some kitschy trip you two planned as kids. He took you because it's what you wanted."

A part of my subconscious I'd covered in thick blankets starts to nod, a part that I've been ignoring since that first night.

"I don't—"

"He took you because he knew you wouldn't give him a chance if there wasn't some kind of reason."

"That's not—"

"He's not pretending, babe," Kate says, voice low.

I ignore that.

I can't handle that, to be honest.

Instead, I continue to tell them about our trip.

"So we left Florida, and we're stopped in Maryland, and he told me to go get a dress that he'll think about taking off of me all night."

Luna goes a bit green, but then again, maybe she just goes pale.

But then her eyes go wide.

"No fucking way," she says in a whisper.

I've known this woman my entire life, and I *know* that face.

Something clicked in her mind.

"What?" I ask, confused and a bit terrified.

"No fucking way, Zoe. He's not . . . but he is." She stands and starts pacing. "But he so is. Dancing, star gazing, the dress . . ."

"I don't . . ." I watch as my best friend shakes her head and moves, leaning into the screen and staring at me.

Everyone else on the call looks just as confused as I do.

"Zo. You gotta do it. You gotta just roll with it. Let him do whatever he's doing."

"I don't . . . I don't know if I can."

"Why?"

"Because... Because it's terrifying. Because there's too much on the line. Our families are friends, and god forbid this goes bad, that's all messed up. And I have that interview and it's... It's not smart. It's not safe."

"What has living safe gotten you?" she asks, her eyes soft.

I know what she's going to say, and I can't handle it

"Luna—"

"Zoe, when was the last time you did something for yourself?"

That's Sadie.

"I—"

"When was the last time you made a decision that benefitted *you*?" she asks again.

"I don't—"

"We can talk about this when you get home, but I need someone to help with Rise and Grind." Rise and Grind is Sadie's coffee and coworking business she started five or so years ago. Kate, who also works there, turns to give her a hilarious *what?* look.

She shakes her head.

"I need it redesigned. I was going to hire a firm to do it, but then you came home, and it felt like a sign."

My heart stops beating.

"You were always so good at that," Hannah says.

"You pretty much helped me decorate the entire bar," Luna says.

"And my house," Jordan says. "Somehow, you made me a girly cave that even Tanner is happy to be in," she says of her overly masculine construction worker fiancé.

"It's what you wanted to do," Luna says, her eyes wide and soft.

They don't fill in the silence I create by not answering, instead waiting for me to say something.

"It's not realistic." I continue picking at the muffin but not eating.

The turn of conversation has my appetite gone.

"Says who?"

I laugh. "Says the world. Marketing is respectable."

Sadie scoffs. "Jesus, listen to yourself, Zoe! Respectable. Is that what you want?"

"Is that so bad??"

"Is that route respecting your own hopes and dreams?" Hannah asks, and that one hits in a way I think I could have brushed off one, two weeks ago.

Silence.

Hannah has always been wise beyond her years, and this is another example of it.

"Look, I see the panic," Luna says. "Don't overthink this just yet. Keep it in mind. Just . . . enjoy tonight. This is the last night. Go get a pretty dress. Make Zee pay for it. Go get your nails done a pretty color."

"I have an interview tomorrow," I say, my voice low and sad even to myself.

"If you interview at a place that won't hire you because you have color on your nails, Zoe, you're too good for that job."

Fair enough.

And strangely, after this conversation, I feel a bit better.

Like the panicked weight that was sitting on my chest is gone.

This past week has been such a whirlwind, and without speaking with my friends to give me validation and clarity, it's been . . . confusing.

Freeing but also baffling.

And now, I'm still confused, but I think . . . I think there might be a light at the end of the tunnel.

"I love you guys," I say.

"Oh fuck, she's really a new person, sappy Zoe," Sadie says with a smile.

"Fuck off."

"Go buy a dress, Zoe," Hannah says.

"And send us pictures!" Jordan says, clapping her hands.

And then, after telling them all thank you and promising to send my top contenders for a dress to them for final review, I sign off and head to the boutique.

THIRTY-EIGHT
THAT'S WHEN
-ZOE-

"You got it?" Zee asks as I hop in the car.

I'm high on life and the idea of even a shred of a future that could maybe, possibly include Zander and me.

"A dress you'll want to take off me has, in fact, been acquired," I say, but then my mind travels into overthinker territory, wondering if maybe that's a bit too forward.

I mean, what if the dress is actually hideous?

The girls all voted on this one, with Sadie actually threatening to drive down here and kick my ass if I didn't buy it.

She's kind of insane, and I'm pretty sure there's a chance she'd actually do it if I didn't buy it.

"Stop. You could wear a goddamn tee shirt to your ankles and I'd want to take it off you."

How does he do that? See where I'm overthinking and counteract it so easily?

I shake my head and smile at him.

"I even got my nails done," I say, wiggling my fingers at him. I went out of my normal comfort zone and got them painted pink. "Not my normal color—I'm more of a nudes kind of girl—but it feels .

. . fun." I stare at them, liking the pink but also a hint self-conscious. "It doesn't feel very me though. I'm not a fun pink girlie."

"You are fun, Zo," he says, his brows furrowed.

"Not really. I'm kind of predictable. Boring."

"Maybe the new, contrived version is. But you? You're fun." There's a pause as he looks me over. "But they look pretty, pip." He smiles at me, and I just *know* he's going in for the kill.

I was right, of course.

"Can't wait to see how they look when you're playing with your pussy for me tonight."

"Zander Davidson!" I say, slapping his arm.

But as he drives off, I can't fight the smile.

And, of course, the tingle.

"You talked to Lune?" Zander asks as we head toward the hotel.

My gut drops.

"What?"

"You called Luna while you were out, right?"

"I don't . . . How . . ."

"She called me freaking out over something. Then Tony called me." I look at him, confusion fully taking over now.

"Why would they call you?" My brow is furrowed, and Zee just smiles at me.

"Because they know," he says, turning into the hotel's lot. "They know what you don't."

"Know what?" I ask, digging through my purse and avoiding looking at him.

"They know this is real." His words are easy and simple, and he's not even looking at me, instead just parking like this is normal.

"Zander—" I start, my voice low.

"It's fine. We're fine. We're still playing pretend. Just, my sister wanted to make sure I didn't do anything stupid."

"You always do something stupid." Zander puts the Jeep into park, looks over at me, and smiles.

"Exactly."

"Why would she worry about you doing something stupid?"

"Because my sister wants you happy and selfishly wants *herself* happy in the form of keeping you tied to her for eternity. And she's worried I'm gonna fuck it up."

"Why would she think that?" I say, my brow furrowing. "I told her everything was good. That you've been a dream. I just—"

I stop before I say too much, before I give it all away.

"You sticking up for me, pip?" he asks with a smile.

"No, I just . . . You're not *actually* always doing something stupid. You're always worrying about everyone else, making sure they're happy. Shit, look at you taking over the Bulldogs," I say of the peewee team his dad used to coach.

He looks confused.

"What does that have to do with anything?"

"Who would have coached those kids after your dad stopped?" I ask, giving him a face. He smiles. "Exactly. Even if you didn't *want* to do it, knowing you, you would have done it anyway." He unbuckles his seat, leaning forward and taking my face in his hands.

"You know, Zoe, you can keep telling yourself this is all fake, but I know, with that moment alone, that I have a lifetime of you sticking up for me ahead of me, don't I?" he asks, and I don't say anything.

I can't.

I can't because before I can, his lips are on mine, and instantly, I'm forgetting why I should be arguing.

What will one more day hurt, right?

THIRTY-NINE

CALL IT WHAT YOU WANT
-ZANDER-

"Wear this," I say, tossing a small bag at Zoe. While she ran off and freaked out about what she still thinks is pretend to my sister and probably half of Springbrook Hills, I was my own version of productive.

This is not from that.

This is from the little thrift store in North Carolina.

From the day I first had her.

"What is this?" she asks, confused and not opening the bag or the box inside. Instead, she stares at it like it might bite her.

"Something for you. Just something small," I say, putting my hand in my pocket.

I refuse to overthink this. Refuse to tell myself I made a mistake.

"Zee, you didn't—"

"I know I didn't. I did, though." She looks at me with that hint of frustration, and I wonder if she can see my heart beating, if she can see how anxious I am.

The last time I was nervous about a woman, I was standing outside Joe Thomas's house and begging his daughter to tell me to forget the girlfriend I had at the time. Silently begging her to let me kiss her, to make her mine.

Some things never change, I guess.

I tip my chin at her, telling her silently to open the bag. Finally, her little hand goes in, grabbing the medium-sized velvet box and pulling it out.

"I got it in North Carolina."

"The gift for Luna," she says with a knowing smile.

I shrug, neither confirming nor denying.

"Open it," I say, my hands in my pockets as I watch her. I see her eyes go wide as her fingers touch the tiny charm there.

A silver letter A on a delicate silver chain.

"What is this?" she asks what feels like an eternity later, looking up at me but her fingers still tracing the letter.

"A necklace. You don't—you don't have to wear it," I say. It's just—"

"No. No," she says, cutting me off quickly. "I'm wearing it. Are you kidding me? It's beautiful, Zee." Then her fingers stop, and she looks at me confused again "Why an A?"

"Did you forget my name?" I ask with a smile, and I watch as her eyes clear and then go warm, shock and awe covering her face.

"*Alexander*," she says in a near whisper. I smile.

"My dad wanted a strong name. My mom wanted a cool name. I got both." She licks her lips, and I have to remind myself that if we want to get to our reservation on time, I can't act on that lip lick.

"So, an A for Alexander," she says.

"If it were a Z, everyone would think it was for you. I want everyone to know that's my initial around your neck." She blinks.

Once, twice, three times, clearly unsure of what to say.

Instead of addressing my words, though, just like I would expect, she changes the subject.

"How'd you know I'd want silver?" she asks, looking at the three random rings on her fingers, all gold.

She doesn't know.

She doesn't get it.

I guess it's a good thing I have a lifetime to show her.

I look into her eyes before answering.

"You wear gold rings and silver necklaces and earrings. You've been that way since you were little."

"How do you know that?" she asks in a whisper, awe twining in those words. I shake my head.

She so doesn't get it.

"I know you, Zoe. I know you better than I know myself," I say, and then I turn to the bathroom to take a shower while Zoe gets herself ready.

FORTY

STAY STAY STAY

-ZANDER-

I fuck up on the drive over.

I make the mistake of forgetting where we are instead of where I *want* us to be.

"So this interview—is it a video?" I ask.

I should have just stayed in the now.

Acted like tomorrow would never come.

Her fingers go to the hem of her dress, the sexy black thing that hugs every curve on her body.

I told her to get a dress I'd think about taking off all night, and fuck did she do that.

"Yup," she says. "It's a video call. Which is nice because then I don't have to go all the way to the city." She moves her eyes to the window, looking out and thinking. "I guess if I get the job, though, I'll need to fast-track finding a new place there."

"You're gonna live in the city?" I ask. I knew it was a possibility, but the more time I spend with her, the more time I dig out the version of her buried under expectations, the more I hate that for her.

"Yeah. It's expensive, though, so depending on the offer, I might need to find a shared apartment with a roommate."

Jesus.

"Is that what you want?"

"I mean, I'd rather not have a roommate, but it's kind of the price you pay to live in the city."

"So you're gonna live in the city with a roommate you don't want because you don't want to commute to a job you don't love?"

And that's where I fuck up.

I should have kept my mouth shut.

"It's not that simple. I mean—" she starts.

And again, I fuck up.

You see, I might have been raised by a feminist, hippie mom, but I was also raised by Michael Davidson. Michael Davidson, who believes nothing can't be fixed with a little elbow grease, that nothing is ever as complicated as people try and make it seem, and that his opinion on anything and everything is the version everyone should be using.

So I cut her off and tell her exactly what's on my mind instead of pausing and thinking about *Zoe.*

"It's stupid, don't you think?" Her body stills, but I'm too *fucking* stupid to notice.

I'm so lost in the future, so convinced that everything will go my way, that I forget that Zoe isn't quite there yet.

"Stupid?"

"This interview. This whole thing, really. It's stupid."

"I don't understand," she says, her voice low, hesitant.

I should know to stop there.

I grew up with a younger sister and a feminist for a mother.

I should know better.

But how many times over the years have I seen my dad walk in the door with a look of shame, holding a bouquet of sunflowers (mom's favorite), and tell her how damn sorry he is for saying some stupid thing he didn't think through?

"Why are you even going on this interview? It's ridiculous. You don't even want that job. You should just stay in Springbrook Hills and figure out how to do something else."

Her voice changes the next time she speaks, moving from hesitant to annoyed.

The *annoyed* is just covering hurt, though.

"Excuse me?" That's when I get the first hint.

The first clue I fucked up.

But do I back off?

No.

No, I do not.

"It makes no sense that you're gonna, what? Keep working the job you hate? Live in the city an hour from home because you think it's what you're supposed to be doing?"

"Zander, that's not fair."

"You know what's not fair, Zoe? That when I look at you, I see a future. I see my daughter's eyes and my son's smile. I see a fucking lifetime of laughter. I see a woman that I know down to my *bones* I want to be with for the rest of my life. And you're sitting there next to me, telling me you need to mentally prepare for some interview for a job that will make you miserable and take you away from me. That's not fucking fair to either of us."

Silence fills the car, and when I look over at her, her jaw is tight.

She's annoyed.

Or at least wants me to think so.

She's probably more hurt than anything.

Fuck.

I want to apologize.

That's what common sense is telling me to do.

But I'm still burning up with frustration.

So for the five-minute drive, I'm silent.

I let thoughts swirl in my mind, versions of apologies and compromises, sifting through them, trying to decide what will help this situation.

We park in the lot for the restaurant, and I've taken the time to calm myself.

To realize what I said wasn't fair.

That wasn't how this should go, how I want a relationship or arguments with Zoe to happen.

When I turn to look at her, her eyes are straight ahead on the brick wall we parked facing.

"Are we ready?" she asks, her voice low and monotonous.

"Uh, yeah. Look, Zoe, that—"

"It's fine. I'm hungry. Let's go," she says, then she opens her door and steps out into the surprisingly warm winter air.

I follow her, her long legs moving quickly with irritation, so I need to speed up to catch up to her.

"Hey," I say, grabbing her hand finally as we're almost to the restaurant. The sky is cloudy like my mood, and I feel like I'm fucking it up. Fucking everything up.

We have one more night, and here I am doing the literal opposite of what I need to be doing, which is convincing her that this will work outside of this trip.

"What?" she asks, tugging her hand from mine and crossing her arms on her chest.

"I'm sorry," I say. I want to pull her into me, to kiss her, to remind her that she's important and amazing and that I'm just some dumb man who should bow down to her.

But I remind myself that ignoring the issue won't help.

It will probably just make it fester.

And if we're going to do this, I need her to know I'm a good partner for her to settle with. That I'm rational. If we have an issue, we need to work through it instead of brushing is aside, and I'm more than willing to do that. For her.

"I'm frustrated. I'm crazy about you, Zoe. I have been for so long, and I hate seeing you miserable. I hate that you're looking at a job you won't love. A job that will mean you won't be staying in Springbrook Hills. I hate that for you. I hate that for *me*. I want you to have everything, Zoe: your dream job, your dream life. I want you to be happy and satisfied. And selfishly, I want you close. I want to come home to you every night. But I also know that it's not fair to expect you to up and change everything right away." Her shoulders relax just a hint, and I take that as my cue to keep going, to step closer to her.

My hand moves up, touching the side of her face.

"If you take that job, I'm going to figure it out. Telling you now, I know you're playing pretend and you need that to be carefree while we're here, but this is real for me. We are real. You're living in the present, baby, and that's beautiful, but I'm looking at the future, and it's fucking gorgeous. And I'll do whatever it takes to give us that."

Her hands drop to her sides, the tension of her jaw slipping out.

My other hand moves to her face, and I press my forehead to hers.

"This is not how we fight, Zoe. We fight clean. I respect you. You respect me. I shouldn't have said it's stupid. I'm allowed to be annoyed, to be frustrated, but I'm not allowed to take that out on you, okay?"

Her brow furrows.

"Okay?" I repeat.

I want her to know that.

I watched my parents argue my entire life.

But they always made up.

They always talked it through.

When it was necessary, they apologized.

And they never hid it from us, never hid their hushed arguments behind closed doors. I learned the right way to fight without ruining a relationship, and I refuse to mess this up with Zoe because I forgot that.

"Are you real?" she asks, her voice low.

Now my brows furrow in confusion.

"What?"

"Are you real?" I don't reply, waiting for her to continue. "Men don't do this. They don't take accountability. They don't instantly realize they were assholes."

"When they're so in love, they're terrified to lose their woman because they spoke without thinking, fuck yes they do." Her face pales, and I smile. "Pretend, baby. Don't stress about that, not yet."

I see that's not helping, so instead, I do the only thing I can think of.

I kiss her.

I kiss her, and I let her know everything I feel, all of my plans and thoughts and ideas for what we're going to be five, ten, thirty years from now in that kiss.

I don't say it with words because words are going to scare her. All I can do is show her.

And when we break the kiss and her chest is heaving, but the touch of anger is gone off her face, I press my lips to her hair as I pull her into me, and I whisper there:

"You're kind of cute when you're mad, you know that, pip?" She scoffs and tries to push away from me with two hands on my chest, but I hold on tight, only giving enough room between us so I can stare down at her.

"We fight, we talk, okay?" I ask, my face going serious. She just stares at me. "Okay, Zoe?"

And then she smiles. A big smile. A wide smile.

She likes that.

"Okay, Zee."

"Now, let's go eat so I can take you back to the hotel and get you out of that dress," I say, taking her hand and pulling her into the restaurant.

But I don't miss the blush on her cheeks when I do.

FORTY-ONE
SPARKS FLY
-ZANDER-

Her fingers are twined with mine as we leave the restaurant, headed back toward the Jeep and then to our hotel room for the final night of this trip.

Every bone in my body hopes it won't be our last.

As we're walking out, I can't help but wish I could fit something more into this last night.

One last way to convince her we're good.

One last moment off her bucket list.

And then, like it's a sign from above, the sky opens, rain falling in buckets.

"Ahh!" Zoe shouts, hands going to her hair that's already clinging to her in wet strands, as if her little hands will help shield it at all. "Let's go!" she says, turning toward the lot we parked in.

But I grab her hand, tugging her into me before she can go.

"Zander!"

"We're already soaked, baby," I say, an arm wrapping her lower back, another moving into her soaking hair. "Might as well make the most of it."

And then my lips are on hers.

She doesn't put up even a hint of a fight, her arms wrapping my neck, lips moving on mine in a sweet moment I hope she'll never forget.

I know I won't.

The kiss breaks and her eyes are still closed as the fingers on one hand move to brush wet strands away from her face, then I start to move, swaying to music that's not playing.

"What are you—" she starts with a smile, but I shake my head.

"Dance with me, Zoe."

"In the rain?"

"Everywhere. Anywhere," I say, and the words sound like a whisper in the loud rain.

I expect her to argue.

I expect for her hatred and fear of spontaneity to take over, for her to say she's too wet or too cold or people might see.

"Okay," she whispers, for real this time, but I'm always so fucking in tune with Zoe that I can hear her.

Anywhere, everywhere.

And so we dance.

We sway on the sidewalk, dancing in the rain to music that's playing in our heads, people running for cover all around us, but my eyes never leave Zoe's.

And hers never leave mine.

It's only when she shivers finally, the rain cold, winter getting closer the more north we head, that I dip my head, water running down my nose as I take her earlobe into my mouth.

"Is it time to take that dress off you?" I ask, my face in her neck.

She shivers again, but it's not from cold.

"Yeah," she whispers.

And then I take her hand and we walk in the still pouring rain to her Jeep.

FORTY-TWO
FALSE GOD
-ZANDER-

We walk back into the hotel, and it feels like a near mirror to the first time I had Zoe.

Walking in, Zoe nervous, me on my way to change her damn mind.

Except for this time, she's shivering from the cold rain, and I just know this is my last chance to show her who we are before we go home.

"Come on," I say, moving toward her as she walks into the room. "Let's get you out of this."

Her smile is nervous before she speaks. "Trying to get me naked so quickly, Mr. Davidson?" she says.

"Your lips are blue, Zo. Trying to save you from hypothermia," I say with a laugh.

"Oh."

I shake my head, moving her toward the bed once the wet dress is off, leaving her in just panties.

Light-pink lace panties that I can't wait to peel off her.

Jesus, this woman is a dream.

My dream.

Pulling back the sheets, I motion until she crawls in, her ass swaying as she does, my cock hardening further as I tuck her in.

"You're not coming in?"

"You're my priority, Zoe. Get warm while I get undressed." Her eyes rove my body as I strip slowly, not because I'm trying to give her a show, but because my button-down and pants are so wet, they're nearly impossible to take off. She giggles a sweet sound as I struggle with my pants.

"Are you laughing at me?"

"It's pretty funny watching you," she says, her teeth still chattering a bit as I open the blanket and climb in naked, pulling her cold, damp body to mine.

She shivers again.

"You're so cold!" she says in a shriek and a giggle. A sound that reminds me just how crazy I am for her.

As if I need *another* reminder.

"Warm me up, then," I say, pressing my lips to her neck.

Her body softens near instantly, arm moving over my shoulder, leg moving over my hip.

And then I put my lips to hers.

It's not insane, passion-driven, crazed with lust and the need to consume her.

It's slow.

Sweet.

Like we have all the time in the world.

Her hand moves into my hair, twining with the wet strands, and I move a hand up and down her back, chasing goosebumps.

Slowly, almost imperceptibly, the kiss begins to change.

It could happen over seconds or minutes or hours, but slowly, her breathing quickens.

Slowly, her hips tip up, trying to get some kind of friction.

Slowly, my hand moves to her ass, grabbing her there.

Slowly, her lips move from my lips to down my neck, sucking and kissing and nipping.

We don't speak as my hand moves between us, feeling how she's already wet for me.

We don't speak as her hand moves between us, grabbing my hard cock and running it along her wetness.

And we don't talk as I slide into her, both of us letting out a sound of pure satisfaction.

And then we don't speak as I start to move into her, her arms and legs wrapping me as I do.

But I keep kissing her.

I kiss her, and with each thrust, with each kiss, I try to tell her everything.

Everything she means to me.

Everything we're going to be.

Everything we need to be.

Until it becomes too much, until I can feel her starting to tighten around me, when I feel my balls starting to tighten.

That's when I roll until I'm over her, her eyes drifting shut with pleasure at the orgasm that's just out of reach.

"Look at me, Zoe," I say, my breath coming in pants as I slowly fuck her.

She doesn't look at me.

Her eyes are somewhere on a wall behind me, avoiding looking into my own, slowly drifting shut then opening again with pleasure.

But it's not the pleasure that's keeping her eyes away from me.

It's what she doesn't want to see.

I know this better than I know most things.

Somehow, I know in my gut that Zoe knows if she looks at me right now, as I thrust into her slowly, she'll see something that will undoubtedly scare her.

Something that she's, for some reason, convinced herself she's not ready to see, but it's so long past due at this point.

"Fuck me, Zander," she moans, her legs tightening around my hips, her dull nails digging into my ass.

But I shake my head.

I won't.

I can't.

"I'm not gonna do that, Zoe."

A frustrated noise comes from her, and I smile.

"What are you doing then?" she asks, and with that, I move one hand from the bed next to her head and move it to the side of her face, my thumb cupping her chin until she's forced to look at me.

And it takes over her face.

Pure fucking beauty when she sees my eyes.

Sees what I've been trying to tell her, to show her, for a week.

For years, if I'm being honest with myself.

I'm so fucking in love with this woman that I can't breathe.

"I'm making love to you, Zoe."

"Zander—"

"No more *Zander*. No more pretending. This is real, Zoe. Us? We're real. If you wanna play pretend, just know you'll be doing it for the rest of your life. I'm not letting you get away from me, Zoe." I mean that.

I might have an uphill battle in front of me, but I'll be pushing that rock up that hill until it becomes my goddamn gravestone.

"Zander—" The word is scared, still tinged with lust and unfulfilled pleasure, but scared all the same.

My words terrify her.

But there's no more time for kid gloves.

"You'll never hurt. You'll never feel lost because I'll always be holding your hand. You'll never be alone. Never again. I'll make all of your dreams come true, Zoe. I just need you to give me the chance."

I keep staring at her, waiting for her response.

But she doesn't argue this time.

I pull out slowly, entering her just as slowly, and she moans low, eyes drifting shut.

The thumb under her chin moves, pressing on her neck just enough to have her eyes shooting open.

"No. You keep your eyes open. They do not close, not this time. You're gonna watch what you do to me."

"Zander," she moans, tightening around me.

And I wonder in the back of my mind what's doing it to her—the hand? The need to keep her eyes open? Or is it just us?

"Don't you see it, Zoe? How wild you make me? Don't you feel it?" I thrust harder this time, hand moving tighter on her neck, her eyes going wider, her pussy gripping tighter. "You were made for me, Zoe. If you didn't figure that out over the past thirty fucking years together, you need to realize it now, with my fucking cock in you, when you fit so fucking perfect around me."

"Zander!" she moans, voice frantic.

"I know, baby. Find it. Find it, take me with you, and keep your eyes on mine as you do."

And then she falls, screaming my name, gripping me tight, and taking me with her.

But the whole time, her eyes stay on mine and I can see it there, clear as day.

She knows she's mine.

Hours later, we're lying under the warm sheets, bodies naked, rain pelting the windows.

It's cozy and comfortable, but I can tell she's back to overthinking.

Zoe is *always* overthinking.

"What happens when we get home?" she asks into my neck, and I'm taking that as a good sign.

Zoe who didn't want this to continue wouldn't need to ask. She'd just know it would be over. Zoe who doesn't *want* it to end asks.

"This is a fairy tale, right? We're playing into it," I say, trying to keep it light.

"What happens when it ends, Zander? How do we—"

"Don't look at the end. Don't worry about it. Just give me this," I say, cutting her off. I look at the clock and smile, running my hand through her hair, fingers catching at knots she didn't brush out after our moment in the rain and definitely not after the last two hours in this bed. "It's midnight."

She moves her head up to look at me with a smile.

A carefree one.

She's no longer worried, not sitting in the panic of *what-ifs* and *what happens whens*.

Good.

That's also a good fucking sign.

Right?

"What's with you and midnights?" she asks.

Midnights have been my favorite time since I was thirteen—the first time Zoe woke up at midnight for a glass of water and ran into me.

But not the last time.

Even now, when I get home after a night shift, a twisted part of me wonders if she were mine, would she be waiting for me? Would she be sitting in my kitchen with a bowl of cereal, sleepy eyes because she woke up twenty minutes ago on instinct, knowing I was on my way home to her?

"When you used to sleep over with Luna, you'd always come downstairs and get water in the middle of the night. Always woke me up, and then I'd come out and talk with you. Those are some of my favorite memories."

"You're a creep, you know? I was four years younger than you." She smiles like it's silly, but I shake my head, a hand moving to her face, so she gets what I'm saying.

I need her to understand this.

"Even then, you were one of my best friends, Zoe. Ten years of you not being mine, and anytime we were together, I felt fucking whole. I liked talking to you even then. Liked the chaos that came out of your mouth when no one was looking."

"Chaos doesn't come out of my mouth anymore."

"You won't let it. Won't *let* the chaos out." I press my lips below her ear.

"That's not true."

"It is. But that's fine. I'll make it my mission, Zoe. Drag the chaos out of you. Make you happy if it's the last thing I do." I roll her until she's below me. "And you'll micromanage my chaos so I don't burn myself out before I can get you into bed." She smiles.

"You do that, you know. Overcommit yourself. Peewee coach, helping at the Center, helping at Camp Sunshine. Taking up extra shifts." Her hand with those pretty pink nails she keeps looking and smiling at when she thinks I don't notice moves to my face, brushing the thick, longish hair back.

This feels . . . different.

"I like to help. I'm single, so I've got no one waiting for me at home." A stab to my gut, but her smile grows, easing the ache.

"Would that be my job, then? Keep you home? Give you a reason to come home to me?"

"Knowing you? You'd be right there with me, helping whoever needs it around town."

"Probably," she says with a smile, and I move again, rolling until she's on top of me.

I love this.

I love how easy it is.

How we just *work*.

We were always meant to work.

I know if we have a dinner date and I call her to tell her I picked up an extra shift to help out one of the guys, she'd be fine.

That, I can say, I've never had. Someone who gets me and gets my job and doesn't take personal offense to the long or strange hours.

And with her, my future looks so damn bright.

"You know the best part of being with you?" I ask, and she blinks at me, her eyes sleepy now. I roll one last time until we're both on our sides.

"What's that?" she asks with a yawn.

"You're with me *knowing* me and that you'll be living with this shit for the rest of your life." Her brow furrows. "I've had women, Zoe. None of them would ever get that about me. They couldn't stand the night shifts and the early mornings and then coaching the Bulldogs. Family dinners and breakfast at the diner. Drove them all crazy."

"Well," she says with a pause, her little brow furrowing, and I can't help but press my lips there. "They were dumb to give up on you."

And it's then I know that even though the next few days will be an uphill climb, I've got Zoe Thomas.

FORTY-THREE
TREACHEROUS
-ZANDER-

"Welcome to New Jersey," I say, looking at the sign as I drive past it and with my words, it's like a cloud fills the car.

"Welcome to New Jersey," Zoe says, her voice low and sad.

A million responses run through my mind, but I don't speak.

The trip is almost over, but I know we have a full mountain to run up before she's comfortable with this.

With us.

I still have a lot of convincing to do.

That's fine.

I will happily spend my entire lifetime convincing Zoe Ann Thomas to give us a chance.

Instead of speaking, I grab her hand, so much smaller than mine, nails tipped in pretty pink—a symbol, in my mind, of how far she's come from her comfort zone—and lift, pressing it to my lips.

And then I squeeze her hand, the same calming cadence, the same reliable way.

One, two, three.

In my mind, it's all three versions of her.

One hand squeeze for the little girl who would chat with me at midnight.

She taught me that it's the smallest moments that will stick with you.

One for the girl who turned me down, who wasn't ready for us.

She taught me to be patient, that waiting for what I wanted would make it all the sweeter.

And one for the woman who took a leap of faith and drove around while I tried to convince her to fall for me.

She taught me that you're never too old to play pretend.

She tries to tug her hand away, but I hold tighter, keeping it on my lap.

"Stop," she says under her breath, tugging once more.

I let her go.

"Zoe—"

"We can't play pretend forever, Zander." My brows furrow as I keep my eyes on the road, confused.

"Why not?"

"That's not how life works," she says with an irritated sigh.

"Says who?" Zoe scoffs like I'm being stupid.

Doesn't she see the only thing stopping us is her stubbornness?

"Says . . . everyone."

"I think you're just scared," I say, my voice low.

I haven't straight out accused her of anything yet, except for right now.

This moment.

And I'm not sure why I'm shocked when she doesn't answer.

An hour later, we're stopped outside her parents' house, parked behind my car.

The trip is over.

My gut sinks with that knowledge.

"We're home," she says.

"We're home," I agree. I look at her and see her eyes are looking out of the windshield, avoiding mine.

A long minute passes before she speaks again, still not moving to look at me.

"What now?"

"What now?" I parrot, confused. Finally, she looks at me.

"Yeah, Zee. What now?"

"Well, now we unpack your shit, get you ready for your interview. Then we figure out how to move forward with whatever you choose."

"We?" she asks, her voice low and unsure.

My brow furrows because I don't understand how she doesn't *get* it.

I thought we were past this, thought we had an understanding.

"Well, yeah. You're mine, Zo." She sighs and it feels like the sound fills the car, ricocheting around.

"That won't . . . That doesn't . . ." She's not even forming a full thought, but I need to end it.

I can figure out where it's headed.

"The fuck it doesn't." Her face goes soft, almost with pity, and my stomach churns.

"Zander, be for real—"

"I spent my entire life watching you grow up. Spent the last twelve years watching you jump from asshole to asshole—" She takes that chance to cut me off.

"To be fair, you jumped from girl to girl just as well." I roll my eyes at her, even though she's not wrong.

I'm just *frustrated*.

The image in my mind made this easy. We'd get back and we'd figure it out and it might not have been sunshine and daisies, but it would be fine.

Simple.

At the end of the day, I know to my bones that Zoe is my person.

"Yeah, well, whenever I was single, you were happy with some douche. Whatever. Now you're mine."

"This makes no—"

"Stop." I sigh, trying to make sense of things in my mind.

To make a new plan.

"Look. You have your interview in two hours. Let's get you through that without any issues and then we can figure it out."

We have a lifetime.

"Okay," she says, and the word sounds fake.

Like what you tell someone when they say you should get together sometime and you agree, knowing damn well you'll never actually make it happen.

"Where are you having your interview?" I ask.

"What?"

"Your interview. You're not going to the city, right? It's video?"

"Oh. Yeah."

"So where are you having it, pip? Here?" I tip my chin to her parents' house.

She shakes her head.

"At Rise and Grind." Sadie's coffee shop has coworking booths where she could easily have a professional call with privacy. It makes sense, when compared to her childhood bedroom with her mother standing at the door, trying to eavesdrop.

"When will it be over?"

That's what happens next.

I need to take this one step at a time. I need to be rational.

First, the interview.

Then, we talk.

"They blocked my calendar off for two hours."

"Two hours? Jesus." I shake my head, not being able to wrap it around sitting at a computer screen for two hours straight, talking to a stranger. "Well, I'll pick you up after."

"What?"

"From your interview. I'll pick you up." Her confusion would be cute if it wasn't frustrating as all hell.

"Why . . . Why would you . . . ?"

"Because you're mine and I take care of what's mine."

I swear it feels like I'm talking to a wall.

It's like as soon as we hit the very corner of New Jersey, the safe, picture-perfect version of Zoe snapped back into place.

A tiny part I refuse to acknowledge is terrified that now that we're home, there won't be any way to break back in.

To convince her to make *pretend* real.

Shit.

"I don't need you to." Her shoulders straighten and I see her now: the version who feels the need to do everything, to impress everyone. The uptight version who wears her hair in tight ponytails and wears tops buttoned up to her collarbone.

"I want to," I say softly, grabbing her hand. She sighs.

That sigh cuts me, the exasperation in it.

"Zander, you don't have to."

"Zoe—"

"This has been fun, Zee. Really. But I need to . . . focus."

Focus.

And not on figuring out what *us* looks like, I'm sure.

I let a long beat go by before I speak.

"What are you saying?"

"I'm saying . . . I'm saying you don't have to pick me up. I can drive myself. I can . . . I can do it without you." She sighs and my gut drops.

"Zoe."

"I need time."

Another shift that feels detrimental to everything we built.

"Time." The word feels heavy on my lips.

"Time. Time to process." Her hand moves between us. "This. Us."

"So you're saying there's an us?"

I smile, hope filling me.

There it is.

No matter what Zoe says, no matter what she thinks she needs or what she thinks she wants, there's a fucking us.

I just need to be patient.

I need to convince her.

"I'm saying I am so incredibly confused and being in a car with you isn't helping. Being isolated with you isn't helping. I need a dose of *reality*. I need to be in the real world, remember that there is more than just road trips and playing pretend."

"Zoe—"

"I can't just go off and start my life over. I have bills. I have student loans. I have *nowhere to live*. I have no job! You want me to drop everything and, what? Stay in Springbrook Hills?"

"I want you to give us a chance. Isn't that what you want? To give this a try? After all this time, you don't think it's finally time to give us a shot?"

"What if that's not enough? It's not that *simple,* Zander.*"

"Is it. It really fucking is," I say as frustration burns in my gut.

I don't know why I'm getting frustrated, really.

I knew that it was going to happen.

I knew she wouldn't go easy—hell, I love that about her. Her spirit, how fucking headstrong she is.

But I'd be lying if a small part of me hadn't hoped she'd just . . . work with me to figure it out.

I can't push her. I can't scare her off.

"Zander, this is—"

"Look, we'll talk about it after your interview," I say, leaning over and pushing a lock of her hair behind her ear.

"I might not be in town after this interview, Zee. If I take the job, I'll need to start looking for a new place in the city as soon as possible. I—" My hands go to her cheeks.

"Shh. Stop. We'll talk about it. If I need to drive to New York every night to sleep in your bed, we'll figure it out." Her eyes go soft with my words.

Hope.

The look gives me all the hope I need.

"Zander."

"Pretend."

"This is real life, Zee." Her words are soft and pained.

"*Pretend*, pip. At least until tonight when we can talk. I'll pick you up after your interview." She stares at me and then it happens.

She shakes her head.

"No."

"No?"

"No. I need time. I need to think."

"Seriously, Zoe?"

"We've spent every moment together for seven days. Give me some space."

"So that's what you need. Space?" I ask, staring at her.

She nods.

"That's what I need."

I have no choice.

Not really.

I know to my bones that if I push, that could mean the end before it starts.

My stubborn fucking girl.

So I nod.

"Okay. I'll give you space."

And then I hop out of her car, grabbing her bags and walking them to her front door.

"Zander—"

"You won't let me take you to your interview. Won't let me pick you up after. Please, pip. Let me bring your bags inside." She bites her lip, looking me over like she's unsure if she should give me that before she nods.

And when I dump them in her childhood room, seeing that her parents haven't changed any of it since high school, I smile.

"Gonna go," I say, standing in the purple room with her.

She bites her lip and nods.

My girl.

Suffering. I hate it. I hate that she's fighting herself, fighting her own desires and what she really, truly wants in order to fit some mold no one expects her to live in.

My work is clear.

Some men would see that as a negative: having to help a grown woman figure out who she is, figure out how to live life for her.

Some men would use that to their advantage, take what they perceive as a weakness and manipulate it until she shifts her priorities to live her life for him.

But not me.

I can't wait to spend a lifetime making sure that Zoe lives life for *Zoe*. That each and every thing she does fuels her soul, brings her all-consuming joy.

And to be a part of that.

So I step to her, grabbing one of her hands, twining the fingers with mine, and closing the gap until our hands are pressed between us, then I put the other one on her cheek.

"I'll be here when you're ready, Zo. Okay?" I ask, then I squeeze her hand three times.

"Zander—"

"No. I'll be here when you're ready. That's it." She sighs, and before she can speak again, I press my lips to hers.

A quick, gentle kiss.

Nothing crazy.

Just a reminder.

Of who I am.

Of who she is.

Of who *we* are.

And then I step back.

"Call me after your interview, yeah?"

She stares at me and somehow, I know.

She's not planning to call me.

So when she nods, she's lying.

"Yeah, Zee."

I stare at her for a few more moments before nodding.

"Bye, pip."

And then I turn, letting myself out of her parents' house and going to the only place I can think of to get the help I desperately need.

FORTY-FOUR
BYE, BYE, BABY
-ZANDER-

"You're back," Tony says when he opens his front door.

I glare at him.

"I'm guessing you're not here to see me."

"Shut up, man."

"Looks like vacation didn't change your attitude." I walk in, brushing past my best friend, and when I turn back as he closes the door, he's cringing at me. "So, I guess you failed your mission."

I sigh, moving to the sitting room and flopping to my back on the couch, putting my hands over my face and breathing deep.

"Who the fuck knows?" I groan through my fingers.

"Well, did you do it?" Tony sits next to me. "Did you put a ring on her finger?"

I think of the straw wrapper ring I twisted around her dainty finger and sigh.

"Nope."

"For lack of trying or . . ."

"Oh, you're back!" Luna says, coming around the corner, but then she stops, her face melting. "Oh. You fucked up."

"I did *not* fuck up. God, why do none of you have any faith in me?" I ask, sitting up and looking at my sister.

"You look like someone killed your dog and Zoe is nowhere to be found, soooo . . ."

"I dropped her off at home for her interview."

"You *what?*" Luna says, her voice appalled.

"I took her home. She has that interview."

"And you *let* her?"

"Luna, I already kept the woman hostage for a full week, not even letting her have her phone. What choice did I have?" My sister flops on the couch with an arm over her head in a huff.

It must be the Davidson genes, the drama.

"You fucked up," she says with a glare.

"I didn't."

"You did."

"No, I didn't," I insist, not even bothering to give any kind of supporting evidence.

"You two are fuckin' ridiculous," Tony says under his breath. Luna's head whips to him.

"You shut up," my sister says to her husband, and in this case, I agree.

"Lune, you think more than five seconds about it, you'll understand Zee *had* to let Zoe take the interview. The woman is stubborn, and God forbid he didn't, there's the chance she'd always think about that what if." Luna rolls her eyes and I smile, loving that my friend is on *my side* and not his wife's.

"Thanks, man," I say.

It's childish, but I totally want to stick my tongue out at my sister.

And then he turns to me.

Well, fuck.

Maybe he *isn't* on my side.

"But you're the dumbass who let her leave, thinking you wouldn't be working to win her." My gut drops.

"The fuck, man, you don't know—"

"You're here, asking your sister for help. Again."

I don't respond.

He's right, after all. I know in my gut we're not done, that I'm going to do whatever it takes to make her mine, to make her *see* she's mine.

But does she know that?

Or did she head into that interview thinking I took her words at face value, that this wouldn't work in the real world?

"You need to fight for her, Zander," my sister says, her voice low.

"Luna, I spent a *week* fighting for her."

"No, you didn't."

"Were you there and I didn't notice?" My sister rolls her eyes to the ceiling and murmurs something about *idiotic men*.

"You weren't fighting for her, Zee. You were pleading your case. Opening the door."

"Dear God," I say, running a hand down my face.

"I'm serious! I don't want to know what you two did on your trip, but when I talked to her, she was happy with—what did she call it?—pretend you were playing." I smile, liking that. Liking that she seemed happy to my sister, her best friend. "But she was nervous. She didn't know what would happen when you guys came home."

"She can't take that job," I say impulsively.

"Glad we're on the same page there." A bit of my anxiety fades with her words.

"She's miserable," I say. Luna nods.

"I know."

"She needs to go into interior design," I say, sure in that. The look on her face when she was flipping through her magazines, the way she would point out things in restaurants or hotels that she liked, things she'd do differently . . . That's where her passion lies.

Luna stops, staring at me.

"What?" she asks.

"It's what she wanted to do as a kid. It's what she likes, but she's afraid no one will take her seriously and even more scared that if she tries it and fails, her parents will be disappointed." Tony scoffs.

"You're trying to tell me *Zoe* thinks that *Joe Thomas* will be disappointed in her?" he asks, also knowing how much the man loves to brag about his daughter.

I nod.

"Does she even know her father?" I shrug and sigh.

"I don't know. There's some shit she's built up in her head around being an only child. It's getting to her. She thinks she's the one who has to make it worth it for her parents. She has to prove herself to them." Now it's my sister's turn to sigh and shake her head.

"She was always that way. Always trying to make sure she was impressive for her parents."

"I know." Her head turns to me, and she looks confused.

"How do you know?"

She doesn't get it either, clearly.

"Because even when she was little and I was too old for her, she was my friend, Luna. Not the way you were friends, but she was always Zoe to me. We would talk about everything under the sky."

"When?!" Clearly, Zoe never shared this with her best friend.

I wonder what that means? If it's a good sign or a terrible one.

On one hand, maybe she wanted it to be just our thing.

"In the middle of the night."

"You are such a creep."

On the other hand, maybe she thought I was weird and didn't want to tell her best friend her older brother was a fucking creep.

I don't think it's the latter, though.

"The girl doesn't sleep. She wakes up at midnight for a snack or water or whatever. Does it because when she was little, that's when Thomas would be coming home. She'd sneak downstairs and eat a snack with him."

Luna's face goes soft, and it confirms my thought that it wasn't a bad thing.

Instead, it was a good sign.

"I didn't know that."

"I did," I say, feeling just a bit smug.

"I can see that."

Silence fills the room, both of us in our own memories, our own thoughts.

"So, I gotta ask. When you were away, did you really do the list?" Luna asks, finally breaking the silence.

I smile.

I smile because even though Luna gave me that playlist, I know she didn't think I would follow through.

I'm the hothead.

I'm the one who laughed at their romantic ideas.

I'm the one who would roll my eyes when Mom went on her tangents about soulmates and the stars and blah blah blah.

But what my sister doesn't understand is, I would be absolutely *anything* so long as it made me Zoe's.

A hopeless romantic. Some idealized oo's romcom character.

A man who would take her childhood love bucket list and bring it to life without her noticing.

"Well, let's see. We watched the sunrise over the water," I say with a smile, ticking off items on my fingers.

'Daylight.'

"Then we danced in a parking lot."

'Fearless.'

"I threw rocks at her window."

'Love Story.'

"We kissed and danced in a rainstorm." My sister's mouth drops and her face softens.

'Sparks Fly.'

"We went stargazing."

'I'm Only Me When I'm With You.'

"I tied a straw wrapper around her finger at a diner—"

"Jesus Christ, you even 'Paper Rings'ed her?!" Luna says with a shout, standing now. I smile.

"I sure did."

"Does she know?"

"Know what?" I ask.

"What you were doing?" I shrug.

"I don't think so."

"Jesus. She's so hardheaded," Luna says with a sigh, sitting down again.

Tony stares at my sister, who literally didn't know that Tony was head over heels in love with her since she was 17 until a literal stalker came and forced her to stay with him.

"Shut up," she says, slapping her husband in the arm.

He just laughs then pulls her into him.

There it is.

What I want. What I'm working for.

"Okay," Luna says finally.

"Okay?"

She stands, wiping her hands on her lap.

"Do you love my best friend, Zander?"

"Luna—" I argue, not sure what to say.

I haven't even really had this conversation with Zoe yet.

"I'm serious. Do you love her?" Her eyes aren't joking any more; this isn't just something she's saying.

Do I love Zoe?

"Yes." *More than she knows*, I think.

"Okay. Good," She says with a nod.

"Good?"

"If you didn't seem like you meant it, I wouldn't give you my secret weapon."

"Your secret weapon?" I ask.

"Come," she says. "But it might mean you're stuck with her forever." It's meant as a threat.

As a test.

But I think I pass when I nod and follow her farther into the house.

Then we begin to formulate our final plan to keep Zoe in Springbrook Hills forever.

FORTY-FIVE
CHANGE
-ZOE-

I turn off the meeting screen and sit back, leaning in my seat.

The interview went . . . fine.

It's everything I *thought* I wanted: a director position with full benefits, a crew of people working under me, and more responsibilities than I had at my old job.

But it's . . . boring.

It's corporate.

It's definitely not creative.

But, I got the job.

They're putting together a formal offer and it should be in my inbox tomorrow.

We're so excited to have your leadership expertise on board.

Leadership expertise. That's what sold me. The ability to *manage* people.

I should feel happy.

I should feel relieved.

I should feel *excited*.

The job is everything I thought I wanted two weeks ago.

VP of marketing for a large firm.

A corner office.

I'd have to live in the city, the job too high pressure to want to worry about a commute, but the pay would be enough to swing a place without a roommate.

And yet I feel . . . stressed.

It's probably lack of sleep, I tell myself, shaking my head.

A good night's sleep in my own bed, alone, and I'll have a better understanding of just how exciting this is.

Standing, I step out of the cubicle and instantly spot my best friend sitting at the barista bar across from Sadie.

"Hey!" Luna says when she spots me. "How'd it go!?"

"Uh, hi," I say, part confused and part . . .

Jesus, I can't be disappointed.

That's not *allowed.*

I can't be upset that a different Davidson isn't sitting there, waiting to hear all about how the interview went.

"Don't look too excited to see your best friend," Luna says with a smile.

"Oh my god, I am! Of course! I just, I wasn't expecting . . ."

"You were expecting to see my brother."

"No, that's not it," I start.

"Bullshit," Sadie says with a smile.

"To be fair, I begged him to let me pick you up and told him he shouldn't come."

My gut both sinks and floats.

Does that mean he *wanted* to come? Even after I told him no? Does that mean that he was going to try and push my boundaries?

Also, if that is what it means, why doesn't that annoy the fuck out of me?

"Why?" I ask. "Why did you tell him not to?"

That's when I reveal my hand and both Sadie and Luna know it.

"Because I need the scoop."

"The scoop?" I ask, sitting down.

"Don't play stupid, Zoe. We need to know what happened on that trip!" Sadie says, starting on my iced coffee without me even asking. I roll my eyes.

"There is no scoop," I say.

"Bullshit. I need to know absolutely everything." She pauses, staring off in space before going a bit green. "Actually, cut out the NC-17 parts, please."

"No way! I want to know the NC-17 parts!" Sadie says with a laugh. "Luna can plug her ears."

Again, I roll my eyes.

"I'm not giving you guys all the details. It told you pretty much everything on the phone *yesterday*."

"Yeah, but you weren't wearing that necklace a day a go," Luna says, her voice low.

My fingers move to the initial around my neck.

"An A?" Sadie asks, confused.

"Zee's real name is Alexander." Her face looks even more confused.

"Really?" Luna nods, but her eyes are still on me. "I went my whole life knowing that kid and I did not know his real name. Weird."

"His initial on a chain around your neck, huh?" Luna says with a smile, and a cog turns in my mind.

Her face tells me that should mean something.

But I'm so deep in my confusion and frustration and pain over my future that I can't quite grasp it.

"It's not that easy."

"It could be," she says, and I roll my eyes.

"The two of you got way too much of your mom and not *nearly* enough of your dad," I say with a sigh.

"Ace is the straight talker. Zee and I live in the clouds."

Pretend. The word runs in my mind on a loop.

"Yeah, well, I can't live with my head in the clouds, unfortunately. I need to worry about bills. And a job."

"How'd your interview go?" Sadie asks, sliding over a drink. I take sip as I think of how to answer.

"Well. I got the job."

"You got the job?" she asks with excitement.

"Yup," I say. "I'll get the formal offer tomorrow and if that looks good . . ." My words trail off.

If that looks good, then what?

"So, are you going to take it?" Luna asks. She says it like she knows it's more difficult that just wanting a job and getting the job and taking the job.

But it *shouldn't* be, right?

A week ago, I would *jump* at this opportunity.

I sigh.

But now . . .

"I don't know. I don't . . ."

Silence fills the air as I try and think of how to explain the chaos that is my thoughts.

"Is it what you want?" she asks, her voice low.

I pause again, still trying to figure out how to answer.

"I *thought* it was," I say, my voice low.

"But . . . ," Sadie says, feeling the word coming.

I grab my drink, twisting the plastic cup to stir it, the ice making a satisfying noise as I do.

"But what if all this time, I've been living a boring life?" I ask under my breath.

Because if I learned anything in the last week, it's that I've been living the last fifteen years of my life for my parents.

And for society.

Trying to please everyone and be impressive and climb some metaphorical ladder.

I realize now every rung has made me more and more miserable.

"That's not a what if, Zo," Luna says, her voice not mean, but cajoling. "That's a definitive."

This actually shocks me.

Because Luna never questions what I do, what choices I make. If nothing else, Luna is the world's best hype girl, always supporting my every move, even if it's not one she would take herself.

"What?"

"You've been living the most boring life known to man," she says, and Sadie nods in agreement.

"I live in the city," I say defensively. Both women roll their eyes.

"Lived. You *lived* in the city. Not that it mattered because you only *worked* while you were there. And you *lived* with the most boring man alive. And you never did *anything* fun." I narrow my eyes at her.

"Yes, I did," I say, crossing my arms on my chest.

"When?" Luna asks instantly.

I stop and think.

Fuck.

I can't think of a single "fun" thing I've done in the city in the last six months, at least.

And I know damn well that if I use the one time in the last year that the girls came to visit and forced me to go to a karaoke bar, they won't accept *that* answer.

There was lots of emphasis on *forced*.

"I just went on a giant road trip!" I say, deciding that was *definitely* fun.

"Because my brother forced you," Luna says, raising her eyebrow.

There's silence because that cuts—the reminder of Zander.

Luna sighs, seeing that and understanding the way only a best friend can.

"I've known you my entire life, Zoe. You are fun and carefree but you're also . . . not. You used to be. And then you graduated and you started working hard, which is amazing, don't get me wrong. If it made you happy, you know I'd be the first in line to encourage you. But you don't seem . . . happy."

"I am happy, Lune," I say quietly. "I've got great friends and a great family. I'm happy." I bite my lip and it feels like I'm trying to keep a lie in, to stop myself from adding a *but*.

"I'm not saying it like that. I'm just saying . . . you used to have too many great ideas for design. You used to walk into a restaurant and start whispering to me what you'd do different." This conversation sounds *so* familiar.

"You've talked to Zander," I say, accusing her.

"I have," she says. "But he just confirmed what I already knew."

I don't ask her to elaborate.

I don't need her to.

"You know, I need to redo this place," Sadie says, wiping down the countertop, repeating what she brought up earlier. "Business is growing and with Kate on staff, I have more time for other things. I did this place on such a tight budget and honestly, I hate half of it."

My heart skips a beat.

"If you have some time while you're here, I'd love to talk to you about hiring you to design Rise and Grind."

This time, my heart stops completely.

"Sadie, you don't have to—"

"I want to. I want to hire an expert. I insist on paying you. You could test it out. See if you like doing that."

My breathing quickens, my palms going sweaty despite the iced drink in my hand.

"And since I know you'd kill it, once you do an amazing job and you set yourself up, I know a handful of other businesses who need design work too. We all meet at the Chamber of Commerce once a month for small business meetings. Every single month, someone asks for recommendations for interior design. So many of the businesses in Springbrook Hills are outdated, and with the new camp and the school getting more funding thanks to Dean applying for grants and whatnot, more people are coming here."

Sweat forms on the back of my neck now.

I can't decide if it's panic or excitement or maybe I'm coming down with a cold.

Who the hell knows.

"The motel needs a whole revamp. I spoke with Edith last week and she's been saving up."

The motel in town is grimy and a little creepy but it's owned by the sweetest old woman.

"She wants it to be in good standing when she hands it off to her son. That way, when she's gone, he can either sell it easily or not have to worry about redoing it."

"You could work with Tanner and Jordan," Luna suggests, her voice low. "I was talking to her recently. They're looking to expand Coleman and Sons. Start doing remodels."

I can't pull air into my lungs.

Have you ever felt like the universe is giving you exactly what you want but you aren't sure if you're ready to take it? Or even more, it's giving you what you didn't even *realize* you wanted?

That's where I'm at.

A week with Zander, two weeks after cracking open the box that was supposed to manifest all of my hopes and dreams and well . . .

Even more, it seems like the universe is giving me what I want and a plan for how to make it happen. A plan for how to make sure I'll be successful.

"We can talk about it later. I can see it's freaking you out," Sadie says.

"It's not—"

"It's okay. Just think about it, okay? And by that, Zoe, I mean all of it."

I know she means Zander.

I know she's not just talking about some job.

But still, I nod.

I nod and I drink my coffee and I tell her and Luna the (PG) stories from my road trip and for another hour or so, I continue to play pretend.

I frame my stories like it was a fun road trip with a man I'm crazy for and that my life isn't in shambles.

As I drive off back to my parents' house, I can't help but wonder if I'm even really playing pretend anymore.

FORTY-SIX
MIDNIGHT RAIN
-ZOE-

On the drive home, though, I can't help but go back into reality.

I only go further as I walk into my childhood home, as I remember that I'm currently living in my *parents' house* and my room is a time capsule of the dreams I once thought were possible.

Into the part of me that can't help but think about the *what ifs*.

The part of me that sees every terrible outcome that could happen—both if I take a leap and if I don't.

I think I need to talk to someone other than my own thoughts.

Luna was no help because she wants me to stay in town.

I know if I talk to Zee, he'll tell me I need to go back to whatever it is that makes me happy.

But happy isn't always realistic or even reasonable.

I sigh and then my stomach grumbles, so I leave my purple room with its collection of posters and memorabilia of a person I don't feel like anymore and head downstairs to find some food.

When I walk into the kitchen, though, my dad is walking in at the same time.

"Hi, Daddy," I say with a small smile, and he comes over to pull me into a hug that will never not feel perfect.

"Hi, sweetheart. Good to see Zander brought you home in one piece. How was the trip?"

Even his name sends a bolt through me.

"All good."

My dad's face contorts with confusion, and he pushes me back and looks me over.

"How was the interview?"

"Good," I repeat, and I'm starting to hate that word.

Good.

It's so much like *fine.* Not great but also not *bad.*

It's just . . . good.

I'm starting to think that's the kind of life I've been living—a good life. A *fine* life.

But last week wasn't good or fine, my subconscious tells me. *It was fantastic. It was freeing. It was freaking phenomenal.*

I kick that subconscious to the side.

She likes to keep her head in the clouds when I desperately need to keep my feet on the ground.

"Good?" he asks, then he uses a hand on my arm to stop me from heading upstairs.

I need to go upstairs.

I need to figure out what I should be doing. I need the chance to overthink everything.

My phone vibrates in my pocket, and I pull it out to see Zander's name.

I hit the ignore button, sliding it back where it was.

He's calling to ask about my interview.

I promised I'd call him, but I can't quite get the nerve to.

What do I say? I got the job, but you're right, and I don't think I want it?

That I want to take a chance on us but I'm way too much of a coward that we'll crumble in the real world?

My dad's eyes move from my hand to me, confusion on his face.

"Interview was fine. I got the job. They'll give me a full offer tomorrow." I sound depressed. For a woman who just got a job, I sound miserable.

I am miserable.

"That Zander who just called you?" my dad asks, tipping his chin to my phone.

I hate how he can see everything. It was the worst when I was a kid and couldn't get into even the slightest bit of trouble without my dad scoping it out.

It probably contributed to my need to stay within the lines, my fear of disappointing him.

"Yeah," I say, moving toward the stairs and away from his questions.

"Are you ignoring him?" he asks, brow furrowed.

Since when is my father so interested in what I'm doing day-to-day and who I'm talking to or not talking to?

"No, I just didn't want to answer it."

He stares at me, and I smile, giving him a small wave as I put my hand on the railing to the stairs.

I'm so close to escape.

So close to my room where I can overthink every moment from the last ten days or so.

"You gonna take that job?" he asks, and I look over my shoulder at him.

He looks older.

So much older than I remember.

Your parents aging is weird because in your mind, they're stuck at a certain age—for me, my dad in my head always looks the way he did when I was ten. No gray in his thick mustache, his head full of thick, dark hair. In my head, he's tan from a summer of adventures and he doesn't have the small gut he has now from my mom's cooking and more time behind a desk.

But when I look at him, I get the reminder.

He's getting older the same way I am.

I shouldn't brush him off. You never know what's going to happen tomorrow.

But I also don't have it in me to have this conversation again. So, I shrug and answer.

"Not sure. It's a good job. Impressive title." His brow furrows further.

"A job you'd like?" And for the first time in I don't know how long—maybe ever—my dad looks concerned.

It hits at something, unfurling a string I didn't know was tied tight.

I take a moment before I answer.

"It's a good job, Dad," I say. That sounds like the right answer to give.

He just stares at me, taking me in, decoding me.

"Okay, Zo."

"I'm tired, Dad. A long week," I say and tip my chin up the stairs. "Gonna go lie down."

"Alright, sweetheart," he says, his big blue eyes that are a clone of my own looking introspective.

But instead of overthinking *that*, I just go, nodding before I head up the stairs.

I don't remember that I was hungry for hours.

FORTY-SEVEN
MISS AMERICANA AND THE HEARTBREAK PRINCE
-ZANDER-

Four hours after when Zoe's interview was, the interview she promised she'd update me on, my phone vibrates with a new text.

I scramble to look at it, dying to see her name.

Instead, it says *Thomas*.

Fuck.

I swear to God, if he's texting to put me on call, I'm going to—

You'd better fix this.

That's it.

And in that moment, my mind runs through all of the moments Zoe and I talked.

The expectations she felt were on her from her parents.

The way she felt like she needs to live up to some ideal for her father specifically.

Her telling me that when she chose to change her major, her father looked relieved.

Her need to be the perfect child for her parents, even at the expense of her own happiness.

And then I hit call.

who the fuck is Joe Thomas to tell *me* to fix a problem
I'm actively trying to fix—a problem that he, in part, made.

He picks up in three rings.

"You gonna fix this?" he says, his voice gruff.

"Are *you*?" I ask.

I'm mad.

I'm mad because I know Zoe will never be mad at her father, but it boils my blood when I think about how she's wasted so much time doing shit she doesn't love.

It's fucked that Zoe isn't designing restaurants and picking out paint colors every day.

It's fucked that she might accept a job she hates because she feels obligated to fit a mold this man helped to create.

"What are you going on about?" he asks. I can picture his face, what he'd look like if he were standing in front of me.

"I spent a week with your daughter—"

"At my insistence."

God, if I convince Zoe to be mine, I'll have to deal with his man at work *and* in my personal life.

Regularly.

I take a deep breath, reminding myself that Zoe's worth it.

"I spent a week with your daughter and I talked with her. A lot. About shit I won't share with you because she should."

"What in the hell are you talking about?"

"Zoe hates her job." Silence. "Zoe hates her *field*."

"She seems to like it just fine," he says.

Either he doesn't pay attention or she puts a good show on for her father.

"Does she? Or does she just seem to be enduring it until she hits some milestone that even *she* can't identify."

"You're speaking in code." My jaw goes tight before I speak again.

"Everything Zoe does is to impress you and your wife. To make you and Mary Ellen proud of her."

Silence.

This time, I don't fill it in, waiting for him to speak instead.

"That can't be true."

"Can't it? Did she ever want to do marketing when she was younger? To run some firm? To even live in the city?"

"I don't—" I don't want to hear his excuses.

"Zoe loves this town just as much as you do. Loves the people in it, loves being close to her friends and her family."

"She lives in New York."

"Her *job* is in New York," I say, my blood pressure rising.

"You just said she hated her job."

"Jesus, you really are dense." I run a hand through my hair.

"Excuse me, I—"

I should remember that this is my *boss* and my dad's best friend, but I can't.

All I feel is indignation for Zoe.

"Look. When she was nineteen, your daughter came home from school after spending a year in a major she enjoyed but you kept scoffing at." Silence. "Doesn't matter how much you told your friends or the men who work with you how proud you were of her, *she* didn't hear that shit. She heard you telling her that it wasn't a stable career, that it wasn't super smart—"

"The entire country had just gone through a recession."

"Jesus, she was nineteen, Joe. She was nineteen and an only child and, you know as well as me, a daddy's girl. She wanted your full support."

Not a single sound comes down the line.

He knows I'm right.

"She told you she was thinking of marketing. She only said it to see what you'd say and you were gung-fucking-ho. Excited for her, told her to switch. She didn't, but the next semester, she had a tough class and decided it was a sign. Now she's spent ten years in a field she hates."

"I didn't—"

"It doesn't matter what you did or didn't do. She took it that way. Joe, I bought your daughter stupid home design magazines at a gas station, big stack of them. She treated them like gold. Read every page five times. She wants that, but she won't chase it because she's too scared."

"Look, I—"

"I'm not gonna listen to your shit. I'm not. Because really, it doesn't matter what you think, if you think you did what you were supposed to do. It's all in the past. But in the present, I'm working on winning her, on keeping her in town. But don't you put that shit all on me as if I'm not working on making her realize she needs to be with me while also cleaning up the mess you made."

Silence again.

"Now. I've got a plan. I need your input on said plan. Are you gonna give me shit, or are you gonna help me make your daughter really fuckin' happy?"

I count to ten.

Ten long seconds before Zoe's dad responds.

But when he does, I'm flooded with relief.

"What do you need from me, son?"

FORTY-EIGHT
YOU ARE IN LOVE
-ZOE-

Hours later, I'm back to staring at the stupid fucking One Direction poster in my bedroom.

It should be a crime for anyone to be smiling like that when I feel like my world is falling apart.

And really, it's my own fault. I did this to myself.

I told Zander I needed to go to that stupid interview for a job I don't actually want.

I told Zander we wouldn't work in the real world.

I told Zander it was all pretend.

And, in all fairness, I told Zander he didn't have to pick me up after my interview.

I just . . . I guess I didn't think he'd listen to me.

When has Zander *ever* listened to me?

I guess that's not fair either.

He proved over a week that all he *does* is listen to me, take notes on me, on who I am and who I was and who I secretly want to be.

But maybe a week of having to remind me to pretend, of having to reassure me that we'd work and that it was worth the risk got old.

Maybe he thought he didn't want to have to do that for any length of time.

I wouldn't blame him, you know.

It just really sucks that when I was sitting in an interview for what one, two years ago would have been my dream job, a culmination of a lifetime of working to hit the top, all I could think about was Zander asking if I liked my job.

And the fact that I said no.

All I could see was the magazines he bought me at a rest stop, the ones I read over and over in the car, figuring out ideas for designing my next apartment.

Mentally redesigning businesses in towns and homes I know could use an upgrade.

And realizing that I need a change.

Not just dumping my boyfriend and quitting my job just to move onto more of the same.

It's not living in the city.

It's surely not avoiding Zander for the rest of my life.

The reason my mind blew up when I found that MASH list was because it made me scared to see in black and white just how unhappy I was.

How far I had let myself get from my dreams.

But I can't change any of that at ten at night.

It will have to be a tomorrow task.

Tomorrow Zoe will do all the things tonight Zoe is terrified of.

Maybe.

In the meantime, I should do something *productive.*

I should work on an email to turn down the job offer.

Or maybe make a plan to test drive an interior design business, a proposal for Sadie.

Or . . . maybe I should start smaller.

More realistic.

I should unpack.

That's what I need to distract myself.

The bag is right where Zee left it when he walked my shit up to my room, right next to the door.

Three bags, only one of which I even ended up opening.

Sighing, I pad over to them and sit crisscross applesauce before one, unzipping it and starting to go through it, making a pile for clean laundry and another for dirty.

I'm about halfway through when my fingers hit it.

A familiar worn tee.

Zander's coach tee that I slept in.

Like that, seeing my name on your back.

He'd said it coming up behind me while I brushed my teeth in nothing but that tee. His words had sent a chill down my spine in a very different way than I'm feeling now.

That's because I'm a very careful packer.

I know *everything* I put in this bag and where I put it.

I did *not* put this into my suitcase.

What the fuck?

I grab it, my level of insane and obsession to the point that I'm prepped to put it to my nose to see if it smells like him, but . . .

It's not just a shirt.

There's something inside it.

The shirt is wrapping paper.

Carefully, I grab it, trying to keep everything contained in the oversized tee because for whatever reason, it's not just one thing in here.

It's a few.

Placing the tee on the floor, I stare at it, afraid to unfold the sleeves to see what's in there.

But I do because I can't fight the curiosity.

And for a moment, I wish I didn't.

On top, there's a note written on the back of a receipt from a gas station.

It's in thick, dark, man's handwriting, messy but still legible.

For our tree.

I'd be confused if I couldn't see what was under it.

Seven ornaments.

Seven ornaments for a Christmas tree.

My hands shake as I reach for them.

The first one is a little bell with the name of the town we stayed in Georgia on it.

A heart that says *Virginia is for Lovers.*

A Mickey ornament from our day in Disney.

Another just says *Baltimore* in big bold letters.

Another is clearly from a gas station, probably one of the days I spent forever trying to get ready in the bathroom.

One for every stop we made.

Oh my fucking god.

The last one is from the thrift store in North Carolina.

I remember touching the delicate blown glass with my fingers and smiling at Zander.

"When I was a kid, every trip we went on, my dad would buy a Christmas ornament," I'd said.

"An ornament?"

"Yeah. My mom would pack it away, and then every year, we'd remember all the family trips we went on. Putting the tree up was fun because we'd talk about all the places we'd been, even if it was just ten ornaments from the shore or the Poconos." I'd shrugged, moving on. *"Just a good memory, you know?"*

It's a tradition I always thought I'd continue with my own kids if I ever had them, but I didn't tell him that part.

I never told *anyone* that.

But somehow . . . he knew.

He knew, and he took it upon himself to buy that ornament.

And then six more.

God, I love that about him. How well he knows me, how he can read me better than anyone ever could.

In the silence of my childhood room, the realization hits me like a train.

I'm in love with Zander Davidson.

And not in a little girl way, the way that was pretending, the way that believed in fairy tales.

In a way that I know if took the leap, we'd be together until we left this Earth.

And I'd never be lonely.

I'd never have some standard to live up to because he loves whatever version of me I'm willing to give him.

I'd never have to make my dreams smaller to impress him because he wants them to be as big as the sky.

In this moment, I realize I'm so crazy in love with Zander Davidson, and I need to show him and tell him and give him the shot before it's too late.

And it's then I start to make my plan.

It's then I decide it's my turn to make the grand gesture and to tell Zander I'm ready to play pretend forever.

Fuck it.

Fuck it.

Maybe he was right all along.

Maybe I need a change.

Maybe I spent so long making sure everyone would be proud of me and happy for me, I forgot I need to make myself happy.

Life wasn't meant to be lived safely.

If was meant to be *lived.*

And I want to live my life with Zander.

That much, I know.

And if it works for another week or another lifetime, I want that time with him.

I can pull myself together if something happens to us and we don't work.

I can figure out how to avoid family functions for the rest of my life if needed.

But I can't live with the *what if* of Zander Davidson for the rest of my life.

The boy who humored me in the middle of the night, talking about silly kid stuff.

The guy who saved me when I was nineteen and didn't push it when I told him no.

The man who saw I was struggling and forced me out of my comfort zone.

That's who I want.

And I think it's my turn to go get him.

FORTY-NINE
HEY STEPHEN
-ZOE-

"Hi, Dad. Bye, Dad," I say, passing my dad in the kitchen as I head out the door, keys in hand, ready to go find Zander.

"Where are you going? It's eleven," my dad says as if I'm seventeen instead of nearly thirty.

"Out. Be back!" I say, taking a step toward the door.

"Zoe, you can't—"

"I'm an adult, Dad. I can. Be back soon!" *Or not, if things go my way.*

"Be back by midnight!" he shouts out behind me, and I wave him off, ignoring his words.

I need to get out of this house.

Even if Zander isn't game to play more-than-pretend, the decision is made.

Tomorrow, I'm declining the offer.

Tomorrow, I'm meeting with Sadie to talk about redesigning Rise and Grind.

Tomorrow, I'm going to research the shit out of how to create a business. I have more than enough marketing ideas to get myself clients, but I need to actually have something to market.

As I start my Jeep, I ignore how it smells just a bit like Zee and think more about how proud he would be of me.

That I'm taking my own future into my hands.

That I'm excited about something.

That I'm ready to start doing things *for myself.*

It doesn't take long for me to get to the other side of town where Zander lives.

But I sit in my car for a full ten minutes, deep breathing and preparing to do this.

I have to do this.

I need to take this step, to show him how serious I am.

I know Zee lives in the first-floor apartment.

I know where it is.

Based on the details Luna gave me, I can kind of sort of figure out where his bedroom is.

So, when I'm standing in front of a dark window, I don't even second-guess.

I grab a handful of rocks and take a deep breath.

What better way to tell Zander I want to give this a try outside of our trip than to repeat what he did for me a week ago?

With that thought, I throw the first rock.

Tink!

Nothing.

I throw a second, hitting the upper left-hand corner this time.

Thunk!

Again, nothing.

A third hits the window dead center with a satisfying *clank.*

That one has the light in the room turning on.

My stomach is somewhere near my feet.

I can't breathe.

The panic worsens as the window starts to lift.

"Who the fuck is out there?" a deep voice asks.

An *angry* voice.

But . . .

Not a voice I know.

Fuck fuck fuck fuck.

"I'm gonna call the cops—"

"No! Please, don't! I'm so sorry. I—"

"Who are you?" the voice says, the curtains moving to show a big man I've never seen before.

Holy fuck, could this get worse?

"My name's Zoe?" I say, panic taking over. "I'm so sorry. I'm looking for Zander. I—"

"Zander?"

"Yes! Is he there?" I ask as if maybe he's in another room and this guy is visiting.

"No, he lives next door." I can now see the man's head as it tips to the left at a different *fucking* apartment.

Oh my god.

"Oh my god. I'm so, so sorry."

"You're standing in his spot, though." I stare at him, confused.

"What?"

"His parking spot. All of them are assigned. That's Zander's. The kid's not home."

Not home.

Oh my god.

His car isn't here.

Why wouldn't I have looked for his *car* first?

I am not cut out for this life of spontaneity and romance.

"I'm so sorry. Please. Uh . . . go back to sleep," I say with an uneasy smile, backing up with my eyes on Zander's blacked-out apartment.

He's not home.

Where the hell is he, then?

At eleven at night after he's been away for a week?

Where could he be?

But I guess it doesn't matter, does it? Because he's not here.

So I get in my Jeep and head back to my childhood home, where I'll wonder if I fucked it all up by telling him I needed time and space.

FIFTY

THE OTHER SIDE OF THE DOOR
-ZOE-

I'm staring at the clock, watching it, waiting for it, prepared to feel wrecked when I don't feel that squeeze of my hand at midnight.

I think that's when I'll start my cry.

That's when I'll give into the urge, let the tears and disappointment and frustration come once and for all.

When midnight hits and I'm not with him.

I don't get the chance to mourn, though.

Because as I watch the seconds tick to the new day, the moment it hits 12:00, there's a clink at my window.

I stare there, confused.

Then again, a clink.

It's all so familiar.

Too familiar.

I wonder if maybe I'm already deep into my crying coma and I'm hallucinating or dreaming, but then I stub my toe as I stand and take the two steps to my window and realize I wouldn't be able to feel that if it were a hallucination, right?

I *think* that's how that works, at least.

But then I wonder if maybe I *am* having a hallucination.

Just a very, very vivid one.

Because down in the grass outside my house is Zander Davidson.

Another tiny click, and I realize what's happening.

For the second time in a week, Zander is throwing rocks at my window.

I open it, the creaks filling my quiet room and the cold rushing in, but none of that matters.

"What are you doing here?"

"Coming to get you," he shouts up in a hushed voice.

"What?"

"Jesus, Zoe, let's not do this again. Come downstairs."

"Zander—"

"Please, pip." I can see in the light from my parents' front porch that his eyes are soft, kind.

Pleading.

And really, how am I supposed to say no to that?

To him?

So I sigh, throwing a jacket on top of my ugly ass pajamas (no one mopes around in sexy silk) and padding down the stairs.

My dad is sitting at the kitchen island, just a single light on.

"Daddy?" I say, pausing.

He sighs, looking at me.

"He outside?" he says, his voice gruff. I blink at him. "Zee. Is he outside?"

I stare before answering.

"I, uh . . . yeah."

"Good." My dad stands, his body moving slower than I remember as a kid, back when I would wake in the middle of the night and eat a bowl of cereal with him when he got home from a night shift.

That's where my habit of waking up in the middle of the night came from—hearing my dad come home, needing to check on him.

Just like the midnights of my childhood vacations where Zee and I would talk about random shit, those are some of my favorite core memories as a kid.

"I don't—"

"Don't make the kid stay outside. Bring him in. Your mother sleeps like the dead. I'll go up, give you two some privacy."

I'm so lost, but even more so when he pulls me into his arms.

"I always wanted the best for you, Zo. If that means marketing in the city, I'll be overjoyed. If that means being a stay-at-home mom, would love that for you. If it means something else, I'm sorry if I never told you, Zoe, baby, but I would be researching color combinations just so I had something to talk to you about. I never made that clear, and that's on me."

My body freezes.

"You're my girl. My only girl, my entire world. But honey, that does not mean—" He moves, pushing my shoulders back and bending just a bit until we're face-to-face. "That *does not mean* that your mother and I are supposed to be your whole world. You're supposed to live your life for you, Zoe."

"Daddy—"

"I'd say we can talk about this in the morning, but you know me well enough to know I do not like this shit, heart to hearts and life confessions. Just know that you have that boy's full heart, and he has my permission. Just know that never—and I mean *never,* Zoe—would you do a single thing that I wouldn't be proud of. You could start finger painting and not sell a single fucking one and I'd brag about you till I was blue in the face. I'd buy every single one under aliases just so you'd feel good and keep going. And I am so fucking sorry I never made that clear."

My tongue comes out to lick my lips, and my eyes start to water.

Where is this coming from?

Why is he saying all of this *now?*

I refuse to give myself the answer I think I already know.

"No. No tears. Could never handle that, my baby girl crying, and that's not changing any time soon. Now go—go let that boy in, probably freezing his goddamn balls off in the fuckin' cold."

He's not wrong.

The low is something like twenty-seven degrees tonight.

"Just hear him out, okay?" my dad says before squeezing my shoulder and turning around.

I watch him pad to the stairs, frozen in place, before I call his name softly.

"Daddy?" I say, feeling like I'm ten again and he's going upstairs after a long shift. He stops, turns, and looks at me.

"Yeah, baby?"

"I love you," I say, my voice cracking as I give him a tight smile.

He nods the way he always did when I was a kid, and right as he turns back around, I see the wet in his eyes.

"Love you to the moon and Saturn, Zoe."

And then he's gone.

My hands are shaking as I walk to the front door, unlocking and opening it.

And there he stands, hands in his pockets, breath coming out in white clouds.

"Hey," I say, my voice low.

"Hey."

It's strange, staring at him like this after spending so long with him and only him.

It's not like he's a stranger.

It's like my mind and body can't figure out where he's been for the past ten hours and why he's not kissing me.

"Can I come in?" he asks.

"Fuck, yeah, you must be freezing. Come," I ramble, moving to the side.

He smiles that smile I love most of all as he walks in. I close the door behind him and then shove my hands in my jacket, unsure of what to do with them.

I want to hug him.

I want to touch him.

But . . .

"What are you doing here?" I ask, staring at him.

"Can I ask you a question?" he says, and my heart might just explode at the reminder of familiar, sweet words. "A little late, but you took forever to come down." There's a smile on his lips.

"What?"

"A question. It's past midnight, but . . ." His words trail off as he shrugs.

"What are you doing here?"

"Getting what's mine."

"What's yours?"

"You, Zoe, if you didn't understand. You're what's mine," he says with a smile.

What in the fuck is going on?

"That doesn't . . . It doesn't make any sense." I step to the side then toward the kitchen, where one dim light shines.

I want to see his face.

I also want *space*.

I lean my hips into the kitchen counter, facing Zander, my arms crossing on my chest.

"Why not? Because I'm telling you right now, all those crazy dreams you had as a little girl? I'm gonna make them happen for you." He steps closer, but there are still a few feet between us.

It feels like an ocean.

An ocean I created with no idea how to drain it.

"That's not how it works, Zander," I say, reality choosing to be the bearer of bad news.

And then he does something I never in one million years would have seen coming.

He reaches into his coat pocket and pulls out a folded piece of paper.

Paper with a heading that reads, *My Love Story Bucket List*.

A paper I started when I was ten and finished when I was nearly thirty.

A paper that I worked on two weeks ago, drunk at my best friend's house and about to blow apart my entire, safe life.

A list that took all my favorite songs, pulled every romantic line I loved from them, and turned it into a checklist for what I wanted from whoever stole my heart.

"It does, Zo," he says, handing it over to me.

I snatch it from his hands, and I know then that this whole week hasn't just been a random mess of impulsive decisions.

Rocks at my window.

Star gazing.

Paper rings in the diner.

The sunrise.

The dress he'd want to take off me.

Dancing in the parking lot.

The A necklace.

Even the questions.

The questions.

He did it all to make this come true.

"Where did you get this?" I ask, my brow furrowed as I read the lines in the dim light of my parent's living room at midnight.

"Lune." My head snaps up to him.

"Luna?!"

"She gave it to me. Told me it would help my mission." I don't even have the mindset to ask about the *mission* because I'm so lost in the idea that Luna gave her brother the super-secret list I started when we were kids.

"I'm going to kill her," I murmur under my breath, wondering if I went over there, could I jimmy her lock and open it to strangle her in her sleep?

"I knew about it already, though," Zander says as if that changes anything. "Years ago, Tony and I found it in her room. You've added to it, but . . . it's all there." His hand moves toward the paper that I'm still reading, but any reply, any outrage that he had seen all of my girly dreams flies when I see different handwriting.

"What's this?" I ask, pointing to the bottom.

"My additions."

"'New Year's Day.' 'The Very First Night.'" My mind moves through the lyrics of both songs—squeezing my hand three times. Riding in the car when we fell in love.

Jesus.

What is he saying right now?

Or more, what has he been saying all along?

"'How You Get the Girl?'" I read off the paper, my bow furrowing.

That one I don't quite get, can't pin it into a part of our story.

"For better or for worse. Forever and ever." I look back up at him, and he's digging in his pocket.

I'm actually scared of what he might pull out this time, how it will either tear me apart or . . .

"Let me put you back together, Zoe. The old version, the good version." My heart stops.

And because I'm me, I overthink, jumping to the worst conclusion.

"Are you saying you don't like me?" I ask.

Because the reality is, I'll never be the old Zoe ever again.

Not really.

I don't think anyone can go back once they've changed. Even if they make every effort to return to who they once were, a small part of them is forever different, irreversible.

Is Zander saying that if I figure out a way to turn back time, he won't like that tiny part of me? That there will always be something inside of me that he resents?

"You know I love you, Zoe."

And then my heart stops full-out.

"I love this uptight version of you, and I love the version that used to play dress-up with my sister and tried to turn me into a toad. I love the version that agreed to go on a road trip with me and the version that started to let go of perfection after just a day or so. I love the version that played pretend with me, but I also love the version that won't admit it was never pretend. Because it never was, pip. Not with us."

"What do you mean you love me, Zander?" I ask because my world is toppling over, and maybe I was wrong.

Maybe you *can* feel pain in dreams and hallucinations. Maybe I am sleeping, living out a fantasy.

Maybe when I wake up, I'll be hungover at Luna's, Tony getting ready to take us to the diner and feed us grease and carbs.

The last two weeks will have been some dream I conjured up.

"Don't play dumb, pip. I've loved you as long as I can remember."

"I don't—" He stops me, continuing to speak.

"You weren't having a midlife crisis, Zoe. You just miss the old you. The fun, carefree girl who would come downstairs and tell me about her wild ideas in the middle of the night. The one who didn't have expectations to live up to, the one who didn't want valedictorian, the one who always saw the good in people. The one who wasn't chasing some dream she thought someone else had for her."

"Zander, I—" He cuts me off with familiar words.

"Can I ask you a question?"

"What?"

"Can I ask you a question, Zoe?" His hand is still in his pocket but no longer fumbling, like whatever he needed he found and it's in hand.

"I don't—"

And then it happens.

It fucking happens.

It's then I wonder if I really am in some chaotic dream state.

Or maybe a coma.

A coma might explain this.

Because at that moment, Zander Michael Davidson gets on one

knee, his hand leaving his pocket and holding up a plastic ring with a heart on it.

My breath stops.

"Where did you get that?" I whisper in awe.

The ring is one he gave me when I was six after he won it in some crane game down the shore in Ocean View. He'd been trying for some baseball card set and instead got the junky ring, handing it off to me like it was trash.

He was so annoyed about it because he had spent his last quarter trying to get it.

I, of course, had been over the damn moon, letting that thing turn my finger green for a month until my mother forced me to take it off.

Once I did, I closed it into the little gumball machine container it came in, snapping the lid on and putting it into Luna's and my pink dream box for safekeeping.

And promptly forgot about it, mostly.

"Luna," he says, giving me an answer I already knew.

"I'm going to fucking kill her," I murmur under my breath.

"It was mine, technically," he says, and I put my hands on my hips, annoyed, emotions so volatile right now.

"You gave it to me," I say, and his smile spreads across his lips.

I'm sure this all looks so strange from the outside.

Me in a winter coat and pajamas, barefoot in the dark kitchen of my parents' house, Zander on one knee holding a damn gumball machine ring that's over twenty years old.

But then his face softens.

"Let me give it to you again," he says in a near whisper, my heart stopping.

"What?"

"It was always meant to be us, Zo. I've spent a week plotting out our perfect future, seeing if it really is the same as what you wanted when you were ten. You want to live here. You want to be an interior designer or do something creative. You want three kids—"

"I said two."

"Yeah, but you want three," he says with a smile. My heart skips a beat with that smile. "You want to live in a white house with a red door and a wraparound porch so you can sit out front and watch the kids play while you daydream about rearranging our living room for the fifth time. You want a puppy that will nip at the heels of whoever is closest, keeping them in line."

I can't breathe.

It's all making sense.

Zander has spent a week giving me everything childhood Zoe wanted and learning everything modern-day Zoe needs.

"I always loved the version of you that was carefree. But this week cemented that I am head over fucking heels for this version of you. The one who loves fiercely and is afraid to let those she loves down. The version that wants everyone to be happy, even if it means she's not. The dreamer. I want to give both of you everything you ever wanted."

"Both versions," I whisper. He smiles.

"Every version, Zoe." I lick my lips, staring at him. "So I just have one more question for you."

The remaining breath in my lungs leaves in a shaky exhale.

"Zoe Ann Thomas. Will you marry me? Be mine forever. We can figure the rest out so long as I have you."

The ring glints in the dim light, the pink heart-shaped gem still shining.

"I didn't get a real ring," he says, his smile nervous now. It's strange seeing it—Zander nervous.

He's the most self-assured person I know and now he's kneeling in front of me, *nervous*.

Because of *me*.

"We can go tomorrow or the next day or whenever. I knew you'd want to pick out your own ring, anyway, since you'll be stuck with it forever."

His words make no sense at all.

And yet they just show me he knows me.

I so *would* want to pick out my own ring to make sure it would be something I'd want to actually wear until the end of time.

"Zander, what are you talking about?" I ask because I still can't wrap my head around it.

"It's the last midnight question, Zoe."

My heart stops.

I get it now.

The MASH card.

That stupid box Luna hid under her bed.

My playlist.

He added his own songs to it.

The questions about how I wanted my life to look.

Will you marry me?

It all slams into me at once, making some form of convoluted sense but still, so confusing all the same.

"Zander," I start, my breathing uneven. "You . . . You have to ask my dad first."

His smile widens, and I realize then that I didn't say no like common sense would deem.

"Already did," a deep voice says from behind me.

I turn, and there stands my dad in his pajamas, my mom with squinty, tired eyes in her robe.

"What the hell is going on?" I ask because now the world is most definitely imploding.

"What should have happened years and years ago, Zoe. I'm making you mine in a way you can't run from."

"When did you ask my dad?!" I say in a panic.

"When you were refusing to call me after your interview," he replies, still on one knee, still holding the stupid plastic ring, a single eyebrow raised in challenge.

He's right.

I ignored him after that interview, so confused because I thought I'd feel relieved to have a job offer that was exactly what I thought I wanted, and instead, I felt sick.

Unfulfilled.

Lonely, even.

I didn't answer because I was scared that I'd say fuck it and tell Zee we should run away from reality again.

"We can talk about that later. Talk options. If you wanna do marketing in the city, we'll figure it out. If you wanna do something else, I'll make it happen. If you wanna stay in town and start popping out kids, I'm game. But this comes first," he says, tipping his chin to the ring.

My dad clears his throat, and oddly enough, I smile.

It is funny, after all, Zander telling me if I want, I can start popping out kids tomorrow in front of my dad.

Funnier, though, is how I don't cringe at the idea.

"Come on, Zoe," he whispers, then he reaches for my hand.

His is warm but clammy. He's nervous.

So damn nervous.

For what?

That I'll say no?

As if I could.

"I came to your apartment before." He furrows his brow, confused. "Threw rocks at your window." He shakes his head.

"I wasn't home."

"Yeah, figured that out when your neighbor opened the window and threatened to call the cops." Zee's eyes go wide. "I was at the wrong window," I say low and embarrassed, and the tension and nerves break as he tips his head back with a laugh.

And the sound fills me, swirling around me with joy and happiness and comfort.

It's then, I know.

I never had a chance.

Whether it was ten years ago, or a week ago, or five years from now, I was always going to end up his, wasn't I?

Zee squeezes my hand once, twice, three times, and I come back to the universe, a new understanding taking over me before he speaks again.

"I want it all, Zoe. I want all of your midnight secrets, all of your fears. Everything you wanted when you were ten, eleven? I want to give it to you."

"I wanted a pony with cotton candy pink hair." I say the words low and confused because, of course, that's what goes through my mind during this monumental moment.

He gives me a small smile.

"Then I guess I need to buy us some land."

Easy as that.

I want a pony; we need land.

He would give me the moon if he thought it would make me happy.

That much, I know.

My heart swells to the point that I'm concerned it won't fit in my chest any longer.

And so I give the boy I've loved for as long as I can remember the answer I've always known.

FIFTY-ONE
TODAY WAS A FAIRYTALE
ONE YEAR LATER

-Zander-

She's walking toward me on her father's arm, and I can't help but think this is definitely payback for when I made fun of Tony for crying when he married my sister.

My eyes water as hers lock onto mine.

I can't breathe.

She's gorgeous.

Her hair's wild and natural, dark against a white dress.

Her bouquet of daisies is a nod to her favorite of the eras.

But her face.

God, her face is what has me.

Pure fucking sunshine and happiness.

Not a moment of hesitation.

It's like she's five and I'm nine, and we're playing a game in my parents' backyard instead of in a church her mother insisted on.

Like she's wearing a pink bathing suit and a colorful beach towel over her head instead of a sleek white dress and a lacy veil.

I don't listen as her father tells the crowd he's the one handing her off to me.

I just keep staring at her, watching him pull the lace veil from her face, lean in, and press a kiss to her cheek with watery eyes.

She's so fucking beautiful.

And she's mine.

Then her water-blue eyes lock to mine again.

But she's nervous.

So nervous.

Not because we're getting married. The crowd, the expectation, the planning, they've gotten to her.

So before the officiant even tells me to, I reach out, grabbing her hands in mine.

And I squeeze them.

One, two, three.

She smiles, nerves falling away, and in their place is comfort and love and everything good in the world.

It's just Zoe.

And me.

The way it's always meant to be.

FIFTY-TWO
KING OF MY HEART
SIX MONTHS LATER

"Morning, pip," Zander's throaty voice says as my body wakes.

Every morning.

This is how I wake every morning when Zee is still in our bed.

Morning, pip.

I think back to that very first morning he said it, back when we were playing pretend (or, as Zee likes to say, *pretending to play pretend*), and how I thought I'd like to hear that every morning.

And now I do.

God, now I do.

Isn't that just beautiful?

The hand on my belly tugs as his body moves, rolling me to my back with him on top, his smile huge.

God, I love this fucking man.

I don't love the *Top Gun* style mustache he grew because Tony also grew one, and now it's become a battle of the 'staches.

I should tell him I won't let him go down on me with it.

But I also like watching him use a little comb every morning to neaten it up and the way it moves when he smiles.

I'll let it stay for now, I think for the millionth time in six months.

"Morning, honey," I say with a smile, my own voice still croaky.

He does the move that, even now, still gives me butterflies, doing a push-up and kissing me before straightening.

"Morning sex?" he asks, and I slap his shoulder.

"The house is full of people we are both related to by blood or marriage, Zander," I say under my breath, ignoring the way my pussy clenches.

"I'll lock the door."

"Zander Davidson!"

"I chose the room farthest from everyone," he says, his smile growing.

We're on the annual family vacation with both of our families, just like when we were kids, except with a much bigger house now that there are *couples* and *adults*.

And he's not wrong—the room we're in is almost completely opposite from where everyone else is sleeping.

He dips, the push-up giving me flutters, his face going into my neck before he speaks there.

"I had a dream about you," he murmurs, and his mustache scratches my skin as he speaks, sending fire down my spine.

Ah, yes. That's the other reason I've been letting the 'stash stay.

"Zander," I say, but this time my voice is breathier, less stern.

And with it, he thrusts his hips into mine, knowing he won.

"We'll be quiet," he says. I think about what the day looks like, knowing it's a full one.

"Zander," I repeat, but any fight has left my voice.

"It's barely even five, Zo. No one will be up for a while."

And there it is.

He will always wake up for me. My own personal morning person.

"Go lock the door," I whisper, tipping my hips up into his already hard cock.

I have no willpower.

He gets up almost gleefully, running to the bedroom door and locking both the doorknob lock and the little chain. He makes it halfway back to the bed before he turns back around, grabbing towels from the attached bath and stuffing them at the crack of the door. I smile as I watch him, shaking my head, and then he's running to me, leaping into bed like he's sixteen instead of thirty-five.

His hands instantly move up his oversized tee I wore to bed, grazing over my hips and continuing on until the material is off and he's tossing it to the ground.

Then he tackles me down into the mattress, forcing a giggle from me.

His hand moves to my mouth as his smile grows, his voice quiet when he whispers into my neck.

"You gonna stay quiet for me?"

But as he speaks, his hand moves over my stomach, up my ribs, a thumb swiping over my nipple.

I let out a shaky breath.

"Zoe," he demands, his fingers pinching on that nipple, sending a jolt running through me. "We can only do this if you stay quiet, baby."

"Make me," I whisper, and he smiles.

My man loves a fucking challenge.

His body rolls over mine before he covers my mouth with his, lips moving over mine, tasting me as his hand travels down, down, down my naked body.

"You gonna be quiet for me?" he asks, a single finger tracing over my already wet pussy, not entering, just playing there.

Featherlight.

"Zander," I whisper, bucking my hips.

His lips press to the crook where my neck meets my shoulder before he looks back up at me, repeating the trail of his finger.

Torture.

That's what this is.

I'm barely awake, already so ready for him, and he's torturing me, his skin on mine, his finger barely playing with me.

"You gonna be quiet, pip?" I moan again with his words, with the way they vibrate in his chest, the way they vibrate against my nipples, the way his fingers just keep dragging along me.

"Yes," I whisper.

Not because I think I can.

Not because I'm any good at not moaning when his hands are on me.

But because I desperately need more.

And I get it when a single, thick finger slides into me.

"Fuck," I whisper.

Not because I'm being cognizant of sound.

But because it feels so damn good, I've lost most of my ability to speak.

"Good girl, stay quiet," he says, then he slides in another finger.

I moan, this one stuck in my throat.

"That's it," Zee says as I lift my hips to get his fingers in farther. "That's it, take what you need, Zoe." My eyes drift shut with his words.

I could listen to him for an eternity, listen to his voice urging me on, telling me I'm doing good, that I'm taking him well, that he likes what I'm doing.

It's probably my people pleaser. She's been in hiding since Zee and I finally became an *us,* Zee teaching me that I don't need to live my life for anyone else's approval, but he's just fine with her coming out to play when it's just the two of us.

He encourages it, even.

"I need more," I whisper, and he lets out an approving chuckle.

"What do you need, Zoe?" he asks, and he slides in a third finger.

The stretch is exquisite, especially as he continues to move into me and out and as he shifts so I can feel his hard cock on my leg.

I don't want his fingers.

"I want you to fuck me, Zee," I moan. This time, the words are less quiet, less hushed, but the groan he lets out tells me I passed whatever test he set up for me.

"Play with yourself while I get ready," he says, and I don't even wait until his fingers are fully out of me before I start to strum my clit with my own fingers, tipped in a lilac purple. He moves off me, and I moan again when I watch his hands move to his mouth, watch him clean my wetness from them.

He's not looking in my eyes though.

His eyes are on my pussy, on my fingers playing with my clit for his amusement.

"Fucking look at you," he says, and my head tips back, my hips arching into my own fingers as I dip down, sliding one in and then out, dragging the wet up to my clit to repeat the process.

The sound that comes from my husband is feral.

But I'm so lost in what I'm doing, I barely register it.

I barely register how he gets off the bed.

Barely register how he takes off his boxers or how he climbs back into the comfy bed.

But I do register when his teeth bite my neck and he growls there.

"On your stomach," he says.

Instantly, I obey, rolling over, my head to the side so I can glance behind and look at him.

Sitting on his heels, his hand is on his cock, stroking, taking me in.

Fuck, I love this man.

"Tip your hips," he orders, and I know what to do. I accentuate the dip in my back, my hips moving, legs spreading just a bit as he groans, watching me.

"That's it. Goddamn," he says under his breath, running a hand up my inner thigh before running a finger through my pussy.

My hips buck.

"Still, Zoe."

I moan quietly.

"You gonna be quiet for me, baby?"

I nod.

I would do quite literally anything to get him right now. His body lines up over mine, his breath against my ear. "You gotta be quiet, Zo."

"I will, Zander. Please."

That's all he needs.

His hand moves between us, grabbing his thick cock and rubbing the tip up and down my wet before notching the head and sliding in.

Slowly.

Torturously fucking slowly.

A low moan falls from me.

"Fuck, you feel that? You feel how this pussy was made for my cock, Zoe?" I nod against the pillow, another moan bubbling in my chest.

"More," I whisper.

I need everything.

"You need me to fuck you?"

Another nod. He chuckles as I clamp around him, but with that, he starts to move, pulling out and thrusting into me hard.

"Oh, shit," I moan into the pillow, feeling him hit my G-spot with each thrust, my ass trying to tip back farther, trying to get him deeper, to get what I need.

"Stay fuckin' quiet, baby," he murmurs into my ear as he fucks me, laying his chest onto my back, his cock sliding in with each stroke. The way we're positioned, he goes almost unbearably deep, pulling deep groans from me with each move.

"Zander," I moan.

"Quiet, Zoe."

"Honey," I moan.

His hand moves, covering my mouth.

"Stay fucking quiet while your man fucks you," he whispers, slamming in harder, deeper this time and hitting me square in the ache he's created.

I moan into his hand and he stops moving.

"Zoe, you don't fucking stop, I'm gonna make myself come and leave you hanging."

He would never, that much I know.

But still, I clamp on him and nip his finger to tell him just how I feel about *that* idea.

He groans into my neck then moves to bite my earlobe.

"Face in the pillow, Zo, hand on your clit. Make this quick," he says, his whisper raspy.

I do as he asks, one hand moving to where my clit is swollen and begging for attention, the other moving to the pillow, and I bury my face there.

And then he moves.

He starts fucking me now, no longer holding back, his cock slamming into me with such force, I feel my body moving up the bed with each move.

I scream into the pillow as he does, as my hand works, as I get closer and closer to the edge.

But that's not what gets me there.

It's not my hand or his thrusts.

It's his voice in my ear.

It's the words he says when he lines his chest to my back, leaning over me and growling in my ear.

"Fucking get there, Zoe. Right now."

Because my body is so incredibly linked to his, my pleasure only erupts with his permission.

And then the world falls apart.

The scream dies in my chest, stars exploding in my eyes, my pussy clamping down on him, a second rush coming as I feel him pulse in me, as he bites my shoulder, groaning there as he comes.

And as always, it's fucking exquisite.

———

He rolls off me, and I groan into the pillow.

"You good?" he asks, and I turn my head to glare at him, pulling another deep laugh from my husband. "I thought you were supposed to be the morning person in this marriage?"

"I am. I just can't function when you fuck me into another hemisphere." His smile widens with pride and I shake my head.

"Come on. Let's go shower."

"Let's?"

"Honey, if I'm gonna be around our families all day with you slapping at my hands anytime I try to touch—"

"PDA in front of my parents is disgusting, Zee!"

"Your parents have more PDA than anyone I've ever met in my entire life. In fact, your dad is probably ready to help pay for our divorce because he definitely thinks you don't like me enough," he says, and I roll my eyes.

He's not wrong, though.

"Zander—"

"Come," he says, standing, then he leans over and slaps my ass.

Hard.

"Zander!"

"Shower time, pip. Let's go. Get in quick, clean off, and I'll let you sit on my face before we have to go out and be normal, functioning members of our families."

I stare at him.

I stare at him because I kind of want that, even though I just came and came hard.

I want to clean off and then sit on Zander's face and let him make me come again.

He sees that, too.

He moves a hand to my wrist, tugging until I'm standing, pulled up to him with a hand wrapped around my naked back.

Zander's lips are on mine, kissing me deep and long until I'm more than ready for our shower.

Hey, reader!!

In this last section of the epilogue and Zander and Zoe's story, there is a mention of pregnancy. If you are struggling with infertility, miscarriage, or if for *any* reason you don't enjoy reading about that topic, you can skip the last few passages and know that Zander and Zoe have their own happily ever after.

You are loved, you are important, and you are seen.

Love,
    Morgan

FIFTY-THREE
THE BEST DAY
TWO YEARS LATER

It's nearly midnight when Zee walks in the door.

My stomach moves to my heart.

I have no idea how he's going to take this. No idea at all.

"Hey," I say, my voice low, my hand in my pocket.

"Hey, you're up," he says with a smile, putting his things down and walking right to me.

The way he always does.

Even if I'm in bed, asleep before he comes home (a rare occurrence), he heads to me first, leaning down and pressing his lips to my temple before moving on with his night, whether that's eating leftovers or taking a shower or whatever.

His arm wraps around my waist, and he presses his lips to mine.

"Late night?" he asks into the top of my hair.

I don't respond, and his brows furrow.

"Everything good?" he asks.

My eyes are on the clock behind his head.

It strikes midnight, and I take a deep breath, putting my hands to his face, the scruff there, his hair still that longish length my dad hates.

"Can I ask you a question?" I ask, and I can hear my words shake just a bit.

"What—"

"It's midnight," I say, as if that explains everything.

And it does for us.

"Yeah, pip. Ask away," he says. His face still holds concern, but some of it has dropped with the familiarity of this routine.

I breathe in deep, trying to remember the words I practiced for hours.

One hand moves to the pocket of my hoodie, the one with *Coach* on the back and the Bulldogs mascot on the front.

My fingers wrap around the stick, and I lick my lips, locking my eyes on his.

"If it's a girl, how do you feel about Taylor?" I ask.

It sounded funny and silly when I practiced the line all night, hours after I took the test, and then ran two towns over to get four more to make sure I wasn't seeing things.

I wasn't, of course.

We've been trying for six months.

The longest six months of my life, it felt.

But this month seems to be the one, I suppose.

"What?" he asks, confused, but then I pull my hand out from my pocket, wrapped around the handle of the capped pregnancy test.

I give Zee a watery half smile as I hold it between us and shrug.

I had words.

I planned words to say. An entire monologue, even.

But they're all gone now.

They flew from my mind now that his eyes are wide, locked on my hand, now that his mouth has dropped open.

"Are you . . . ?"

I nod.

"You sure?" he asks, words soft.

I nod again.

And then it happens.

The most gorgeous look comes over my husband's face, a mix of love and joy and awe, and it's everything I hoped it would be and nothing my anxiety told me it could be.

He's *happy*.

"You're pregnant," he whispers.

I nod, my eyes watering further, a single tear falling.

And then Zander wraps his arms around my waist, my hands going around his neck as he lifts me off the ground, spinning me as a sound of pure fucking elation comes from him.

I laugh as he spins me, filing this moment in my mind as a core memory.

When he stops, he kisses me, pressing his forehead to mine but not letting go.

"I'm gonna be a dad," he whispers. I nod.

I don't think I can speak anymore.

"Know you love her, but if it's a girl, we're not naming her Taylor, Zo."

And then I burst out laughing.

EPILOGUE

Never Grow Up
Seven years later

A sliver of light comes into the dark room, but I don't look up to see who is there.

I *know* who it is.

Right now, my eyes are locked on my daughter.

The most beautiful thing I've ever seen in my life.

Dark hair and bright blue eyes like her mother, dimples from her dad.

She's the twin of her older brother, who's already three.

Her oldest brother, Mikey, is all me, the firstborn and nearly six.

Our middle boy came right after, Joey having just turned four when she came into the world.

But Allison is the baby.

The last one, Zoe keeps saying.

Her entire tiny hand is wrapped around my finger as I rock her in her room.

The fact that she's already four months old tears something inside of me, something I know from the boys will never repair the right way. An old injury that will ache when she smiles, that will hurt when I flip through old photos.

"She's dead asleep, Zee," my wife whispers from the doorframe she's leaning on. I look up at her, and she's got a small smile on her lips.

"You're supposed to be sleeping," I whisper.

"Was waiting for my husband to come back to bed." I wiggle my eyebrows.

"Number four?" I whisper with a smile.

She shoots me a look that could kill.

"Allie's the baby. Let her have that," she says, and her argument is sound. My baby girl. The spoiled princess. The first girl on both sides, Luna and Tony having two boys of their own, and Ace living the rockstar life with his girl. "Come on, honey," she whispers, softer now. "Let's get to bed." Allie's nose scrunches in her sleep, my heart skipping a beat as it does.

But then she settles, snuggling into my chest, and I look at my wife.

Her eyes roll, and she shakes her head softly before she speaks.

"Five more minutes. Then you both need to go to sleep."

I smile and nod and kind of feel like our six-year-old, being given five more minutes to play video games before Zoe makes him brush his teeth and go to bed, but I don't care.

I've got Allie.

The five minutes fly by as they always do. Eventually, I lift my little girl, pressing my lips so gently to the light whisps of dark hair on top of her head before placing her into her crib gently.

"Never grow up, princess. Okay?" I whisper.

She doesn't reply, simply snoring lightly as I tiptoe out and click the door shut.

Two years later

It's Sunday dinner at our house.

Some nights, it's at Mr. and Mrs. Davidson's.

Sometimes, it's at my parents.

Sometimes, we all pile into Tony and Luna's house.

This week it's our turn.

Zee ran out with the boys for last-minute groceries while I stayed behind to clean up, getting the house ready and putting food together before everyone arrives.

Allie is sitting on her play mat in the kitchen, my little helper, and smiling her big, toothy grin.

Despite her dark hair and my blue eyes, I think she's *all* her daddy.

I also know her daddy is going to *lose his mind* when he sees her.

Which will be any minute as I hear him in the garage, the boys yelling about ice cream and Grandma.

"You need me to put these in a vase?" Zee says, walking in with a bouquet of daisies, the boys behind him carrying bags with food and drinks.

God, I fucking love this man.

We have three kids—one more than I wanted in my manifesting box, but the same number I daydreamed of when I thought of my family as a kid.

The universe always knows.

Plus, the third was because Zee wanted his princess.

Our first two, born nearly back-to-back with 18 months between them, were my boys—the two sweetest, kindest, boys you could ever find. Protective and honest to a fault.

Their dad to a tee.

It took three years for Zee to convince me to give it one more go, to try for our girl, and then we got her.

"What the fuck is that?" he says, walking over to his princess.

"Don't you dare, Alexander," I say of the little pink bow in her hair. "It's adorable and goes with her outfit."

"Ooh, she used daddy's big name," Joey says under his breath to his brother, and they both giggle.

Mikey for Zee's dad, Joey for mine.

Best friends and now, brothers.

"I do not care. My girls do not put their curls in hair ties, Zoe."

"It's not a hair tie; it's a bow."

"Zoe—"

"Zee, if it's not up, it's in her face and she gets *food* in it." He takes a step closer to Allie, and I know it's game over.

"Great, then she gets an extra bath. You love baths, don't you, princess?" he says. Her eyes are locked on his face, her smile wide because her favorite person on the planet is talking to her.

"BATH!" she yells and claps.

Zee stares at me before carefully taking the bow out of her hair.

"Much better," he says, moving her wild curls to the side and out of her eyes. Then he takes the little pink bow that went perfectly with her outfit and tosses it in the trash.

I look at the ceiling, shaking my head, but I can't help but smile.

It's been like this since that road trip.

My eyes scan the living room, stopping on the frame that holds two tickets to a concert from 2009 in it.

It doesn't go with the design of our house, not even a little, but I wouldn't change it.

I could create an award-worthy home decor design (and I have— some of my work has been in the fancy magazines Zee once bought me on a road trip to make me fall for him), an entire space, and would still hang that frame, even if it throws the whole thing off.

It means *everything* to me.

But as my eyes move around the living room, I stop on the tree in the corner.

My enemy at the moment.

"Can you take the tree down?" I ask for the fifth time in three days.

"Babe, Christmas was three days ago.

"And that tree's been up for over a month.

"And?"

"And it doesn't *go*," I say through my teeth.

I had to rearrange the furniture to make the thing fit in our living room, and I can't wait to shift everything back to the way I like it.

"I like it. Like seeing the ornaments," he says, walking over to me.

The ornaments.

Dozens of them now.

One for every trip we've made, every stop along the way.

An entire Christmas tree of memories, starting with that that very first road trip.

"Yeah," I murmur because I do too—I love pulling them out and I dread putting them way.

But it's *past Christmas.*

"We can keep it up as long as we want," he says, his face in my neck.

"It's a *Christmas tree,* Zander."

"And this is our house. We get to decide when we take down the Christmas decorations."

"You're just saying that because you don't want to get on the roof and take the lights down."

He laughs because I'm right before pressing his lips to mine.

"January. We'll take it all down in January."

And as much as I want to argue, I can't.

He's right.

We make the rules in our own place.

And what's another week remembering just how he won me?

———

Twelve years later

"Please, I don't need you guys to come with me!" Allie says in a whine.

There is no winning.

I wish she would just accept that once and for all.

"Allie, baby, no."

"Daddy—"

"I was a fourteen-year-old boy once. No."

"Dad!"

You know she means business when she goes from *Daddy* to *Dad.*

"Allison."

And I know *Zander* means business when his baby girl moves from Allie to Allison.

So does our daughter, whose jaw goes tight.

"Why can't you just . . . you know, drop me off around the corner?"

"One day you'll be older and you'll get it. Until then, you can just hate me. Endure it or don't go. I don't care either way."

"How am I going to explain to Jaxton that my *dad* is going to go to the movies *with us?!*"

"What kind of name is *Jaxton,* anyway?" Zee asks.

"Your name is *Zander,* Dad." I bite my lip, holding back a laugh.

"But it's short for *Alexander,* which is a normal fuckin' name." Sometimes it's like these two are siblings rather than father and daughter.

I love it.

I also really need to cut in before it escalates.

"Zee, honey. Let me handle this, okay?" He glares at me, but I push him to the side. "Allie, honey, you'll get it when you're older."

"No, I won't."

"Get that, but promise you will." She glares at me, but I see it in her eyes.

I see that she knows she's not going to win.

The whining is about to commence.

"But how am I going to *explain* it?!"

"You don't. You just *go to the movies with me and your mom.*"

I bite my lip.

Really, the girl should just be happy that he's even letting her go out with a boy before she's sixteen.

"You know, your grandfather didn't let me date until I—"

"Yeah, I know, Pop-pop wouldn't let you date until you were sixteen, but you're ancient, Mom." I blink.

I blink again.

I blink a third time, my mouth opening just a bit.

Zee tips his head to our daughter, who has gone just a shade paler.

"If I were you, princess, I'd apologize to your mother and take the offer she's handing you before she loses it and tells you you're not going at all."

Allie stands there, jaw tight.

I blink again.

I admit it—I'm faking it just a bit.

It was kind of a funny joke.

But if I can convince her to just take the offer, tell a little white lie and make her think she's hurting her sole ally . . .

"Fine," she says with a huff. "I'm sorry, Mom."

I smile.

"The movie is at six," she says through gritted teeth, staring at her dad.

"Perfect. We'll pick your boy up at five. Gives me plenty of time to glare at him."

And as she walks off, her hands flailing as she mumbles under her breath about how uncool her parents are, I laugh into my husband's shirt.

Four Years Later

"Now what?" I ask, staring out the window as Zander drives us out of the city, headed back to Springbrook Hills.

We just dropped Allie off at school—NYU.

And now I have no more babies in my house.

No more after-school snacks, no more juice boxes. No more arguing over who gets the TV remote or whose music is too loud.

I can take a shower without worrying if there will still be hot water.

I can walk around my own house without worrying if I'll get caught naked by one of my kids.

I can buy the snacks I like without someone eating them before I get a single taste.

But the house will be empty.

Zander doesn't reply, instead tapping the screen of the dash until music starts to play.

"New Year's Day."

"It's going to be so quiet," I whisper, my voice cracking, the words wrapping around me the same way the quiet piano notes do.

His hand moves out, grabbing mine.

And then he squeezes.

One, two, three.

I like to think of it as our kids.

Mikey, my oldest, the most like me—an overachiever who's in California, slaving over a tech start-up, chasing some crazy dream.

Joey, my wild child, the most like his dad—a protector through and through, the one who came home from school to punch a boy who called his sister ugly last year.

Allie, my baby. The perfect mix of us both. Stubborn and beautiful and a total spoiled princess.

"This isn't the last page, pip. We're just starting a new chapter. I'm excited to do it with you," he says, and with his words, I know even though I'll probably cry my eyes out every time the house gets a little too quiet in the next few weeks, I'll be okay.

WANT MORE ZOE AND ZANDER?

Want more Zoe and Zander? Maybe... what happens when she doesn't listen and he *does* leave her hanging?

Grab it here!

ACKNOWLEDGMENTS

Writing acknowledgments is weird.

There I said it. (Again.)

I love my people and I hope I tell them that enough day to day, but I also know this book would be absolutely nowhere without those people, so I want YOU ALL, dear readers, to know how much they mean to me.

So here we go.

Forever first, thank you Alex. Every time I think about this writing journey I think about the time you told my dad I wasn't going back to work after Ryan was born and you said, *she's always loved to write, so we're going to see where that takes us.*

Thank you for always, always believing me. For bringing my Coke Zero and buttered bread and chicken nuggets to my office when I'm stressed and for being the blueprint for all book boyfriends. Here you go, I accidentally wrote a boyfriend named after you.

Next: Ryan, Owen, and Ella. I actually hope you never ever see this acknowledgment, but if you do, please, close this book and never speak of it.

But still thanks for letting me be your mom, for letting me live my dream, and for singing *All Too Well* in the kitchen with me.

Thank you to Madi, the word's most amazing cover designer. Thank you for coworking and crying sessions and alllll the Taylor Easter eggs. Thank you for being kind and open and honest and utter fucking sunshine. The world knew I needed you in my life and I'm honored to be in yours.

Thank you Lindsey. Thank you for understanding my anxieties, for being the world's best, kindest most amazing cheerleader and letting me vent without judging me. I love you to pieces.

Thank you Norma Gambini for taking my typos and turning it into a real book. It's been a year since we started working together and I'm so grateful for you.

Remember to leave space in your schedule when you're unbearably sought after.

Thank you to Shaye, who will always tell me like it is and is literally the biggest champion for indie authors I've ever had the utter pleasure to know.

Thank you to Good Girls PR for making this launch the crazy success it is. (Manifestation, babyyyyy!)

Thank you to Chelsie for sprinting and bouncing ideas and being a giant ball of joy and kindness. You're next!!

Thank you to Steph for sitting there while I brain dump story lines and watching as I slowly string things together. I can't wait to see what you come up with in the next year.

Thank you to my beta ARC's who receive this story and point out typos without holding them against me.

Thank you to my ARC team, the true stars of any hint of success this book will receive. You accept my crazy stories, read them, and share them with the world. I can't thank you enough.

Thank you to Booktok - yes, the whole damn thing - because without you, this would all be a pipe dream. It's easy to see the shitty parts of the platform but when you push that aside, there's a glorious, supportive, beautiful mix of people who are so kind and amazing. I'm honored to be a part of it.

But most of all: thank YOU, dear reader. When I first started writing, it was a crazy, delusional dream at best. I thought I would write a book and put it up and no one would read it. I just needed to get it out of my brain and onto paper. Little did I know it would just be replaced with three more stories and people would actually give it a chance.

I'm sure I'm missing people which will haunt me and my anxiety for years, but thank you. From the absolute bottom of my heart. I love you all to the moon and to Saturn.

WANT MORE SPRINGBROOK HILLS?

If you're looking for spicy small town romance, Morgan Elizabeth has you covered! Check out these releases:

Get book one, The Distraction, on Kindle Unlimited here!

The last thing he needs is a distraction.

Hunter Hutchin's success is due to one thing, and one thing only: his unerring focus on Beaten Path, the outdoor recreation company he built from the ground up after his first business was an utter failure.

When his dad gets sick, Hunter is forced to go back to his hometown and prove once and for all that his father's belief in him wasn't for nothing. With illness looming, distractions are unacceptable.

Staying with his sister, he meets Hannah, the sexy nanny who has had his head in a frenzy since they met.

When Hunter's dad gets sick, he's forced to leave the city and move back into the small town he grew up in at his sister's house. Ever since he watched Hannah dance into his life, he's finding himself drifting from his goals and purpose - or is he drifting closer to them?

She refuses to make the same mistakes as her mother.

Hannah Keller grew up watching what happens when a family falls apart and lived through those consequences. When it's time, she won't make the same mistake by settling for anyone.

But when the uncle of the kids she nannies comes to stay for the summer, she can't help but find herself drawn to the handsome, standoffish man who is definitely not for her.

Can she get through the summer while protecting her heart? Or will he breakthrough and leave her broken?

Out now in the Kindle Store and on Kindle Unlimited

He was her first love.

Luna Davidson has been in love with Tony since she was ten years old. As her older brother's best friend, he was always off-limits, but that doesn't mean she didn't try. But years after he turned her down, she's found herself needing his help, whether she wants it or not.

She's his best friend's little sister.

When he learns that Luna has had someone stalking her for months, he's furious that she didn't tell anyone. As a bodyguard with Garden State Security, it's his job to serve and protect. But can he use this as an excuse to find out what really happened all those years ago?

Can Luna overcome her own insecurities to see what's right in front of her? Can Tony figure out who is stalking her before it goes too far?

Out now in the Kindle Store and on Kindle Unlimited

She was always the fill-in.

Jordan Daniels always knew she had a brother and sister her mom left behind. Heck, her mom never let her forget she didn't live up to their standards. But when she disappears from the limelight after her country star boyfriend proposes, the only place she knows to go to is to the town her mother fled and the family who doesn't know she exists.

He won't fall for another wild child.

Tanner Coleman was left in the dust once before when his high school sweetheart ran off to follow a rockstar around the world. He loves his roots, runs the family business, and will never leave Springbrook Hills. But when Jordan, with her lifetime spent traveling the world and mysterious history comes to work for him, he can't help but feel drawn to her.

Can Jordan open up to him about her past and stay in one place? Can Tanner trust his heart with her, or will she just hurt him like his ex?

WANT THE CHANCE TO WIN KINDLE STICKERS AND SIGNED COPIES?

Leave an honest review on Amazon or Goodreads and send the link to reviewteam@authormorganelizabeth.com and you'll be entered to win a signed copy of one of Morgan Elizabeth's books and a pack of bookish stickers!

Each email is an entry (you can send one email with your Goodreads review and another with your Kindle review for two entries per book) and two winners will be chosen at the beginning of each month!

ABOUT THE AUTHOR

Morgan is a born and raised Jersey girl, living there with her two boys, toddler daughter, and mechanic husband. She's addicted to iced espresso, barbecue chips, and Starburst jellybeans. She usually has headphones on, listening to some spicy audiobook or Taylor Swift. There is rarely an in between.

Writing has been her calling for as long as she can remember. There's a framed 'page one' of a book she wrote at seven hanging in her childhood home to prove the point. Her entire life she's crafted stories in her mind, begging to be released but it wasn't until recently she finally gave them the reigns.

I'm so grateful you've agreed to take this journey with me.

Stay up to date via TikTok and Instagram

Stay up to date with future stories, get sneak peeks and bonus chapters by joining the Reader Group on Facebook!

ALSO BY MORGAN ELIZABETH

The Springbrook Hills Series

The Distraction

The Protector

The Substitution

The Connection

Holiday Standalone, interconnected with SBH:

Tis the Season for Revenge

The Ocean View Series

The Ex Files

Walking Red Flag

Bittersweet

The Mastermind Duet

Ivory Tower

Diamond Fortress

Made in the USA
Las Vegas, NV
23 September 2024

95674451R00203